A Wild Red Rose

by

Lynn Shurr

The Roses Series, Book Two

A Wild Red Rose

COPYRIGHT © 2014 by Lynn Shurr

Cover Art by *RJ Morris*

The Wild Rose Press, Inc.
PO Box 708
Adams Basin, NY 14410-0708
Visit us at www.thewildrosepress.com

Publishing History
First Yellow Rose Edition, 2014
Print ISBN 978-1-62830-241-7
Digital ISBN 978-1-62830-242-4

The Roses Series, Book Two
Published in the United States of America

She headed for the cluster of students
who surrounded the bullfighter, and they gave way before her, though someone groped her in passing. She didn't care enough to turn around and glare with Clint Beck in her sights. Renee stroked his arm down to the hand holding a pen signing autographs. That got his attention.

"You want an autograph, honey?" Clint Beck turned his blue eyes on her. They were the shade of deep ocean water, not the sparkling Irish blue eyes that Bodey Landrum always said was his best feature. His hair was a short, crisp, dark blond, dampened with sweat. Not really tall, he had the compact, muscular body of a gymnast and the tan of an outdoorsman.

Clint grinned, showing a good set of white teeth. No way could she tell he'd lost a few doing what he did, his dentist was that fine. He wondered if she wanted one of those big bazookas signed. Wouldn't be the first time. While bullfighters didn't have the cachet of bull riders—or the money—they were coming into their own these days.

"No, darling. I want to give *you* something." Renee took his pad and pen, wrote her name and number, tore off the sheet, and buried it deep in the pocket of his shorts. She tied the tails of Bodey's shirt around her waist and sauntered off, giving Clint Beck a good backside view of what she had to offer.

Praise for Lynn Shurr

"Shurr is a wonderful storyteller."

~The Romance Studio

~*~

"Very easy reads, well written, combined with conflict, believable plots and secondary characters that make the story come alive."

~Jane Lange, Romance, Reads & Reviews

~*~

"Lynn Shurr's stories have that distinctive flavor...and make you eager for another taste."

~J.L. Salter, author

Dedication

For Lisa Patin Mallet, the first to reply.

But people like us don't deserve true love.
~Renee Niles to Bodey Landrum,
Always Yellow Roses by Lynn Shurr

Chapter One

Rainbow, Louisiana
Ten months after Bodey Landrum married
Eve Burns, not Renee Niles Bouchard Hayes

Bodey Landrum, retired World Champion Bull Rider and reformed womanizer, quietly opened the door of his bedroom. The screaming had stopped about four a.m. At six, he'd sneaked out to get his Famous Bull Riding Academy of Rainbow, Louisiana rolling for the day. Now, he'd come in to swill some badly needed coffee and check on Eve's condition.

Snoring lightly, his bride of ten months lay stretched on the king-sized bed. Her long, white-blonde hair, damp and darkened by a recent shower, spread out across the pillow. One plump, blue-veined breast protruded from a white terry bathrobe, and that little devil, Shea Patrick, pumped away on the rosy nipple. Bodey felt a small surge of envy and a slight tightening in his jeans.

Damn, two more weeks before he could touch his wife the way he wanted. Shea released the nipple with an audible pop and snuggled into the soft cushion of his mother's breast. Bodey tiptoed across the room and raised the milk-groggy baby to his shoulder. A few firm pats and his son released a small, but manly, burp. Bodey laid the child on his back in the cradle custom-

1

made of saddle-colored oak to fit the southwest décor of the bedroom and drew a light cotton blanket over the tiny legs. Eve had been right to persuade him into attending the prenatal and parenting classes, or he would have panicked more than once during the past four weeks since the birth.

Bodey knew Eve would be blaming herself for the rugged night they'd both had. After a pregnancy nurtured by bland and boring foods, she'd succumbed to a large plate of Mama Tyne's barbecued ribs and spicy cowboy beans. Shea Patrick, proudly named for his granddaddy, kept them up for hours with his gas pains. Bodey took a moment to admire his offspring. The dark curls and little cleft in the chin said he was Bodey's boy, through and through. Maybe, he'd get Eve's long legs though. Nothing wrong with being under six feet, but still.

Bodey turned toward his wife. He ran a finger lightly across the top of her exposed breast, usually encased in ugly nursing bras day and night. Eve moaned in her sleep in a way he cherished. Reluctantly, he covered her with the robe and began a quiet exodus toward the bedroom door.

Then, some sonofabitch laid on the doorbell. Bodey eased the door shut and ran as fast as he could in cowboy boots down the long hallway and across the great room, dodging the leather chairs and sofas in his way. He sprinted like a downed bull rider making for the barricades and fearing for the worst. He'd left this week's class of wannabe rodeo clowns in the capable hands of Clinton O. Beck and Snuffy Jones, but things could go wrong. Why else would someone keep pressing the bell like that? They'd have to be a jackass, otherwise.

Bodey reached the door and flung it open. Make that description "some bitch" and "a piece of ass". Renee Niles Bouchard Hayes lounged against the frame, her elbow pressing the bell. She wore nothing but a very small bikini top on her over-inflated breasts and, Bodey suspected, a very small bikini bottom under the tropical-print towel wrapped around her provocatively rounded and tight hips. Renee had already oiled up, and one strand of her brilliant red hair lay glued against her cleavage with the lotion. Her emerald green eyes, as fake as her boobs, gave Bodey the once over from his boot tips to his tousled black hair.

"Must be hard going without sex while the little woman recovers from childbirth," she said.

"What do you want, Renee?" He had fallen into her grasp before, but not since she'd tried to get between him and Eve. Never again.

"Oh, I'm just so bored. I thought I'd come over for a swim and keep Eve company—even if all she can talk about is babies."

"Doesn't your mother have a pool?"

"Sure, but then I'd have to talk to my mother. Come on, Bodey, let me in."

"Eve and Shea are sleeping. Go on home. Shoo! I need to get back to the bullring."

"In the middle of the morning? I'll bet that bunkhouse you built for your students is entirely empty then."

"We have a class going on, yes. I'm headin' over there right now. Git."

"May I come watch? I do love seeing a man on a

wild bull."

"No, you distract the students. Besides, we have a clown and bullfighter group this week. Not your type of thing at all, Renee."

"Pretty please." Renee tapped the doorbell with her elbow again. Bodey thought he heard the baby let out a small squawk in the back of the house.

"Okay, come along, but you got to cover up."

Renee opened her arms wide showing off that impressive bosom again. "This is all I brought besides my sunglasses."

"Oh, hell. Stay here."

Bodey trudged to the kitchen and entered the small laundry room. He sorted through a hamper of soiled clothes and came up with a wrinkled, blue chambray shirt that didn't smell too heavily of cow. He turned, and there was Renee right where he didn't want her, crowding him in the small space.

"Since you're here, put this on."

Renee took Bodey's shirt, gave it a sniff, and finally shrugged into the sleeves. The buttons didn't close over her chest, but the long tails covered her torso to the knees. She dropped her towel into the hamper.

"Now am I decent enough to consort with clowns?" she said while rolling the long sleeves up past her elbows.

"Not hardly, but I have no more time to waste on you."

She made Bodey squeeze past her breasts to get out the door and trailed him all the way to the bullring built on the pasture behind the last of the barns. A bunkhouse that could sleep twelve sat farther up the hill away from the scent of the animals. The building had a deep, inviting porch filled with rockers, four private showers and commodes, a long line of sinks and mirrors, and a well-equipped lounge where lectures were held and DVD's of bull riding shown on a large, high-def wall-hung TV. In the evenings, the students were welcome to use the pool and poker tables and help themselves to snacks and soft drinks from the kitchenette. Bodey had a strict "no liquor" policy, and sometimes, Renee just had to take home men who wanted a stiff drink or were stiff in another way. Bodey never thanked her for her services to his Academy.

Renee strolled over to the fence of the bullring, put her feet up on the lowest rung, and hung her substantial breasts over the top rail. The shirt rode up and showed her tanned thighs and two rounded buttocks to the class of clowns seated on the bleachers shaded by a metal roof. She noted when all eyes swung from the short man in the center of the ring to her backside.

Snuffy Jones had been clowning for a good thirty years and knew when he was being upstaged. He'd just dropped his baggy pants to reveal his heart-covered drawers and gotten nary a laugh. Looked like he needed to make Miss Big Boobs part of the act. He pulled up his pants by their red suspenders, thumped his hands over his heart, and crawled on his knees toward the large breasts. Arriving in their shade, he took off his crushed derby hat, plucked a bent plastic daisy from the band, and offered it to the pretty lady with a soulful look on his painted face. When she laughed and accepted the pathetic gift, he jumped up, flashed his underwear again, and made his bowtie spin.

"And that's how you bring the audience into your act," Snuffy announced to a round of applause. "But we all know the real reason I'm out here groveling in the dirt is to distract a bull from a fallen rider. If I was you, lovely lady, I'd get down off those rails and take a seat because here he comes."

Renee's cousin, Rusty Niles, manager of the bull riding academy, opened the gate on cue. The huge black bull, irritated at being confined in the chute, charged into the ring looking for trouble. A man Renee had hardly noticed left his place by the chute and followed Bodey's stud, Black Tuesday, out into the ring's center. This guy wore a wide-brimmed, white cowboy hat, a large, loose T-shirt covered in stars, stripes, and advertising, long shorts, kneepads, and a good pair of running shoes. The bull, intent on Snuffy Jones, paid no attention to the man on his heels.

Snuffy waved his sorry hat and called, "Here bully, bully, bully."

Just before the bull arrived in the same space as the clown, Jones dove into a rubber barrel. Black Tuesday savaged the barrel with his stubby, clipped horns. The audience could see the clown holding on to hand grips as the animal rolled the object of his fury around the ring, finally getting his horns under the barrel and tossing it a good five feet. Jones stayed tucked inside.

Before the bull could gather for another charge, a white cowboy hat slammed across his muzzle. Black Tuesday turned his head and focused on a new victim, the man in running shoes, who stepped deftly away as the animal swept by trying to side hook him with a horn. Meanwhile, Snuffy Jones gathered himself, picked up his barrel and waddled back into the center of the ring.

"Yer mother's a cow!" he called out, waving his

arms.

Black Tuesday paused to consider the insult while the man in shorts circled the ring. The bull decided to make another try at the barrel. Snuffy Jones flopped the barrel on its side and hunkered down for another beating. Just as Black Tuesday arrived and lowered his head for another toss, the T-shirted bullfighter leaped on top of the barrel, grasped the bull's horns and vaulted onto the animal's wide, black back. He did a handspring off of Black Tuesday's flanks, landed without losing his hat, and wrung the bull's tail.

By the time Black Tuesday pivoted and charged again, the bullfighter was across the ring near the gate. He pulled a large red handkerchief from a pocket and waved it as if it were a huge cape.

"Come get me, you side of beef, you piece of brisket."

The bull came roaring. Clinton O. Beck stepped aside, and Rusty swung the gate open, then closed it behind the irate animal who suddenly found himself in a small holding pen. Game over.

The students surged to their feet and cheered. Renee Hayes looked as stunned as if she'd been hit with a cattle prod.

"Who is he, Bodey?"

"Well, the barrelman is Snuffy Jones, one of the best rodeo clowns ever."

"Not him. He smells like chaw. The other guy."

"Clinton O. Beck, three times World Champion Bullfighter."

"Introduce me."

"Now Renee, you know I hate when you mess with the talent."

"Most of the time *you* are the talent and you're so very taken. Fine, I'll introduce myself."

She headed for the cluster of students who surrounded the bullfighter, and they gave way before her, though someone groped her in passing. She didn't care enough to turn around and glare with Clint Beck in her sights. Renee stroked his arm down to the hand holding a pen signing autographs. That got his attention.

"You want an autograph, honey?" Clint Beck turned his blue eyes on her. They were the shade of deep ocean water, not the sparkling Irish blue eyes that Bodey Landrum always said was his best feature. His hair was a short, crisp, dark blond, dampened with sweat. Not really tall, he had the compact, muscular body of a gymnast and the tan of an outdoorsman.

Clint grinned, showing a good set of white teeth. No way could she tell he'd lost a few doing what he did, his dentist was that fine. He wondered if she wanted one of those big bazookas signed. Wouldn't be the first time. While bullfighters didn't have the cachet of bull riders—or the money—they were coming into their own these days.

"No, darling. I want to give *you* something." Renee took his pad and pen, wrote her name and number, tore off the sheet, and buried it deep in the pocket of his shorts. She tied the tails of Bodey's shirt around her waist and sauntered off, giving Clint Beck a good backside view of what she had to offer.

He did a body check. Nope, hadn't sprained or broken anything during the demonstration. He could hang out with Bodey and Snuffy tonight, hit a honky-tonk out on the highway, or watch a movie in his motorcoach, but since he wasn't too bunged up to screw, the bodacious lady had just given him another option.

The catering service arrived, and slim, yellow-toned Ja'nae Plato from the Rainbow Café put out lunch on the long picnic tables set in the shade. A giant po-boy sliced in sections flanked by potato salad and coleslaw bowls made up the meal. She placed a tray of huge chocolate chip cookies and began filling cups with iced tea. The crowd around Clint and Snuffy thinned and re-formed near the food and Ja'nae, the best looking black woman in Rainbow, and the one least likely to respond to a pass of any kind. Ja'nae was all about building her business, and so Bodey hired her to do the catering, not just because he'd known her as the kid sister of his friend, Leon. Besides, he'd never slept with Ja'nae because Leon wouldn't allow it, a very good thing for all of them at this point in their lives.

Bodey slammed Clint on the back. "You always amaze me. Reminded me of the time you jumped the bull to save my hide a few years back."

"Warn't nothing. Say, I got an offer from your lady friend. Mind if I take her up on it?"

"Not my lady friend anymore, not for some time. Feel free, but be careful. If Renee finds out you're the heir to the Beck's Baked Beans fortune, she'll have one hand down your crotch and the other in your wallet faster than Black Tuesday can throw a rider. That's a dangerous woman when she's between husbands."

"Why Bodey, my man, you know I thrive on danger."

****

Clint Beck took Bodey up on his offer to shower in

one of his mansion's guest baths. His luxury motorcoach was parked behind the bunkhouse and hooked up to electricity, water, and sewage since Bodey knew well how a lot of rodeo folk traveled, but he would hardly shower in a cubicle when he could have jets of hot water massaging his sore muscles. He gave himself a close shave and slapped on a tangy aftershave. Once he'd put on clean boxer briefs, khakis, and a button-down shirt with starched cuffs, he looked exactly like any other well-built man on the street, he thought. He slid his feet into soft Italian loafers, put a matching belt through the loops of his pants and went down to the kitchen to cadge a bottle of wine off Bodey.

Clint walked in on a tender moment between Bodey and Eve. He noted that the great bull rider only stood taller than his luscious, gray-eyed wife when he had his boots on—which didn't seem to bother Bodey one bit. He was laying a long kiss on his missus, and she had bent her head slightly to accept it. Their baby watched, attempting to focus his already bright blue eyes, from an infant seat nearby.

"Ahem. Bodey, could you spot me a good bottle of wine? I couldn't find anything decent in Rainbow at Plato's Liquor and Groceries and don't want to have to go into the city. Miss Renee is waiting."

Bodey didn't break the kiss, but gestured toward a cabinet that, when opened, revealed a state of the art wine cooler fully stocked. Eve pulled away.

"For heaven's sake, Bodey, we have guests tonight."

"Don't stop on my account. I'll be dining at the home of Renee Hayes this evening. I wanted to take along a little offering."

Bodey gave a deep laugh. "You won't need an offering. Renee will have your clothes off before you get to the bedroom. She'll be the appetizer, main course, and the dessert. You better eat something before you go to keep your strength up, but feel free to help yourself to the wine."

"Red or white?"

"White," said Eve. "Renee is always watching her weight. And Bodey is right. No food will be served. Instead of letting Renee have free run of your students and instructors, we should be helping her find a good husband who will satisfy her needs and lead her to a happier life."

"I doubt if there is a man on earth who could satisfy Renee. And what makes you think she isn't happy?" Bodey asked his wife.

"Underneath all that bravado, she is miserable. She believes her looks are all she has to offer, and she kissed thirty good-bye the same year as I did. Everyone knows her reputation, and sure, men take advantage of that, but no one is offering to marry her. Renee has been used and abused by men all her life. She needs to be led in a better direction."

"You are too good for this world, darlin'. She's had two husbands already, both rich—and I don't think she'll ever be a nun." Bodey eyed Clint who had selected a slim green bottle of German Leibfraumilch from the cooler.

"Clint, bro, Renee is going to scent prep school and money all over you if you show up at her place lookin' like that. Cowboy up a little, man. Play the rodeo bum, or she'll pursue you to the ends of the earth. Too bad you already shaved and perfumed yourself. Ditch the I-talian loafers and put on your running shoes. Come with me."

Bodey led the way to his bedroom suite and threw open a closet door. Along the back wall, pegs held maybe fifty western hats and below them sat racks and racks of boots. Western wear of all styles filled the hangers on both sides. Clint wondered where Eve kept her clothes. Must have her own closet. He tried to keep his eyes from straying to what appeared to be two nude paintings of Bodey's wife on the bedroom walls.

"Pick a hat," Bodey ordered.

Clint reached for a worn black felt with a battered silver concha band that sat on a shelf next to a white business Stetson.

"Not that one. That's my lucky hat. I wore it the first time I met Eve—and on other momentous occasions. Here, try this nice straw hat. See if it fits."

Bodey selected a model with upturned sides and quail feathers stuck in the leather band. He stuck it on Clint's head. "Wouldn't be caught dead in this myself, but it looks good on you. Now remember, you're just a good ole boy who can't afford a high-priced Stetson. For God's sake, put one of your bullfighter prize buckles on your belt when you go change your shoes. Roll up those sleeves. You don't know nothing about wine either. Oh, and I'd ask Snuffy if you can borrow his truck."

"The Belly Nelle? You've got to be kidding."

Snuffy's truck, named in honor of Pat Brady's Jeep, the Nellybelle from the old Roy Rogers Show, was a wreck the barrelman sometimes used in his clown act. It possessed a deceptively good engine, however, and could pull his equally disreputable, old trailer anywhere Snuffy wanted to go.

"Yep. She sees you in that sports car you tow around, and you are doomed."

"This seems like a lot of work for a good lay."

"Just tryin' to protect a friend the way he protected me in the arena. That's all."

Chapter Two

Clinton O. Beck, heir to the Beck's Baked Beans and Condiments fortune, graduate of a top prep school and the University of Texas, holder of an MBA from Harvard, arrived at Renee Hayes' door in running shoes and carrying a bottle of fine wine he wasn't supposed to know anything about. She must have heard him pull into the drive since the Belly Nelle was tuned to shake and rattle as part of Snuffy's act. Clint prayed Snuffy would stay in visiting with Bodey and Eve and not decide to unhitch the classic Corvette from his motorcoach and go on a bender in one of Rainbow's bars. He'd had to offer the clown a trade of transportation for the night.

Renee opened the door to her home in high-toned Red Horse Acres, a development right next to Bodey's ranch. She started to give Clint a seductive smile, but it froze on her face.

"Is that your truck?"

"Sure is, darlin'. She don't look like much, but she's got a good engine and a big heart. I'd never give her up. My daddy gave her to me when I was just a pup." Clint tried his best to imitate Bodey, but maybe he was laying it on too thick. "Want to see her up close?"

"Ah, no. I'm not dressed for it. What's that printed on the side?"

"Her name, the Belly Nelle. It's sort of flakin' off, but I meant to honor Pat Brady's Nellybelle from the old Roy Rogers show. You remember."

"No, I don't. I'm not that old. Eve and I are the same age."

He'd hit a nerve there. "Didn't mean to um—say you were. You sure look fine."

She did, too, in a pornographic, wet dream sort of way. She wore one of those outfits women, or sometimes men, purchased at shops with names like *In His Dreams* or *Fantasy Time*. A sheer baby doll top covered tiny black lace panties and an underwire pushup bra barely hiding her nipples. She had high-heeled mules with fluffy feathers across the toes on her feet.

Clint didn't think he'd ever seen an outfit quite like it in real life. The women he took up with once he got out of college generally wore jeans and boots and just got naked. After a while, they grew tired of following him around the circuit, hoping that he wouldn't be too sore or injured to have sex. Tonight, he felt fine. Hot dog!

"May I—can I come in?"

"Hurry! I think I see my father walking up the hill. Remember, we can't do it in the backyard until after dark. Tara-on-the-Bayou looks right down on my place."

"Huh?"

"My parents' house—up there." She pointed to an ostentatious, columned mansion on the crest of the hill. "My daddy developed this area and got the best lot."

Renee grabbed his open collar, thrust Clint inside, and slammed the door, but didn't try to drag him any

15

farther. The second the door locked, she began rubbing those big tits against his chest and grinding her hips against his crotch. Renee dived straight for his open mouth with the tip of her pointed tongue. Clint figured he went from zero to one hundred in less than ten seconds.

When she twined her arms around his neck and wrapped her legs around his waist, he put his hands under her buttocks for support and accidently laid the chilled wine against her thighs. Cooled off rapidly, Renee abruptly dropped her feet to the floor.

"Uh, I brought wine."

"Let's go put that somewhere for later."

Clint turned toward a kitchen set off with a breakfast bar and high black leather and chrome chairs.

"Not there."

She spun Clint around. He got a glimpse of a living room possessing a plush couch that resembled a pair of huge red lips. Slick black pillows rested upon it. All the tables—coffee, side, and dining—were rectangular glass set on black iron stands. An entertainment center with television, sound system, and DVD player rose like a black monolith in one corner. Blood red drapes covered floor to ceiling windows. Not exactly homey. No, sirree. More modern bordello in style.

Renee took him in the opposite direction down a hall hung with paintings of nearly nude males, a black man with bulging muscles accented in purple and one that sort of resembled Bodey Landrum if he'd taken steroids or modeled for male porn magazines. Clint was pretty sure his friend had not done either, but when he paused to study the picture, Renee yanked him into her boudoir, another fantasy room he hadn't seen outside of

Vegas. The silky, tiger-striped wallpaper and bed coverings should have seemed tacky like Elvis Presley's jungle room, but suited her feline personality just fine. She'd placed live jungle plants near a sliding glass door opening onto a terrace furnished with loungers big enough for two and covered in hot tropical colors. Inside, the room was dim with recessed lighting. The bedstead made of faux bamboo had a filmy netting hung over a frame open to the mirror on the ceiling.

Clint swore the temperature must be ten degrees hotter than the rest of the house. Maybe it was only him. Regardless, he would be more comfortable if he took off his clothes right now. Might be the plan.

Renee took the wine from Clint's hand and sat the bottle on the dresser, also made of fake bamboo. "Do you like what you see?"

"Every single bit of it. Hot in here."

"Then, let's get you out of those clothes."

****

Bodey was right. Clint should have eaten something in advance. Round one went fast and furious, but Renee soon had him pumped up for round two. That woman knew more tricks than a bareback rider—which she had been part of the time. Her pelvic muscles were so strong, he swore at one point she'd nearly squeezed off his dick, but no, she'd merely milked him of every ounce of his vital fluids.

Thankful for his gymnastic training and his stamina, he'd needed both in excess tonight. Now, Renee wanted to play the "name that scar" game. Women, when they got up close and personal to his body, always did. He answered her questions as briefly as possible—"Cheyenne Frontier Days—zigged when I should have zagged", "Houston Stock Show—a mite too slow", "PBRA finals—took a hit for Bodey." Man, after all that exercise, he was parched and starving.

"Mind if I go out and look for some grub, Tiger?"

"If you find anything, bring some for me. We can eat together in here."

Though it seemed a little silly considering they were alone, Clint pulled on his pants to go forage in the kitchen. He got a plate that appeared to be platinum-ringed wedding china from a leaded-glass cupboard and filled it with what he could find. The refrigerator yielded a bunch of red grapes in fairly good condition and two kiwis that looked disturbingly like a man's balls until he cut them into slices. He found a bag of cheese cubes that might have been left over from a party. Cheddar, Swiss, and jalapeno, he thought. The bread drawer held Melba toast rounds, but no bread. He arranged the fruit and dry toast around the edge of the platter and dumped the cheese cubes in the center. That would have to do because not much else appeared to be available.

Clint started to take two matching wine glasses from the cupboard, but stopped himself. Tonight, he was only a lonely, unsophisticated cowpoke. Balancing the plate on his fingertips, he returned to the tiger's lair. Sitting up with the striped sheet barely covering her privates, Renee rested on a mound of pillows with a motif of jungle leaves.

"Dinner is served, Madame—but first the fine beverage." Clint set the platter on the dresser top and worked the cork out of the wine bottle. "Bodey's stuff. Woo-eee, no cap."

He took a swig and passed the bottle to Renee. She

put her lips to the rim and swallowed in a way that made him randy all over again. He should eat first before he passed out and humiliated himself.

Placing the platter between them on the bed, they nibbled and talked. He told her another brief scar story ending with, "Yeah, Bodey and I—Bodey and me had some real good times." Years of prep school grammar and diction lessons tripped him up now and then.

"What do they pay you for such dangerous work, my championship bullfighter?"

"Oh, about $150,000 a year, plus some special prizes if I win a competition. But what with paying my travel expenses and havin' a little fun on the road— Vegas can sure suck you dry—some years, I can barely pay my taxes. Got a bit put aside for a doublewide on a piece of land I own, and this is gonna be my last year of bullfighting. I promised my mama and daddy I'd quit and come into the family business after ten years."

"What sort of business does your family own, Clint?" Renee nibbled on a cheese cube like a pretty white rat, but he could tell the income of a bullfighter had disappointed her.

"We got a grocery business in San Antonio. My dad made me work with him every summer—after school, too, stocking shelves and such. We lived over the store."

All but the last parts were true. He'd been at boarding school most of the year, but in summer he'd traveled with his father, sitting in on board meetings around the world, very much the Beck's Baked Beans crown prince. Beck's Spicy Beans were very popular in South America, and he'd gotten to practice his Spanish, but in the end, too little playtime caused him to rebel.

He'd gotten the MBA to please his father, then simply couldn't do the corporate heir routine anymore.

He wanted freedom, the open road, and danger, not a corner office for the rest of his life. He'd tried bullfighting on a bet, was damned good at it thanks to years on the gymnastic team, and he'd saved lives—which was more than baked beans ever did. His mother urged Gunter Beck to let the boy have his fling. Gunter Beck made his son, Clinton O. Beck, sign a valid contract stating that ten years hence, or any time before that period ended, his son would report for duty to the family business or have his trust fund revoked.

Mostly, he didn't give a shit about his trust fund, but his mother hinted more and more often that his iron-willed father needed help with the business whether Gunter would admit it or not.

"My mama says, marry a man with a grocery store and you'll never go hungry. Might not get rich, but you won't starve. Maybe I should buy you some groceries before I leave," Clint said as his past flickered through his mind.

"I don't need groceries. I dine out with men and otherwise don't want the temptation of food around. I have to watch my weight."

Clint had spied the exercise equipment in a spare bedroom when he'd passed along the hall with the tray. The machines were as heavy duty as the ones he worked out on between bullfights.

"I don't see as you got any weight problem, except for being a little top-heavy. They ain't real, I guess." He stared mournfully at her naked breasts.

"Well, to be honest, no. After my divorce, I felt very insecure. Gerry, my second husband, bought them for me. He said I didn't need them, but I did need a lift, so I went all the way. Don't you like them?" Renee peered down at herself, thoughtfully rolling a small piece of cheese into a little ball with her fingers.

"They sure are pretty, but they make me sad."

"How so?"

"Guess you'll never nurse my babies with those titties."

Renee, horrified, exclaimed, "I don't plan on nursing anyone's babies! Eve will ruin her figure, wait and see. You did use a condom? I know I put the first one on you, but what about the second time?"

"Didn't mean to spook you. 'Course I used a condom. We don't know each other that well a'tall to go without. You are on the pill, ain't you?"

"No."

Clint took a turn at being horrified. He'd been in a hurry and hadn't gotten the second one on as snugly as he liked.

"I use a diaphragm and a spermatocide. The pills make me retain water and give me nausea."

"Oh, good. I didn't know anyone used those anymore. My mama said I came into the world because of a loose diaphragm, the best mistake she ever made."

"You're an only child?"

"Heck, no. I got older sisters, both married with kids. Takes the heat off of me to reproduce until I get hitched."

"I'm not interested in marriage."

Now, that was a damned lie according to Bodey. What Renee meant was she didn't want to be the wife of a bullfighter or help to run a grocery store. That sort of irked Clinton O. Beck. He'd be plenty good enough for her if she knew his real net worth. Somewhere along the line, this fabulous woman had been spoiled for the ordinary pleasures of life and turned into a man-eater. He had half a mind to teach her people could be happy without great gobs of money. He met them every day when he was out on the circuit, some of the best people on earth. Yet another reason why leaving the rodeo for the conniving business world depressed him.

Renee set the platter aside and kicked off what little covering she had. She stretched her body out full length. Clint watched. He'd never known a woman who had endured a Brazilian wax before. Must have hurt like hell. Most of the girls he knew had bikini waxes to go with low-slung jeans and sexy underwear, but nothing like this. The remains of her pubic hair were a dark auburn shade, not as light and bright as the hair on her head, but she'd been born a redhead for certain. He couldn't remove his eyes from that little fringe.

Renee took the small ball of cheese and placed it on her navel. Her stomach was so flat the bait didn't roll off but sat there in the small dip, a tiny temptation.

"Enough talk," she said. "Here mousey, mousey, come eat me."

Clinton O. Beck found himself happy to oblige.

****

Just before dawn, Renee lowered a motorized screen over her terrace to keep the mosquitoes off their bare bodies. They made love outside on the hot pink cushion of one lounger, then switched to the orange-covered one leaving some damp spots behind, to watch the sun rise over her garden.

Thick plantings of bamboo on three sides of the yard kept the first rays from penetrating, but eventually, pots of hibiscus with blooms of red, lemon, and peach emerged from the gloom. An interesting piece of statuary sat in the center of a small, grassy area. Clint assumed it was a takeoff of the Mannekin Pis he'd seen in Brussels, but instead of a small, chubby child urinating into a fountain, the statue of a full-grown man, life-sized, with the body of a Greek god, pissed into an elegant copper birdbath. Both of his hands directed the spray of his giant penis. Water dripped from the sides of the birdbath onto a circle of ferns reminding him a little of Renee's Brazilian wax job. For a minute, words failed Clint Beck.

"Never seen nothing like that before," he finally managed.

"I studied art in college. The statue is based on a drawing I once made of a—friend." She'd almost said her personal trainer, the one her first husband had caught her screwing.

"My first husband, the heart surgeon, Elias Bouchard, hated it. I had to put the thing into storage for a while, but Gerry didn't mind. He made his money off of oil royalties, and for an older man, was very broad-minded. Too bad he didn't last. Had a heart attack practically on top of me. Mixed Viagra with his medication. Even Elias couldn't bring him back."

The sun of a Louisiana June boiled up higher into the sky. Clint had a feeling all this information about her rich husbands might be Renee's way of telling him this had been fun, but now she had to get back to serious spouse hunting. He should return to Bodey's place, too, and try to get some sleep and a good breakfast before schooling the newbie bullfighters in their moves.

Whatever possessed him to say, "May I come over again tonight? I think I might have an interesting proposition for you." Damn, he should have said "deal".

Renee didn't appear to notice the big word usage. "I'm always up for interesting propositions, Clinton O. Beck, but don't call before three. I need my beauty rest."

"Darlin', you couldn't get more beautiful."

She smiled like a cat full of cream and ready for another full saucer.

Chapter Three

"You're going to do what!" Bodey Landrum shouted as Clint Beck helped himself to an oversized portion of scrambled eggs from the breakfast buffet in the bunkhouse.

"I thought I'd take Renee around on the circuit with me for a few months, try to break her of some of her bad habits. Not that sharing my bed will be any hardship."

Bodey lowered his voice since all the students craned their necks to listen in. "If Renee sees that fancy rig of yours, that old Corvette like the one I got back in Texas, she'll do a computer search to see what you're really worth. All those *Millionaire's Son Fights the Bulls* stories are gonna pop up, and you are doomed. I know she Googled me. If I hadn't been so in love with Eve, she might have taken me down. Before you know it, you'll be married to her."

"Would that be such a bad thing? You know I live for danger." Clint put two bran muffins studded with raisins on his plate and picked a ripe banana out of the fruit bowl. He passed over the bacon and home fries.

"Yes, yes, it would. She's a man-eater, not your ordinary house cat."

"I have a plan. I'll trade rigs with Snuffy for a while—and keep her away from computers if that will make you happy."

"Have you ever been in Snuffy's trailer? It's a health hazard. There is a reason why he got the Snuffy nickname."

"I'll clean it up. We'll only use the thing for a month or two."

"And when someone on the circuit calls you the 'Bean King', what are you going to say?"

"I've got an explanation all worked out. There's nothing in my program biography about Beck's Baked Beans, just a blurb that I went to UT and once tried out for the U.S. Olympic gymnastics team. After that, it's just a list of awards and honors."

"You know, I thought I was brave man, but Clint, you take the prize buckle with this one."

****

Snuffy Jones showed even less enthusiasm for the idea than Bodey. "Let you use the Belly Nelle and my trailer? Well, I don't know. We been together a long time. That would be like letting you sleep with my wife—if we weren't divorced."

"Say, I'm doing that rodeo for special kids up in Casper for you, no charge, in a week. You didn't have to beg me to take the time from my busy schedule. Just let me use The Tin Can and the Belly Nelle until then. You can take my motorcoach."

"What about the Corvette?"

"Ah, I promised Bodey he could use it. What do you say, Snuff?"

"Maybe I can endure the separation for a good friend who's saved my balls from bulls a few times."

"Great. Only one favor. Be sure you spit your chaw into a cup while you use my rig."

"You got it. I have to move out some of my stuff."

"I'll help you before we start class."

Snuffy's ancient metal-clad trailer had been rolled by a tornado in Kansas and battered by hail in Texas. The barrelman had painted her affectionate nickname, The Tin Can, on her side. Clint hauled the case of beer and three bottles of whiskey over to his luxury motorhome while Snuffy gathered up his street clothes, costumes, and make-up kit. The Tin Can's refrigerator held only leftovers from the generous meals provided by Bodey, so Clint loaded up his groceries, too, along with all his bullfighting gear and a week's worth of clean clothes. Bodey would store his surplus and more upscale clothing. With the transfer completed, Clint figured he still had a lot of work to do before he would be able to coax Renee through the door.

After working in the bullring all morning with the students, Clint skipped lunch and sought out the nearest K-Mart about ten miles away from Rainbow for an array of cleaning supplies. He looked over a display of Martha Stewart sheets and picked a couple of sets in red. If Martha said that was good taste, then it was. The tiger print throw and pillows he got didn't bear her name. He found some narrow floor runners that looked like fake Persian rugs to cover the snuff-stained beige carpet in The Tin Can. He couldn't stand the thought of walking on it barefooted. Once he got back, he realized he should have gotten some new curtains to replace the sorry, striped, grease-streaked ones hanging over the small windows. They'd probably been there since before Snuffy's wife, Ruth Ann, refused to travel anymore and left him years ago. Too late for another trip now. Clinton O. Beck had a toilet to scrub.

The stains in the bathroom proved to be permanent,

but Clint had the satisfaction of knowing he'd disinfected all surfaces his flesh or Renee's was likely to touch. He put out an air freshener hoping it would compensate for the aroma of used snuff that seemed to hang in the air, the cloudy mirror over the sink, and all the other imperfections of The Tin Can. The mattress on the foldout bed proved to be better than expected and probably newer. Fresh sheets made it look good, if he did say so himself.

Snuffy poked his head in the door, searching for some forgotten item. "Wouldn't hardly recognize the place, Clint, all duded up for a woman. I like that tiger skin blanket. Do I get to keep this stuff when you're through with it?"

"You bet." Clint could see Snuffy puckering and looking for a place to spit and grabbed a paper cup in a hurry.

"How about the mountain bike you got on that rear rack. I get to use it? I figure I can store my custom barrel back there, too."

"Sure, use the bike. I'll be getting my exercise another way."

"You're spoiling me, Beck. I plan on leaving tomorrer evening and get on up to Casper to visit with my kid. See you there."

"That's a promise."

****

After the bullfighting class ended for the day, Clint took a box of files over to Bodey for safekeeping.

"Papers that might reveal my net worth. Keep 'em safe for me, Bodey."

"You bet. What about your laptop?"

"The Belly Nelle has a bunch of secret

compartments, not to mention trapdoors."

"Good, then you can escape Renee if you have to run."

"Cut it out. I promise to bring her home a changed woman."

Eve Landrum, who had been rocking her baby and obviously listening in, said, "Clint, be careful with her. I don't think Renee is as strong as she seems. Tricking her is wrong."

"Yeah, right. Like she didn't try to trick me or half a dozen other men," Bodey snorted.

Clint left it at that and went to convince Renee Hayes to ride the circuit with him.

****

Renee allowed herself to be persuaded to go along fairly easily. After two rounds of very hot sex, she regarded a fingernail she'd broken on his back and said, "What else have I got to do? Give me a day or two to get ready."

She admitted the sad truth about not having anything else to do, though pronounced the fact so casually Clint mistook it for boredom. After Eve snatched Bodey away from her, two other well-researched marriage prospects slipped through her fingers in the last year, each one now engaged to women in their early twenties. Sure, those men had been willing to try to the goods, but neither closed the sale with her.

Renee didn't even have her art classes to distract her anymore, she thought resentfully. Eve Landrum had been her instructor and stopped giving lessons a month before the baby came. Mrs. Bodey Landrum showed no signs of returning to her small studio on the other side of Rainbow. She'd quit her waitress job after marrying the great bull rider, but honored her teaching contract at Mt. Carmel Academy until the Christmas break to allow the school time to find a new riding instructor and art teacher. Early on, most of the older women who had taken painting classes from Eve nodded wisely and said Eve had signed up for the mommy track and would be showing a baby belly any day now. How right they were. That howling kid must have gotten its start on the wedding night. Bodey built an art studio next to the house for Eve's own pleasure, but she wouldn't be instructing others anymore. Some people had all the luck.

What was Renee Hayes supposed to do with no place to paint, and no one to listen to her schemes? How selfish of Eve to abandon her best pupil, especially when she'd taken that lecherous fraud of an artist, Evan Adams, off of Eve's hands for a while, and let the way wide open for Bodey to step in and claim her.

Getting away would be good. Who knew, maybe she would bump into a Texas millionaire at one of those rodeos or a bull rider as rich as Bodey Landrum. In the meantime, she'd have a man with a gorgeous bod and lots of stamina for entertainment despite his country yokel personality. If nothing else worked out, she'd fly home from wherever she wound up once she grew tired of Clint.

Her preparations for the trip were simple. She packed a small suitcase since Clint said he didn't have much room to spare in his trailer and stuffed her most essential items—make-up, condoms, her diaphragm and spermicidal jelly, spare contacts, a touchup kit for her hair color, and a pile of credit cards, most of them near their limit—into an oversized leather satchel. She expected Clint to pick up the tab for anything else in return for her company.

The shock arrived when the Belly Nelle returned to her driveway hauling a trailer that looked like something cartoon characters, mouse, a duck and a parrot, would take on vacation. She knew her mouth hung open but couldn't seem to close it.

Clint spread his arms wide. "My home away from home, princess. Climb aboard."

She did, not sure why, but she did. The interior, a decorator's nightmare, possessed a strange odor that a cheap floral air freshener couldn't hide. She felt the urge to bolt.

"Thanks for packing light, Renee. You can see I don't have much room, but that there bench folds down into a pretty good bed."

"Oh, none of my clothes take up a lot of space, and I have everything I really need in my satchel. You can buy me anything I've forgotten later."

Renee pretended an interest, opening cupboards and the refrigerator. "You certainly like Beck's products. I believe you have every variety of beans they put out, plus the complete line of pickles and their spicy brown mustard."

"Yeah, well, there's a story behind that. See, I do like their foods. One time, just once, I mentioned in front of Snuffy that maybe I might be related to those rich folks somehow, and maybe they'd sponsor some bullfighting competitions. He about busted a gut over that. Calls me the Bean King, now. So do a lot of the guys. I have to put up with a bunch of flatulence jokes, too. It's embarrassin'."

Half a truth was better than none, Clint figured. His mother kept him well-stocked with the family products, which were certainly high quality and very nourishing for a reasonable price. He had asked his father to sponsor a bullfighting competition, but his dad lowered his head and bellowed like one of the bulls Clint fought, "Are you out of your mind!" He hadn't asked again.

"Now, the announcers call me Clinton O. Beck, the Bull Bomber. I like that better."

"So do I." Renee felt a tiny twinge of pity for this nice, unassuming, well-built, sexy guy. "Come on Bomber, let's try out the hide-a-bed."

They rocked The Tin Can on her old springs for an hour, then Clint helped her into a pair of short shorts so tight he'd had trouble getting them off. They got back to the business of moving on.

Renee wanted to say good-bye to her mother, and Clint had to gas up and get some fresh food for the trip, so they towed The Tin Can up the rest of the hill and parked in the circular drive before Tara-on-the-Bayou.

"Want me to come in and meet your mom so she'll feel better about you going off with a stranger?" Clint offered.

"No, thanks. I just want to leave a note with your name and that we are heading off to Casper, then Glendale, Arizona. Where after that?"

"Wherever the road takes us, baby, but we'll be in Cheyenne at the end of July."

If they lasted that long, if she didn't find someone better, Renee thought. She let herself into the phony mansion and looked around for her mother. The maid dusting in the den said Miss Prudence sunned out by the pool—of course.

Renee found good old Mom basking, basted with coconut oil, and out cold. The pitcher of luridly pink cosmopolitans sitting on the table next to her lounger told Renee her mother had fallen off the wagon again. A life of tennis and sunbathing had stained Pru Niles' skin the color of leather and wrinkled her hide to the toughness of an alligator's back. She wore a bikini but possessed the sex appeal of a skeleton. Years of alcohol abuse and bulimia kept her extremely thin. Her short cut of dyed red hair only pointed up her sunken cheeks and bad teeth, slightly exposed like those of a dried out mummy, except Mrs. Niles snored, miraculously not dead yet.

Renee didn't bother to wake her parent, but she slammed the door to the house harder than she intended. She got a notepad and paper in the kitchen and wrote out her itinerary, gave them Clint's name, reminded them she could be reached on her cell if they wanted to get in touch—as if. She stuck the note to the refrigerator door where her father would find it just as Pru Niles staggered in.

"Wadda you want, Renee? I heard that door slam exactly the way you used to do back in your teens. You think by now, you'd let a woman get her beauty rest."

"I want nothing from you, Mom. I'm leaving on a trip. I asked Dad to make sure my gardener is keeping up the yard. My cleaning lady will come once a week to dust and water the plants. I'm off with a new friend of mine. His name is on the note. Don't know when I'll be back." Renee didn't bother to hide her scorn for the woman who gave birth to her. She stared at the emaciated form before her with hard, green eyes.

"Don't know how I raised such a piece of trash. You'd go off with any guy with a big dick and a little money. Must of got running around from your father. He's down the hill doing that Parker bitch right now."

"Sally, my friend, Sally?" Not Sally who had always been the most decent member of her old Academy clique, the Sexy Seven, if you didn't count her cousin Rusty's wife who had never really belonged.

"No, the old bag, my former friend, Sally's mother. Since her husband left with his secretary, she thinks my husband is fair game. But, you know what? Jed promised he'd never, ever leave me, so she's in for a shock. The Niles men keep their word even if they do screw around on the side."

"Dad didn't make me what I am, Prudence. Think about it when you sober up. Meanwhile, I'm outta here—with a guy who's good-looking, brave, and—simple and sweet and almost poor."

"Like the nigger yardman you screwed for a while, the one caused your divorce from Elias? Or was it the personal trainer. I forget since you had another husband since then. You really can't hold on to them, can you, Renee?"

"Gerry died on me!"

"Yeah, right on top of you in bed, naturally. Poor old geezer, you screwed him to death."

Knowing from years of sparring verbally with her mother that she would not win the battle of words because all Prudence said rang with truth, Renee retreated through the house. She slammed the front door harder than she had the back. Climbing into the cab of the Belly Nelle, she slammed the truck door, too. The vibrations sent a cascade of small, stuffed animal toys sliding into her lap from the dashboard. Clint stared as Renee buried her face in her hands.

"Ah, maybe if your mama is real against this, you shouldn't go."

"She doesn't care where I go or with whom. What is with all these stuffed toys? You must have fifty of them shoved in here." Renee began pushing the plush unicorns and blue teddy bears back into the heap on the dash.

"Snuffy—and me—like to give 'em out to little kids at the rodeos. Besides, I'm a devil with the claw machine. Passes the time, you know." Clint sorted through the stack. "Here, looks like you could use a furry friend to cheer you up, too."

He handed her a tiny tiger with green glass eyes. Renee blinked. In high school, boys hopeful of getting in her pants spent all their cash trying to win the huge pink poodle or the enormous stuffed panda at the booths of passing carnivals. In college, they wooed her with bouquets of expensive roses or jewelry full of diamond chips. After graduation, men who sought her favors gave her cars and rings with colored gems, usually emeralds. She had no idea why such a small, cheap toy made her feel as warm and happy as when her father had given her similar items in her childhood. She blinked her eyes a few times to hold back some sentimental tears.

"Now, don't cry. There's plenty more where that came from. Take your pick if you don't like the tiger but it reminds me of you."

"No, I love the tiger. My contacts are bothering me." Renee tucked the little beast deep into her satchel.

Clint swung the truck and trailer out of the

driveway and went down the hill, passing through the brick pillars with the rust-red iron horse heads on top that marked the entry to Red Horse Acres.

"Swanky place," Clint remarked. His family owned an estate so big and venerable you couldn't see any neighboring houses. "Maybe you should see an eye doctor when we get back."

"I don't really need them. They are for effect."

"Effect. You mean you don't really have green eyes? So what color are they?"

"None of your business, Clinton O. Beck. Do you want to tell me what the O in your name stands for?"

"No, ma'am. The only way you will find that out is when the preacher says it on my weddin' day."

"I'll bet Snuffy knows. I could ask him."

"Yep, he knows, all right, but he won't tell because I know his real name. It's a standoff, you see."

Clint parked his battered rig in front of Plato's Liquor and Groceries where he'd attempted to buy a fine wine a few nights ago. At least, the gas wasn't overpriced considering the small size of the town. He got out and swiped a credit card, careful not to use his American Express platinum, at a relatively new pump. The front of the store looked to be a hundred years old with its gray and sagging cypress boards, but its protruding back was a long metal building stuffed with all the needs for a small community. He thought he'd seen some homemade bread in there on his last trip, and he did need to stock up on fresh items.

"Want to come in and shop with me?" he asked Renee.

"It's what I do second best."

She slid down from the truck seat and climbed up

on the old porch. A couple of bentwood chairs sat on either side of an antique cracker barrel with a checker game set on its top. This was Ja'nae Plato's doing, preserving the rustic charm of Rainbow, Louisiana. Her Unc Knobby, who owned the place, wanted to tear down the old entry, Renee knew, and put up a neon sign and some aluminum siding that would never need painting. Not that any of the Platos had painted the store before, but Ja'nae, a force in the community, prevailed. Beyond the front door, the grocery was just another warehouse-like building with florescent lighting and long rows of coolers and canned goods. Renee and Clint went down a small ramp and got a grocery basket to wheel around.

Clint headed for the dairy aisle and loaded a half-gallon of skimmed milk, a jug of orange juice, and two dozen eggs. He recognized the cheese assortment from Renee's refrigerator and tossed in a bag of the chunks, then headed over to produce. Bananas were a must. He filled filmy plastic bags with some other fairly fresh and firm fruit, including a pineapple that could ripen on the way, and picked over the home-grown tomatoes, choosing a few red ripe and half a dozen partly green, to go with the bags of salad he threw in the cart. In the cereal aisle, he selected a box of shredded wheat and Cheerios. For cold cuts, he settled on the 96% fat free ham and smoked turkey. And, what the heck, some lean bacon. Crisp bacon was one of those simple pleasures in life he didn't often allow himself with keeping an eye on his cholesterol.

Renee showed little interest in his choices until they got to the gourmet section, more of Ja'nae's work, near the registers. She tossed a jar of Louisiana caviar into the basket. Clint picked it up, checked the price, and put it back.

"That's big money for some salty fish eggs. Got to watch my budget."

Renee pouted and wandered away to the liquor display. "Want some beer or wine or anything harder?"

"Nope. I rarely drink. May have a beer or two after an event, but that's about all. If I hit the bottle, I'd have a lot more scars than I do."

"Makes sense." Secretly, she was relieved. Drunk men were often abusive men, and how well did she really know Clint Beck? She looked into the basket and saw he had added a jar of locally-made organic strawberry preserves and two loaves of herbed wheat bread baked by the Herbarium tea room down the road.

"That's fancy bread for a cowboy. And those preserves cost almost as much as the caviar."

"Yeah, but this stuff is good for you and tastes better, too."

"So you are a connoisseur of caviar?"

"I been to some fancy affairs. Don't care for it. Let's pay up and get on the road."

Renee seized the cart and swung into line at the register, cutting off two elderly nuns who were getting a treat of their own. Each clutched a chocolate ice cream bar. Clint wrestled the cart away from Renee. "After you, Sisters."

"In fact, just put those ice creams on my tab," Clint told the dark-skinned cashier.

"Why, bless you, son," the nun with watery blue eyes said. "Is this a friend of yours, Renee?"

"Yes, he is, Sr. Helen. He's a rodeo bullfighter, and we're going on the road together. That's his truck and trailer outside." Renee gave the nuns a defiant glare and latched on to Clint's muscular arm.

"Yes, maybe you should hang on to him. He seems to be a kind and generous gentleman," remarked the chunky nun with the chopped off salt-and-pepper hair showing around the edge of her short veil. In a slightly gravelly voice, Sr. Inez added, "We'll pray you have a safe journey."

"Thank you, Sr. Inez. Clint, we need to get going."

"Sure, honey. Nice meeting you, ladies."

The two old nuns hobbled out of the store. They were sitting in the bentwood chairs and licking their ice creams when Renee and Clint finished hauling the groceries into the trailer and took off for Wyoming. Renee flicked a wave at them as the Belly Nelle pulled onto the blacktop road.

"I think we failed that child," Sr. Helen said, watching as the trailer rattled away.

"She was a nice girl, sort of a tomboy, always hanging around the stables when she first came to the Academy. Then, she turned twelve and had no more time for horses. Boy crazy in the worst possible way." Sr. Inez caught a dribble of chocolate ice cream sliding down the stick of her treat with her tongue.

"Well, they all go a little crazy when those hormones kick in, but I felt something might have gone wrong at home. Of course, Mrs. Niles is a drinker, but she seemed to keep it under control when her girls attended school with us. Renee's father spoiled her with expensive gifts, too." Sr. Helen finished her fudge bar and tidily disposed of the stick in a brass spittoon placed on the porch for decoration and sometimes used for its original purpose.

"No, I always felt there was something more. I asked her once if she wanted to talk to me about anything. She said I couldn't help, no one could." Sr. Inez missed a drop of chocolate that splattered onto the front of her short-skirted, plain habit.

"God could help her. We must put her in our prayers, Nessy. Also, that nice young man. I hope Renee doesn't damage him."

Chapter Four

When they got onto the highway, Renee huffed a sigh of relief. "I can't wait to see the last of Rainbow." She glanced in the side view mirror and watched the hamlet disappear behind one of the small hills in the area.

"You know, you shouldn't be rude to nuns or elderly people, Renee. That's what my mama taught me."

"Yeah, well, those two old biddies taught me, not my mother. Sr. Inez could be pretty quick with a ruler in history class if she caught you daydreaming or passing notes. I went to Mt. Carmel Academy from the time I turned six. It's a very exclusive school. My daddy could afford it after he sold his cattle land for development. Bodey's ranch sits on a big part of the Niles parcel, and my cousin Rusty has a little piece, too. At one time, the Niles family owned all the land on the other side of this highway. We fell on hard times after the War Between the States."

"The Becks were already in Texas by then, German immigrants who didn't know nothing about ranching. Some of them fought around here with General Green, a couple of brothers who went home when peace set in and opened a general store." Jeez, he'd almost told her the Beck's Baked Beans story learned at his daddy's knee. "They didn't get rich," he added.

"That old store we were in—Rusty's wife says it has been there in one form or another since Reconstruction. The same with the Rainbow Café across the street. The Platos were freedmen."

"Well, old times don't matter, and good times do. Wyoming, here we come." Clint pumped the Belly Nelle's horn. A loud aaah-oooo-gah sounded turning the heads of a herd of cattle grazing by the wayside and the truckers in the big rigs they passed.

****

Toward evening, they swung into bluesy Memphis. Clint found a campground where they could leave The Tin Can, despite Renee's hints that she'd like to see the ducks at the Peabody Hotel.

"We can see the ducks tomorrow, honey pie, but that will give us a late start. I want to be in Albuquerque for dinner. What say we unhook the Nelle and go into town for some barbecue and blues?"

If that was the best she could get, she would take it. They shared a pile of ribs and a mound of slaw at a place Clint knew called the Rendezvous, down an alley and in a cellar. Great food though. She licked and sucked on those bones as she had once done at the Rainbow Cafe on a prom night date shared with Bodey Landrum.

Clint watched, grinning, and worked a piece of meat out of his teeth with a toothpick. "Keep that up, Tiger, and there will be a bone under the table as well as on top."

"The Peabody is nearby if we want to get a room."

She never gave up, did she? "Gotta watch the budget. Have to say Mama Tyne's wet ribs back in Rainbow are about as good and cheaper. Let's hit some clubs."

They did Beale Street, had beers at B.B. King's Blues Club and the Rum Boogie Café, enjoyed some free street music and acrobatics, wound up at Automatic Slim's Tonga Club where the Renee had two martinis, but Clint cut himself off for the night.

"We got an early mornin', babe, remember?"

Renee put on her pouty look again, but allowed herself be driven back to the trailer. She intended to punish Clint for cutting the night short and the lousy accommodations by turning her back on him in the foldout double bed and pretending to go right to sleep. He simply poked in between her firm thighs and rounded buttocks and rocked against her until Renee figured she wasn't going to get anything out of this unless she turned over.

Clint worked his fingers between her legs and remarked, "You're mighty slick for a sleeping woman."

Hard to resist Clinton O. Beck when she felt full and buzzy. The warm waves he created rose up into her body. Amazing, the skills an ignorant cowboy could acquire on the road—and the stamina. She gave him her special moves in return, sucking him in deeper and working those muscles. She was touched when they finished, and Clint got a bowl of warm water and a bar of the scented soap she'd packed to clean her thighs and lave her pubis. She came again as he washed her, running the terry cloth up and down in her cleft. By the time he'd disposed of the bowl and gotten back into bed, Renee had fallen into a genuine sleep.

Clint couldn't shut his eyes. Guys were supposed to doze off without a care. Yes, he'd used a condom, but he wasn't so sure Renee had done her contraception thing. When she'd worked her muscles, she'd sucked the rubber right off of him. He'd tried to clean up any spillage, and she'd had another orgasm, great for encouraging any stray sperm to come on down. Well, one thing he'd learned in the bullring was not to worry about what might happen and deal with what did happen. Clint rolled over and closed his eyes.

****

Renee woke sniffing the air. The scent of frying bacon overwhelmed the usual tobacco fug of the trailer. She squinted her eyes against the light coming in through the flimsy curtains. Way too close to dawn to suit her usual schedule. Turning the meat in a pan, Clint stood at the small propane stove. Another little skillet held scrambled eggs flecked with green peppers, onions, and mushrooms. On the back burner, a dented metal coffee pot burbled. Clint forked some crispy strips of bacon onto a paper towel.

"Stay where you are, Tiger. I got this all under control. Breakfast in bed coming up."

Renee reached down and plucked up the shirt Clint had worn the night before. It still smelled of barbecue sauce and cigarette smoke from the bars, but she put it on anyhow, leaving the tops of her breasts exposed.

"Aww, you didn't have to dress up for the meal," Clint said as he filled a plate with eggs and bacon and toasted herbal bread just popped from a vintage 1950's toaster. He presented the food along with a scratched and bent fork garnered from a drawer full of eating utensils.

"I never eat breakfast. I'm not usually awake for it."

"Breakfast, the most important meal of the day."

Clint pulled the leopard throw over Renee's bare legs and placed the plate in her lap. "Don't want you to burn yourself. Eat up. We need to get on the road."

The spicy steam from the eggs wafted up from the plate. The bacon beckoned. Renee couldn't remember when she'd last had bacon. Her appetite was enormous this morning for some reason. She raised a crisp, brown strip to her lips and crunched down on it. Salty, greasy heaven. Before she could stop herself, she shoveled down the eggs. Considering how old the gadget on the counter was, it made perfect toast, better than her fancy machine at home.

"Coffee, milk, or juice?" Clint asked. "I usually have all three."

"Just coffee, black. This meal has done enough damage already."

"I like a woman with an appetite, but all we got time for is breakfast." He poured the bacon grease into an empty Beck's Baked Beans can to save for frying eggs and ate his food standing up to avoid temptation.

Clint cleaned up the dishes in the small sink while Renee showered. He could hear her bumping around and cursing in the tiny bathroom and smiled to himself.

They picked up Rt. 40 and made good time on the long, straight highway that put old Rt. 66 out of business. Renee tossed them a salad for lunch at a roadside rest. Clint opened a can of Beck's Hearty Chili with Beans to go with it, but Renee declined a bowl. They would have gotten to Albuquerque before dark if Renee hadn't gotten playful when he stopped for gas and a stretch.

Afterward, she seemed to want a reward, so he took her inside the hideous "trading post" crammed to the ceiling with Indian baskets made in Indonesia and rattlesnake heads encased in plastic paperweights. While he waited in line behind a large family with four kids who couldn't make up their minds about flavors to get his girlfriend a single scoop of low-fat vanilla in a sugar cone and with a chocolate dip, Renee made a beeline for the good jewelry. Ah-ha.

By the time he handed over the cone, she had draped a silver sunburst of a needlepoint Zuni necklace across her shoulders and held up the matching earrings. Each slim setting was filled by a sliver of green stone that came close to matching her unnatural eyes. A bracelet and ring completed the set. The smiling, brown-eyed clerk showing lots of Native American blood in her features stood by the case she had unlocked and waited for the sale like Crazy Horse sneaking up on Custer.

"A set like this is called a parure, a Zuni parure. Don't I look great in it, Clint?"

"Sure do, Tiger." He glanced at the dangling price tags and did a quick estimate in his head. "Get it if you can afford it."

Renee scowled, and the clerk frowned. She cocked her pretty red head and considered. Husband hunting had depleted her resources, and she hated running to Daddy every time she maxed out her cards. Every once in a while, she sold a painting, but erotica seemed to be "out" in Lafayette right now, while Eve's icons and landscapes were "in". Better save what credit she had left on her cards to get home when she got tired of Mr. Cheapskate with the great body.

"Sorry, no deal," she told the clerk. "I'm going to nap in the trailer this afternoon, Clinton O. Beck."

Renee flounced off to sulk in The Tin Can.

"Be with you after I use the restroom, baby," he called after her. "Those beans go right through a man."

The clerk paused as she was about to thrust the jewelry back into the case. "You're Clinton Beck, the Bull Bomber. I saw you perform once. You were fantastic."

"Fantastic enough to get a discount on those earrings? I'd be pleased to autograph the sales slip. But first, is this real Zuni work?"

"Yeah. That's why we keep 'em locked up." She held up the necklace. "Might have cooked the stones a little to bring out the color. I can give you twenty percent off."

"You still get a commission?"

"You bet." The woman smiled broadly. "No more dumb Injuns."

"In that case, I'll take the necklace, bracelet, and the ring, too. Put it in a nice box for me, now." When he and Renee parted as friends, he'd give it to her, but not before.

The tab came close to a thousand dollars, eight-hundred with the discount. While the clerk rang up the sale, Clint gave out autographs to several of the staff members and took his time about it. Once back at the truck, he opened one of the secret compartments from which animals popped when Snuffy performed his clown act and, making sure dirty birds or the miniature donkey hadn't left any souvenirs of their own behind, hid the jewelry case until the right time came along.

Renee sulked until they reached Albuquerque and parked the trailer at a truck stop. She had no way of knowing he should have taken the cutoff toward Las

Vegas, New Mexico, to save time in getting to Casper. Clint hinted he wanted to show her something in this city. He suggested they take the tram up Sandia Peak and dine at the High Finance Restaurant. She mellowed under the influence of a glass of wine and prime roast rib as they watched the lights twinkle in the valley. Renee refused dessert and didn't touch her baked potato. Clint asked for a box and forked the potato and her leftover meat into the Styrofoam tray. Renee appeared to be mortified by his frugality.

"My mama always said, 'Waste not. Want not'."

Lena Beck had spoken those exact words the summer she worked on the *Beck's Barbecue and Grilling Cookbook* and had forbidden her husband to travel. He could just stay home for a change and help her test the recipes. Same went for the boy. The summer Clint Beck turned fifteen was one of the best of his life—the vacation he'd spent with Brandy. His father referred to that time fondly as the Season of Leftovers when the family worked their way through countless dishes intended to serve at least six people. Both the good and the bad concoctions showed up for lunch the next day.

"Tomorrow, you get your choice for lunch—broccoli/cheese baked potato or prime rib sandwich, the best kind of leftovers."

"I'll take the sandwich. You can have the broccoli."

"Deal."

They strolled back to the tram station, the desert air turning chilly high up on the peak. Clint put his arm around Renee and looked up at the stars.

"The lights below, the heavens above, a million

dollar view that can't be bought."

"We don't get skies like this in Louisiana, too much moisture in the air."

"So enjoy this. I'm almost sorry we got to go down into the valley again."

"I'll make the decision to go down worth it for you."

She did. As full and lazy with meat as a lioness, Renee made love soft and easy with Clinton O. Beck into the night. In the morning, they took Rt. 25 and stayed on it straight into Casper, Wyoming.

Chapter Five

After a long and rugged drive north, Clint slotted the Belly Nelle and Tin Can into a trailer space at the fairgrounds arena where Snuffy's Special Rodeo would be held in the morning. Casper, Wyoming, resting in an elbow of the wide and stony North Platte River, was surrounded by bluffs and lorded over by a 3,000-foot peak. The historic part of town still maintained the feel of the Old West.

"This place is smaller than Lafayette, Louisiana," Renee said. "At least they have some buildings over two stories. I wonder what people do for fun around here."

"Well, there's the Mormon Handcart Museum and lots of outdoor activities."

Renee wrinkled her nose.

"We'll have fun in the morning, darlin'," Clint told her.

Renee sighed and trotted off to use facilities that were less claustrophobic than the bathroom in The Tin Can. She barely passed out of sight when Snuffy appeared, patted the hood of the Nelle affectionately. "How's she doing?"

"Fairly well. I got her to eat breakfast and leftovers, admire the night sky, and take a pass on some expensive jewelry she didn't need."

"I meant Nelle. How'd she do in the high

elevations?" Snuffy rubbed an imaginary spot off the old truck's already distressed finish.

"We got here, didn't we?"

"You taking good care of her and The Tin Can?"

"Both are cleaner than they have been in years. Why?"

"Well, I want to use her tomorrer. Some of the retired clowns and me are going to do the old animal act for the kids." The barrelman scratched his unshaven jaw, puckered up and let loose with a squirt of tobacco politely aimed away from Clint.

"Oh, man, I have my laptop and some jewelry hidden in those compartments. Put my stuff in the motorhome before you stash any rabbits or chickens, okay?"

"You afraid your lady friend will steal your stuff?"

"No, not exactly. I just don't want droppings all over the place."

"Okay, will do. Ma'am," Snuffy said as Renee walked up and slid an arm around Clint's waist.

Renee took a good look at the short, skinny man with the hangdog face and a week's worth of chin whiskers. "Have we met?"

"Sure have. You remember." Snuffy patted his heart with his hands and mimed handing Renee a flower.

"Oh yes, the clown who performed at Bodey's school. I didn't recognize you without your face on. I'm Renee. Where are you staying?"

"Over there in that nice, big motorcoach. You should see the size of the shower. I'm leading a life of luxury, but I plan on spending a little time out on my ranch after the show tomorrer."

"We'll be pushing off for Glendale in the morning," Clint said.

"Well, I'll let y'all get settled in. We start early. Registration begins at eight. We'll start with the pony rides. Then, we have the mock-steer roping. The clown act right after the break. We'll end up with the stick horse barrel racing, followed by the real thing. After that, Clint, you're on for the bullfighting demonstration. We end up with the awards ceremony. There'll be more hot dogs and hamburgers than anyone can polish off around lunchtime, so you don't have to go looking for food."

Taking in the wedge sandals, short shorts, and the bulge of her breasts pushing out of a silky yellow slip top, Snuffy stared Renee up and down. He wrinkled his brow as if wondering what possible use she could be outside of a bedroom, then snapped his fingers. "I'll put you down to be a hugger. Sleep tight now." The clown chortled as he walked away.

"Clint, what's a hugger?"

"You know, you give out hugs after the kids finish their races. Hugs, like this." He opened his arms wide, and Renee stepped into them. Clint drew her tight against him and gave her a squeeze. She nestled her head against her chest and sighed.

"Hey, that's a snuggle, not a hug. You got to let go after a hug, or you'll give some of these boys the wrong idea. Now, if you want to snuggle, we got a bed in the trailer."

"What if all I want to do is snuggle?"

"Then, that's all we'll do."

"Really? Tonight, I might want to do something more, but I may take you up on that offer another time."

Renee swayed away from Clint drawing him after her like the Belly Nelle towing The Tin Can.

****

Come morning, Clint fried eggs using some of the bacon grease. Renee wrinkled her nose and accepted only slices of wheat toast slathered with the organic strawberry preserves and the coffee he perked in the old pot. As Clint, eating right out of the pan, mopped up the broken yolks with his bread, Renee twisted a finger in her long red hair and questioned him.

"How come we're living like this and Snuffy has that gorgeous motorcoach and a ranch?"

"Oh, Snuff's been on the circuit a long time. He's been careful with his money and saved up. I told you I'm putting away for a doublewide, so The Tin Can will have to do for now."

"I see." She sighed, not the kind of sigh she'd given him last night. "So, what does a hugger wear for this event?"

"Oh, they'll give you a T-shirt. I'd wear jeans and athletic shoes if you don't have boots. There's bound to be horse manure and cow plop down in the arena area where you have to stand."

"Great. So, all these kids are—ah—retarded."

"I think the term used now is special needs children."

"We didn't have special needs children at Mt. Carmel. I'm not sure I can do this. The idea kind of sickens me, and I'm not good with children anyhow." Renee wrinkled her nose even though she knew it emphasized other tiny lines in her face.

"Renee, they are only kids who want to have some fun and get a hug at the end of their event. Tell them how good they did and don't sweat it. We got to hustle before they run out of T-shirts in your size. Not many of those. Come on now."

Renee came, dressed as Clint recommended and still feeling squeamish. She shrugged into an XXL yellow cotton shirt proclaiming *Snuffy's Special Rodeo* in bright red letters and pulled it over the tight turquoise tank tucked into her snug black jeans. She checked her outfit in the window of the snack bar. The hump of the bucking bull on the shirt sat roundly on the end of one of her breasts and looked extra-extra large as well. It wasn't haute couture. Maybe the hat would help. She settled the straw cowboy hat with the little feathers in the band that Clint had given her on her head. Good, no one she knew would recognize her—if they happened to be in Casper, Wyoming at the end of June, unthinkable for most of her crowd except maybe Bodey Landrum.

She turned to find Clint had disappeared into a crowd of children who remembered him from past appearances. A big woman with a clipboard shouted, "Huggers over here!" That's where she went.

The ring cleared of volunteers who had been giving pony rides. Stepping carefully, Renee took her assigned place and waited patiently while one child after another tried to rope a mounted steer's head. Each awkward contestant seemed to get an infinite number of chances to succeed, and when they did, they came running for their hug. Some whooped, some lumbered, some jerked with uncontrollable spasms in her arms. She tried not to flinch and received hugs as well as gave them. An announcement called for a lunch break, and suddenly she was caught up in a dusty stampede of children heading for food.

Renee climbed up into the bleachers to search for Clint and didn't see him anywhere. She leaned against a railing and remarked to a fiftyish woman with broad streaks of gray in her short, dark hair and an approachable, friendly face who sat nearby, "I don't know how the parents of these kids do it. Must be hard."

"You do the same as with any other kid. Love and protect them, teach them what they need in life to be decent human beings. Try to keep them safe. That's my daughter, Gracie. You hugged her after she got her lariat around the bull's horns on her fourth try. It's not her best event."

Renee saw a thick-bodied girl with the slanted eyes and heavy neck of a Down's Syndrome child coming their way. Probably somewhere in her teens but hard to tell from her childish features, she carried four hot dogs squashed together in her hands.

"I'm sorry," Renee said.

"Don't be. What you see there is love on the hoof."

The girl arrived and held out her offerings. "I got one with ketchup and one with mustard and two plain. I like mine plain," she said decisively. "The mustard one is for my mom, but you can have this one." Focusing on Renee, Gracie held out her offering of food. "You gave me a hug. I am Grace Ann Jones." Gracie poked a finger at the paper nametag stuck to Renee's impressive chest. "You are Miss Reney. You have pretty hair and really big boobs."

"Gracie, we don't say such things to strangers!" her embarrassed mother exclaimed. "Not to friends either."

"I'm supposed to tell the truth always." Gracie

stuck out her lower lip in a hurt pout.

"Thank you, I consider what you said a compliment, Gracie. My name is pronounced Renee. I'm not very hungry right now. You can have the extra one." Renee passed on the crumbled bun and the hot dog dripping ketchup.

"Okay. They're real good."

"What did I tell you, Gracie?" her mother prompted.

"I can only have two." Gracie thrust the oozing wiener back at Renee who accepted it with reluctance. "I got a boyfriend. His name is Tony. Do you have a boyfriend?"

"I guess I do." She saw Clint cutting across the ring in her direction. "There he is."

"I know Clint. Clint is Dad's friend. He's pretty like you."

"And strong and brave and kind." Renee amazed herself by stating her feelings out loud. Usually, she kept her emotions locked down tight. Life was largely a business deal that had to be played with cunning. Never let the other guy know what truly went through your mind, but the closer Clint got, the better he looked. Yes, he was pretty and all those other things, too. Renee sucked on her hot dog and took a bite. Ketchup dribbled down the front of her T-shirt, making her look like she bled from the heart.

He climbed up into the stands and sat next to Renee. "I see you've met Gracie and Ruth Ann. Ruth Ann and Snuffy were married once upon a time."

"Might as well still be," Ruth Ann confessed. "He wouldn't quit the road. I wanted special schools and such for Gracie, and I sure didn't want my son to follow in his footsteps, so I divorced the man. And what does he go and do? Gives me the deed to the ranch outside of Casper. Every time that man swings by, I open my door and say, 'come on in'. I guess we're common law again by now. Didn't stop my boy from putting on makeup and going on the circuit, either."

Gracie finished wolfing down her two dogs. "I'm thirsty."

"Come on, Gracie, let's get something to drink," Clint said, ruffling the girl's clipped dark hair. They walked off arm in arm.

"We had her tubes tied a couple of months ago. Both Tom and I thought it was for the best. She does have a boyfriend, and you know, sex just feels good, so they're bound to try it. I talked to Tony's parents. If the kids still feel the same in a few years, we'll put up a little place for them on the ranch. Gracie knows how to clean, and she can heat up things in the microwave. I try to keep her away from the stove. Tom and I won't live forever. It's best they have someone and a place to be."

"Tom?"

"Tom 'Snuffy' Jones, my one and only."

"Like the old, sexy disco star way back when?"

"He always hated the comparison, but you just can't call your husband Snuffy now, can you?"

"Would you know Clint's middle name?"

"Can't say as I do. Anything starting with an O has got to be bad."

"Oliver, Ozzie, Otto, Olaf?" Renee guessed.

"Could be Obediah, Oscar, or Opie for all I know," said Ruth Ann. "Whatever. If you're looking to marry, you could do worse than Clint Beck."

"But could I marry a man with the middle name of Omar?" Renee joked. What Ruth Ann didn't know was that Clinton O. Beck couldn't afford to keep a woman like Renee Hayes—in more ways than one—and there was no need to tell her.

The two women were still laughing when Clint and Gracie returned bearing sweating cans of soft drinks. Clint tossed a Diet Coke to Renee and popped the top on a Mountain Dew. Gracie gave her mom a root beer and opened an orange drink for herself. The four sat in the bleachers sipping their drinks with Gracie carrying on most of the conversation.

"This afternoon, I get to ride in the real barrel races, not the pretend ones they got for the little kids. My horse is named Pete."

"What kind of horse is Pete?" Renee asked, doing her part.

"Brown," said Gracie. "But my favorite kind of horse is a unicorn. They got big, golden horns. I've seen pictures of them."

"Really? Clint, could I have the keys to the truck for a minute?"

"Snuffy has them. He's using the Nelle for his act. Supposed to start in a few minutes."

"What did you do with the stuff on the dashboard?"

"Put it all in a plastic sack in the trailer. Why?"

"I want to get something. Be back in a minute. Save my seat, Gracie."

Renee went back to The Tin Can, found the sack of stuffed toys and rooted through it until she found the blue unicorn with the white yarn mane. She trotted back to where Gracie sat and held out the fuzzy animal like a grand prize.

"For me? I can add him to my herd. I know he's a boy because he's blue. I'll call him Clint." Gracie hugged the stuffed unicorn.

"Oh, you already have some."

"Gracious, her room is full of them. Tom brings them home all the time." Seeing the disappointment on Renee's face, Ruth Ann added, "But each one is special. She'll remember the lady with the red hair gave it to her."

"Miss Renee gave him to me," Gracie corrected. "She's a nice lady."

Suddenly it occurred to Renee Niles Bouchard Hayes that for a whole half a day, she'd been a nice lady—not a slutty gold digger, as Gerry's family had called her, or Dr. Bouchard's cheating trophy wife. Not a soul in Casper knew her bad reputation, and that felt good. She could be anything she wanted to be, and today, she was a nice lady.

An old truck, the Belly Nelle herself, careened into the arena, her bed loaded to bursting with retired rodeo clowns in full paint and regalia. The announcer called out for the truck to get out of the ring because the barrel racing was about to begin, but unfortunately, the old heap had broken down in the dead center of the oval. Clowns tumbled out, kicking tires, looking at the undercarriage. Snuffy Jones, the driver, got down and opened the hood. Black smoke billowed.

Renee gasped. Their ride to Arizona looked in pretty bad shape. Clint leaned over. "Don't worry, just a little oil sprayed on the engine block. She'll be fine in the morning."

Snuffy announced grandly, "I've found the problem. There's a hair in the engine." He held up a black rabbit that Renee was fairly sure had been pulled out of his baggy pants—an old joke, but the kids laughed.

Snuffy tried to crank the engine again. No luck. A duck seemed to drop from a wheel well. A chicken flew out the window. Smoke pumped from the exhaust pipe and engulfed the truck. The tailgate dropped and inside the truck bed appeared a miniature donkey. That one had Renee stumped.

All the clowns took turns trying to remove the stubborn donkey. Finally, when Snuffy got down on his hands and knees and said, "Pretty, pretty, please", the animal got up and jumped from the back of the truck—which still wouldn't start. At last, the clowns tied the truck's front bumper to the little donkey, put the Belly Nelle into low gear, and pushed the vehicle from the ring with all of them forming a long conga line at its rear.

The children cheered and clapped. Gracie said, "That's my dad," over and over.

Renee sat comfortably in the stands with her thigh pressed against Clint's muscular leg. When the huggers were summoned for the stick-horse barrel races, she went without hesitation, took her place, and gave out embraces returned twofold.

Clint stayed long enough to watch Gracie ride a real horse around the barrels in the cloverleaf pattern. The pace wasn't as swift or the corners as sharp as regular rodeo, but she made good time and held on to the lead throughout the competition. Renee cheered, jumping up and down, only mildly aware of the men who watched her breasts bob. She gave Gracie the biggest hug of all.

Clint went off to gear up for his bullfighting demonstration. Someone had hauled an old red-skinned, white-faced beef breeder of a bull to the event, and Clint's biggest problem seemed to be getting the animal to do anything at all. He jumped it frontwards and sideways and finally backwards, ending up in the animal's face, startling the beast enough to make it snort and paw. Clint darted away, waving the red handkerchief, and the arthritic bull lumbered after him, then paused to bunch up and drop a heap of steaming turds on the ground. The children giggled.

Clint shrugged and pretended to turn his back on the pathetic hamburger stud. The animal took the hint and charged. Clint heard him coming, dodged, and escaped easily to the safety of the rails. The crowd roared. He noticed Renee put her hand over her heart, flutter her fingers, and smile down on him.

The awards were given out with Gracie getting her first place in barrel racing. Gradually, the crowd dispersed. Loaded pickup trucks and horse trailers moved out in clouds of dust. When the dust settled, those that remained, mostly the old clowns, started a small blaze in a metal fire pit near The Tin Can and sat around eating leftover barbecued hamburgers and telling tales of their glory days in and out of the ring— their famous acts and the time one of them rode a goat through a department store when he'd had one too many. They passed a brown bottle. The stories grew more outrageous and further from the truth each time it made a round.

Renee listened as the stars came out in the pure black of the night sky. She and Clint sat in two bent aluminum chairs taken from the trailer and set up nearby under the striped awning with a gaping hole in the center that pulled out from the side of The Tin Can. They passed a single beer back and forth. As the group broke up to return to motorhomes or nearby motels, all of them better accommodations than The Tin Can, most of the clowns paused to say a goodnight to Clint.

One clown ogled Renee. "Little lady, if this guy disappoints, you can count on me. I may not satisfy, but I'll always leave you laughing."

"Yeah, in my day, we didn't suit up in all that body armor he's got. You want a real man, give me a call," an elderly, bald trouper said, flexing a flabby muscle—or trying to. "Don't know how you got Snuffy to let you have the Belly Nelle, but you be good to her. She's a great old gal." He made his exit into the dark.

"Clint, you said the Nelle was a gift from your dad when you were just a pup."

"I lied." At least, he could tell the truth about that. "I totaled my rig swervin' to avoid a pronghorn, and Snuffy loaned her to me. The trailer, too. Didn't want you to think I'm a bad driver, or you might not have come along." And added another lie.

"Just don't do it again. I've been lied to by enough men in my life. For that, you only get a cuddle tonight. Besides, those children really wore me out."

"Yeah, kids can do that. A cuddle it is."

"You aren't going to try to talk me into anything else?"

"Nope. Let's go to bed. And sleep."

The idea was so novel to Renee when in bed with a man, she couldn't seem to close her eyes, even when she had one leg thrown over Clint's warm thigh and her head nestled against his chest. She listened to the steady thump of his heart and thought back over the day. She'd never given or received so many hugs.

"I'm not a person who hugs," she announced to a half-asleep Clint.

"Well, you were today. Good job."

"I think one of the boys groped me."

"I'd grope you, too, if you were hugging me."

"You are, sort of."

Clint reached a hand down and squeezed her behind. "Grope, grope."

"Stop that. I mean hugging and cuddling is not something I do normally. I don't like to be touched unless I'm in control of the situation. When I have sex, I can control men. That's what my analyst said."

"Okay," Clint answered, afraid to go forward. "Guess you weren't hugged enough as a child."

"I was, way too much. Later after I went to Paris with my Uncle Dewey, I didn't want to be touched anymore."

Clint didn't want to ask, but he had to. "He abused you?"

"He didn't make it seem that way. He said in France, an uncle was supposed to train a niece in the ways of the world. He meant sex. He bought me sophisticated clothes, changed my hairstyle, made me a woman, he said."

"How old were you?"

"Twelve."

"Jesus H. Christ! Why didn't you tell your parents?" Wide awake now, Clint held the woman in his arms a little tighter.

"He said he'd tell my father everything. That I'd given him blow jobs and all the positions we used. I loved my dad. I couldn't face his knowing. I think my mom knew. I think he might have abused her, too, when she was a teenager, but she never said anything or tried to stop him. Today, Ruth Ann said parents are supposed to protect their children. Some don't."

Clint felt the dampness on his chest, his sweat or her tears, he couldn't be sure because her story gave him the chills. Her eyelashes fluttered against his skin like a butterfly caught in a net, but she did not cry aloud. "How long did this go on, sweetheart?"

"Until I turned eighteen and moved away to college. He was married, had a daughter younger than me. His wife left him when my cousin turned twelve—and I think I know why—so he came over more often, on all the holidays. He tried to take my younger sister to Paris, too, but I insisted he take me instead. That's the one thing I've done right in my whole life, Clint. I saved Cathy from Uncle Dewey."

"There must have been other good things."

"No. Mostly I've made trouble for men, used them for what Uncle Dewey did to me. Ask Bodey or my cousin, Rusty."

"They know about Uncle Dewey?"

"No. Just that I'm bad, bad to the bone."

"I don't think that, Tiger."

"Well, you're wrong. Wait and see."

Renee turned over, pushed his arm away when he tried to cuddle her again, and bunched her knees up under her chest. She stayed frozen in that position until certain Clint had drifted off and disturbed, he took a long time to doze. He left a little space between them because Renee insisted on it. When she heard his breathing fall into a strong, steady rhythm, she reached down to where her leather satchel leaned against the bed and took out the toy tiger. Tucking it under her pillow like a talisman to ward off evil, she finally rested.

Chapter Six

As if to prove her words, Renee turned sullen and demanding over the next few days. Her attitude made the long drive to southern Arizona through the high country—with its ponderosa pines, down to the lower elevations of the pinon forests, around impressive red rock formations, and across the cactus-studded desert— seem even farther.

She complained about his using the bacon grease in the eggs and would accept only toast, left half her food on her plate if they ate in a restaurant, and told the waitress she didn't want a box. Rough and without tenderness, sex happened every night because Renee claimed she wanted it exactly that way. The aggressor, the initiator, she took him to the floor and clawed his chest bloody. Like being in the bullring without any defensive armor, he dodged and feinted until he dominated, and she purred under him like a great cat when he rammed himself inside her body. They both gained satisfaction big time. The trouble being, Clint thought, he had set out to tame her, and now he wanted to help her. She didn't want or need his help or his pity and seemed intent on proving that. He'd only made Renee Hayes worse, not better.

They arrived in Glendale, right outside of Phoenix, for a Professional Bull Rider's event called the Cheeseburger IslandStyle Restaurants Invitational held at the Jobing.com Arena. The big, comfortable venue kept the searing, dry heat of an Arizona summer outside and gave the riders the best of accommodations within, along with some top prize money.

"Cheeseburgers," sneered Renee. "I guess that's what happens to these bulls when they are all used up."

"Hardly, babe," Clint said refusing to snap back. "This is top rough stock. When they finish their bucking career, most of them will go on to be studs making more tough bulls for the rodeo."

"And what about bull bait like you? What happens when you can't outrun the bulls anymore?"

"Some of us raise cattle, some breed rough stock, some go back to the family business. We get by."

"But you don't get rich like the riders do."

"Not generally. And speaking about being bull bait, I'd appreciate if you wouldn't come on to my friends." He'd introduced her to the other bullfighters and some of the riders. She'd flirted with them all, and a few had flirted back. Most gave her a wide berth. She was Clint Beck's girl, and she had the potential to be more trouble than the next bull they had to take on.

Renee seemed to want to drive him off, as if she couldn't stand his knowing about what had happened to her as a girl. While he rested up for the night's event, she'd taken all the money from his wallet, gone into Phoenix, and had a shopping spree—evidently maxing out all her credit cards after his cash ran out. He woke to a trailer filled with bags of designer clothes and shoes.

Renee held up a chic black dress that would cling to every curve. "Do you like it? I thought it was time you bought me something for the pleasure of my company."

"We're not going anywhere you can use that."

She opened a large oblong box. "You told me I needed boots." They were black, heavily tooled with hearts and roses outlined in white stitching, and probably cost more than all the money she had taken.

"I know I didn't have enough in my wallet for much more than cab fare downtown and maybe one of those dresses, Renee. How did you pay for all this?"

"With my credit cards, which are at their limit. The other fellows said this gig pays really well. If you would give me two thousand dollars, I could go to the bank downtown, deposit a check, and then pay my bills on-line at the public library." She gave him a pretty, baby doll pout with her full red lips.

He wasn't buying it. Clint Beck knew how to tame a tiger or any other animal for that matter. Make them depend on you for their food, shelter, and affection. Lay down the rules and stick to them. Reward good behavior with praise and attention and the occasional treat. He'd start right now.

"Renee, I've enjoyed your company, but some things you got to know. Don't take without asking. Don't expect me to pay for stuff you don't really need. And don't flirt with other men in front of me. If you can't live with that, I suggest you return all this crap tomorrow and use your money to fly home because we won't be near any airports for a long time after this if you stay. Your choice. Now, I've got to get over to the arena and tape up, then warm my muscles on the exercise bike. I hope you're still here when I get back tonight." Clint picked up the duffel containing his knee and shin pads, his chest protector and running shoes, and walked out to fight the bulls, leaving the untamed tiger alone.

****

Clint couldn't worry about his love life when in the bullring. He stood near the gates, waiting for the bull and rider to explode from the chute. This was a high caliber event with some of the rankest bulls known on the circuit. A man could earn a ninety point score on their backs or wind up in the hospital. Earlier, one of the worst animals had gored Steve Darden in the arm before the bullfighters could drive off the big, black beast with the unclipped horns by using swats of their hats and catcalls. Without their intervention, the injury would have been worse, much worse. Steve walked out of the arena under his own power.

During a break, Clint went to chug down a sports drink. He caught sight of Renee positioned low in the stands. Hard to miss with those long waves of blazing red hair, she sat with her feet propped up on a railing. He couldn't help but notice her shiny black boots, topped by brand new boot cut jeans and a stretchy emerald green, rhinestoned top that showed a lot of cleavage and fit like a coat of lacquer on her skin. Wouldn't surprise him at all if Renee carried body glue in that big satchel to keep herself from falling out of some of her outfits. She talked to—no, make that flirted with—the guy next to her, judging by how she rubbed up against him, breaking every rule Clint had set for her earlier in the day. Maybe, she solicited a ride to the airport. He couldn't dare to care right now.

Pedro Sanchez, dark-eyed and full of Hispanic machismo, was slated to go first in the next round of bull riding. He came up along side of the bullfighter and leaned against the same section of fencing. Without turning his broad, handsome face toward Clint, he said, "I drew Cyclonic."

"He's well-named. He'll spin into your hand and won't stop even when you're off his back. If you get a choice, watch which side you land on."

"I wanted to say, I wasn't messing with your girl, yesterday. She comes on strong like Cyclonic." Pedro shifted his dark eyes from the empty bullring to Clint's face.

"I know Renee. Don't worry about it."

"My life is in your hands, man."

"I'll do my job."

Pedro went to get his bull rope. Clint finished his drink and pitched the plastic bottle into a trashcan. Renee had left her seat, but at least the man she'd been seducing still sat there alone. He had to put the woman out of his mind as the next round of riding began. He went to join two other bullfighters by the gates.

Cyclonic stood already wedged into the narrow chute. Pedro balanced up on the side boards getting his bull rope around the uncooperative animal with the help of the wranglers. The rider dropped down on the beast and pounded his gloved hand into the grip. He shouted, "Go," and the gate swung open on long ropes. His sickening, circular ride ended at the six-second mark when he flew off the right side of the bull directly into the vortex of the spin. One big cloven hoof punched down squarely on Pedro's knee. Cyclonic lowered his head to savage the rider with a blunted horn, but the bullfighters arrived in time.

Clint scooped up a handful of dirt and dashed it into the bull's eye. The other bullfighters got between the animal and the downed rider, driving the beast away with swats of their hats. Clint shouted at Cyclonic, waved his arms, and took off across the wide arena. The bull bore down on him like a locomotive on a pickup truck stalled at an unguarded crossing. Clint reached the boards a second before the bull and was scrambling over the top to safety when Cyclonic gave him a butt in the rear that completed the job. He landed in a heap on the other side of the barrier but jumped up immediately and raised his hands to show the gasping audience he'd survived just fine. He fired a wide grin at the TV camera zooming in on him. That thousand-watt smile flashed on all the upper level screens.

"Let's give Clinton O. Beck, the Bull Bomber, a great big hand," the announcer cried out. The crowd cheered wildly.

An outrider got a rope on Cyclonic and held him steady as the medics helped Pedro to his feet and partially carried the limping bull rider to the Mobile Sports Medicine Center. The announcer assured the crowd they would be given updates on the rider's condition.

Clint took only a second to look for Renee. She'd returned to her seat and stood on her feet, not cheering, one hand held across her heart. She appeared to have spilled half a cold drink down her front. Didn't hurt her appearance one bit and might have enhanced it, the way her nipples poked out. The dude she'd been seducing certainly appreciated his close up view. He began patting down her front with a wad of paper napkins and doing a very thorough job of it. Jealousy rose up in Clint like a high bucking haunch. Regardless, the next bull entered the chute, and the Bull Bomber had to go back to work.

The rest of the event went off without a hitch, only a quarter of the riders hanging on for their eight seconds of agony. Pedro Sanchez had been transported to a hospital the announcer informed one and all. No word yet if his knee injury meant the end to a promising season. Clint kept on moving, simply doing his job, but he sank into one of the Jacuzzi baths provided by the medical center before he went back to the trailer. His gluteus maximus was one big bruise despite the padding he'd worn.

A light shone through the thin curtains of The Tin Can. He wondered if Renee waited or if she had been careless as usual and forgotten to turn off the lamp. Probably on her way to the airport by now. Experiencing a twinge of pain in his backside, Clint made his way up the little pull-down step, opened the door, and tossed his bag of bullfighting gear into a corner. There, Renee Niles Bouchard Hayes sat, cross-legged on the foldout bed in all her naked glory with the fake tiger throw covering only her most private part.

"I thought you'd be gone by now with that guy you were rubbing up against at the rodeo. What, he wouldn't part with enough money for your plane fare?"

She ignored his surly remark and glanced over from reading the rodeo program. "It says here, you went to the University of Texas."

"I did—on a gymnastics scholarship. Missed getting on the U.S. Olympic Team by a tenth of a point. My dad was very disappointed in me, all that expensive coaching and driving around to all those meets for nothing. After that, I drifted a while."

All true. He'd gone to Harvard to get that MBA in

order to please Gunter Beck, substituting his dream for his father's version of the future. The summer after he'd gotten his degree he'd thrown over the traces and taken up bullfighting.

"Sometimes, you don't sound so cowboy—like now, like last night."

"Depends on who I'm with. I won't use an education to talk down to a nineteen-year-old bull rider. People are more comfortable with the cowboy persona."

"A persona, is it?"

"Yes, and if you don't like it, you can get on outta here. I still earn only $150,000 a year fighting bulls." Not counting interest from his trust fund and stock dividends, his prize money, some small endorsements, and gigs at bullfighting clinics. Clint raked a hand through his short, dark blond hair. He had no energy left to deal with Renee's moods tonight. If she didn't want his help, she could go, just go, and leave him to cope with his own pain. When he'd seen her all tricked out in those new clothes, flirting with another man in the stands tonight, he knew he'd never tame her, teach her the right way to behave. Bodey had pegged her as a man-eater, and she'd sure taken a chunk of out him tonight.

"Clint, I saw how you saved that rider's life. You aren't paid nearly enough. I'll take the clothes back tomorrow, all except the outfit I wore. I squeezed my soda cup when the bull hit you and sort of ruined any chance for an exchange. You must be sore. Come over here and drop those pants." Renee patted the mattress.

"Look, I'm a little tired and a lot bruised."

Still, he took off his shirt and dropped his pants.

Renee usually enjoyed the revelation of his tight, shapely buttocks, but tonight a "Eeuwww" escaped her.

"I had an eggplant in my refrigerator go bad one time. You're that same color behind."

"I didn't need to know. I don't want to be on the top or the bottom tonight, okay?"

"How about sideways? I'll do all the work. You just enjoy."

"Well, sex does ease the pain—or at least takes my mind off of it." Enjoying her one last time wasn't really giving in, right?

"Then let me take care of you."

Clint eased himself down on his side. Renee slid a slim hand deep between his legs and stroked. She cupped and massaged his balls, working her way upward until he sprang erect between her fingers. She rolled a condom down, stroking as she went, placed one leg over his thigh, and eased herself on top of his penis. Working those marvelous internal muscles of hers, Renee milked him dry. Once she finished him off and withdrew, Clint moaned and rolled over on his front.

"I guess you didn't get much out of that," he said. He also guessed she'd be gone in the morning now that his thrusters were out of order. He almost wished for Renee to disappear so he could end the struggle and get on with his life.

"I got all that I wanted," she answered. "Go to sleep, Clint."

Chapter Seven

Sr. Inez got up from her place before the shrine to the Virgin with the use of her blackthorn walking stick. She helped Sr. Helen arise and handed her a brightly painted cane. They stretched, limped down the aisle of the nuns' chapel at Mt. Carmel Academy, and exited into the thick, hot summer air.

"I saw Prudence Niles at Rainbow Liquor and Groceries today. She was stocking up on booze for the week. Doesn't even try to hide it anymore." Sr. Inez shook her head sadly. "She said she had a postcard from Renee. She and her cowboy went to Casper, Wyoming, to help with a rodeo for special kids."

"That doesn't sound like Renee. I was under the impression she only went to charitable affairs to meet rich men. Do you think our prayers for her are working?" Sr. Helen asked.

"I'm positive, but I believe we need reinforcements. The BVM cannot handle this alone. Tomorrow after dinner, we should go into the pine woods and pray to St. Mary Magdalene at her statue."

"Ah, Nessy, I don't think I can make it down that long and winding path anymore. With all the praying we've been doing in the chapel, even in the air-conditioning, my knees are killing me. I'm happy to offer up my pain to God, but if I collapse halfway there, you won't be able to carry me back to the convent."

"I'll ask the Mother Superior to borrow the golf cart. She does approve of what we are trying to accomplish—the redemption of Renee Niles Bouchard Hayes."

"Very well, then," said Sr. Helen, her blue eyes twinkling, her white head nodding. "You bring a candle. I'll cut some flowers for an offering. And BYOB—bring your own bug spray."

They carried out their plans after the seven p.m. prayers and went into the woods smelling of candle wax, incense, and DEET. Sr. Nessy drove the golf cart, a gift from the father of one of their Academy girls who had given up the dubious pleasure of the sport. Her recklessness behind the wheel caused Sr. Helen to squeak each time they rounded a curve. Petals from the bouquet of white crepe myrtles she held scattered in the artificial breeze the turn created.

"The intention of the winding path is to promote the contemplation of one's sins, not serve as a Formula One race course," she reminded her fellow nun tartly.

"I'd like to get there before the mosquitoes come out if you don't mind. Good thing it stays light until almost nine this time of year, but under the pines the bloodsuckers rise earlier."

Sr. Helen clamped her mouth shut and held on. God saw them safely to their destination at the rather lascivious statue of Mary Magdalene who reclined upon a couch, her long hair undone, her feet bare, her body lush and curvaceous. If the Blessed Mother Leontine hadn't declared it a work of art and a true tribute to the Magdalene, surely some priest would have had it hauled away a century and more ago. She got down from the golf cart rather unsteadily and laid her tribute of flowers by St. Mary's feet.

"Not much in bloom in the summer heat. Sorry we have nothing better to offer. The marigolds are meant for the Virgin, you know." Whether Sr. Helen's apology was intended for her companion or the saint was hard to say.

"The little spray of red roses is a nice touch though," Sr. Nessy assured her.

"Yes, a tough variety of climber, it tries to bloom even when the temperatures hit ninety. The old roses Mother Leontine planted long ago do fare better than the modern hybrids, but this is all the bush had to offer right now. We'd better get started."

Sr. Nessy set the squat pale yellow candle by the flowers and lit it with a cheap cigarette lighter she quickly stowed away deep in her habit again. She'd given up smoking long, long ago, but even possessing a lighter for a short time brought back the old urge to light up again. The scent of mosquito-repelling citronella filled the air.

"Practical and pleasant," she remarked. Getting to her knees rather gingerly in the soft pine needles, she closed her eyes and folded her hands. Her strong voice filled the glade and scared off a plump raccoon just about to start its nightly marauding of the convent's garbage cans.

"St. Mary, hear our prayer. We beseech you, who stayed by the grieving Virgin and went with her to into the garden to see the miracle of the risen Christ, to lend your strength to hers in bringing about another miracle. One of our Academy girls needs your help most grievously. She is called Renee Niles Bouchard Hayes. As you can tell from her excess of names, she has married often, but not in true love and happiness. Please show her the right path to travel in order to gain these most invaluable blessings."

Sr. Helen continued in words so soft they did not so much as startle the flock of sparrows that had hidden in the bushes when Nessy began her plea. "Give the man she travels with strength and everlasting patience. I believe he is a good man, full of the type of kindness Renee has never known. He paid for our ice creams."

"She doesn't need to know that!" Sr. Nessy interjected with her usual force. The tiny birds took flight.

"It's an example of his generous spirit if you please, Sister." Sr. Helen continued gently, "He also has courage, great courage. He is a bullfighter, you know. He will need all that courage and whatever more you can lend him to help our girl. Please do not let him fail. Oh, I am sure if the task is too great for you and Mother Mary, our own Blessed Mother Leontine will lend you her great strength as well. She would never give up on salvation for a Mt. Carmel Academy girl."

"You shouldn't say that," Sr. Nessy whispered as if the statue might overhear. "I mean we should not cast doubt on her ability."

"I am not! This is a great task we ask of her. Calling on Mother Leontine is simply a suggestion. She knows that."

"I suppose."

"St. Mary, hear our prayer," Sr. Helen ended as Sr. Inez had begun.

The last shaft of evening sunlight speared through the pines and illuminated the white marble of the statue. Prettier than any dove, a snowy egret fluttered from the darkness under the trees and landed on St. Mary's voluptuous hip. It wrapped its golden feet into her draperies to secure its perch, then turned one round, dark eye toward Sr. Helen, then Sr. Nessy. Its small head made a single bob, and it flew away to join a flock arrowing toward a night roost in the distance.

"Did you see?" asked Sr. Helen, her voice full of awe.

"Of course, I saw the bird. My hips and knees are going, not my eyesight." Sr. Nessy put her hands on the base of the statue and heaved herself up. "They should put a handicapped bar right here. We aren't the only old women who come here to pray."

"Oh, offer up your pain to God! Didn't you notice the bird wore its mating plumage, those glorious white aigrettes people used to kill them for?"

"Pretty, but what of it?"

"They don't breed this time of year, Nessy, only in the spring. We have experienced a vision and must tell the Mother Superior when we return the golf cart."

"If you insist, but I think your logic is shaky, even if I do back your word."

"No more than your driving. Help me up. I know our prayers will be answered."

Chapter Eight

Clint parked the Belly Nelle and The Tin Can in the huge ring of pickups and horse trailers fanning out around a plain dirt arena shaded by a metal roof. No hookups for water, waste, or electricity here. They'd have to run the generator if they wanted AC and take quick showers. Multicolored buttes rose up in the distance, but the rodeo took place in a small and sweltering valley with a trickle of a stream running through it and a line of heat-stunted cottonwoods as its only foliage.

Food stands had been set up far enough away from the dirt and flies drawn by the rough stock to be sanitary. A line of bright yellow portable toilets stood farther out in the desert. Way down at the intersection of the blacktop and the dirt road to the arena, the small oasis of a gas station was doing big business in fuel and snacks.

"Tell me again why we're here and not in some nice, climate-controlled arena," Renee said, tilting the raffia cowboy hat down almost to the top of her designer sunglasses.

Why in hell was she still here complaining more every mile they went away from Phoenix? He should have left her by the side of the road. A woman like Renee would have no trouble getting a ride back to the city. He simply couldn't do it, no more than he would take a bitch pregnant with puppies by the wrong kind of sire and dump her in the country on her own. Certainly, Renee had survival skills the average dog lacked, but he didn't have it in him to abandon her yet. He patiently explained again.

"Because this is my final year on the circuit, and I'm giving back. I got my start at places like this. Now, I've been Bullfighter of the Year three times, and this year I'm not working for points at competitions. Let someone else have a chance at the title. I'll help the local boys learn their stuff, do a demonstration, put in a personal appearance. They don't get many big names out here."

"I can certainly see why. I don't think this place is on the map."

"People who live here know where the rodeo is. We're still in Arizona if that will help you out any."

"Not really. I guess I'll stand in line for a drink and some food if you're going to be busy."

Renee shifted her satchel because its thick leather strap cut into her shoulder. This morning the lock on the door to The Tin Can had broken, and she refused to leave her most vital possessions inside to be stolen by anyone who came along. She wore wedge sandals, cropped white pants riding low on her hips, and an equally cropped yellow boat-necked top showing more belly than anyone else at the rodeo. Male eyes shifted her way as she passed, and female eyes squinted and judged. She could care less.

"I could eat first. What are our options for lunch?"

"The usual at these affairs—hot dogs, corn dogs, hamburgers." Renee sighed.

"Look over there, an Indian taco stand. Get me two

with extra lettuce and tomato. I'll stand in line for some drinks while you do that." Clint thrust a twenty-dollar bill into her hand and watched Renee move away, rolling those hips like the waves in an ocean out here in the middle of the desert.

What to do about Renee? Despite his backside injury requiring a pillow beneath his butt for the drive, he'd slept well last night. His brain felt sharp today despite that unsettling dream lingering in mind.

He'd fought a huge bull striped like a tiger with clawed feet instead of hooves. The creature almost had him, nearly devoured him with a mouth full of sharp teeth, when three women appeared between him and the slavering animal. One wore a blue veil, the next had unbound black hair that fell to her waist, and the third with pale eyes dressed like a nun. He tried to save them from the strange bull by shoving them to safety and offering himself to the vicious claws instead, but his hands passed right through the trio.

"No Clint," the blue-veiled one said. "We have come to save *you*," the second lady answered with an almost saucy look on her beautiful face. "You must keep trying," the stern nun demanded. "We will give you extra strength and patience." They disappeared and where the beast once stood scratching the earth, ready to charge, a tabby-striped kitten appeared. It bounded to his feet, rubbed against his ankle, begged to be picked up—and he did, holding it close to his chest.

Clint shook his head to get rid of the vision, but it remained firmly lodged in his memory unlike any other dream. His mother, a devout Catholic, would say he'd been visited by the three Marys. He wondered what she'd think of Renee if he ever brought the woman home. Just couldn't imagine doing that unless Renee's behavior improved considerably. For that, he'd have to go with his plan and bend her to his will, not break her, but teach her to mind her manners. "Ladies, you'd better deliver on that patience and strength you promised," he mumbled to himself.

Clint took his place in a loose line moving along far more quickly than the one for tacos. The man in front of him paid the cashier, thrust his wallet back into a hip pocket and attempted to grasp six long-neck bottles of beer in his two hands. Quick as a sidewinder, a small brown hand lifted the wallet as the man started back to a group of friends who had staked out a space with a beach umbrella and a few folding chairs.

Clint ignored the woman asking for his order. He left the line and followed the child who had the sense not to bolt and call attention to himself. The kid ducked behind a large SUV. When Clint came up on him, he was shoving the folding money from the wallet into the pocket of worn, blue jean shorts covered by a plain, white T-shirt. As Clint's hand descended onto the small shoulder, the boy ditched the wallet under the SUV and dug in his sneakers to take off. Clint secured him, clamping a hand around the kid's neck and forcing him down into the pebble-studded dirt.

"Get the wallet. Now put back the money. All of it!"

"I found it, Mister. Yeah, I shouldn't take the money. But me, I got two baby sisters who need milk."

The boy was all wide, innocent, dark eyes and thick, black hair cut in bangs across his forehead. He wasn't scrawny enough to be starving, either. He probably had at least one parent and maybe both his sisters also working the crowd. Clint double-checked his own wallet, which he had the sense not to keep in a hip pocket.

"I'll see this gets back to the owner."

"You gonna let me go, Mister?" the kid said in a small, pleading, pathetic voice that had most likely worked before on softer hearts.

Clint would bet the child often left with donations and a pat on the head. Baby sisters, my ass. "I might if you'll do me a favor first."

The boy looked wary. "I don't drop my pants for men. I seen that *Brokeback Mountain* movie."

"Well, you shouldn't have, but that's not what I want."

Clint began to frogmarch the small thief back toward the arena through the messy maze of trucks parked any which way. In the process, he returned the wallet to the group under the beach umbrella, saying he'd found it by the beverage stand. By this time, he held the boy's hand like a loving uncle.

Clint spotted Renee. Bent over inspecting a display of intricately beaded necklaces and turquoise bracelets set out on a blanket by an enterprising Navajo woman, Renee and her nicely rounded ass were hard to miss. She held a cardboard carrier filled with three tacos.

"See that beautiful woman over there?"

"The Anglo lady with the big *muchachas? S*i."

"Watch your mouth. I want you to steal her bag. Might be hard. She's got it crosswise over her breasts now."

"*No problema.*"

"I'll chase you into the parking area. You meet me back there on the far side of that old trailer and hand over the satchel. I know for a fact she doesn't have much money in there, so don't even think about really taking off with it. I can catch you, and I will turn you in this time if you cross me. Do what I ask, and I'll give you enough cash so your daddy will let you take the afternoon off to enjoy the rodeo. Deal?"

"You want to be a hero, fine by me."

"Go." Clint released the boy, who bore down on Renee like a cattle dog on a stubborn cow.

As she straightened up, shaking her head, "no" regretfully, and turned away, the kid circled behind her back. Coming on fast, he knocked her face first into the ground. The tacos went flying. The thief neatly stripped the satchel over Renee's head as she struggled to get up and tore off into the parking area.

"Clint, he has my bag!" she shouted.

"I'm on it!"

Clint sprinted after the boy, who put on a good show, ducking down and weaving among the vehicles. Both of them breathing hard, they rendezvoused behind The Tin Can. The kid handed over the satchel, and Clint dug two-hundred dollars out of the money belt Renee had no idea he owned. They made the transfer.

"Wish you hadn't knocked her down, kid."

"Had to get the bag over those mountains, Mister." The small thief shrugged.

"You're quick, agile, and smart. Watch the bullfighting demo I'm giving this afternoon and consider a more honest career when you get older, okay? Enjoy the rest of the day." He gave the boy a friendly swat on the rear, and the kid took off.

Clint felt under the front bumper of the Belly Nelle and found the lever releasing the doors to the compartment behind the cab that had once held a miniature donkey for the show in Casper. He climbed into the bed of the truck and added the satchel to his stash of good running shoes, a laptop, and the box of jewelry. The space still smelled a bit like burro, but was otherwise clean—as Snuffy had promised it would be when they renewed their deal to let Clint keep the truck and trailer for the rest of the summer.

Not winded after the chase but pretending to puff a little, he went back to Renee. She crouched under the Navajo woman's tarp. The woman, wearing a full-skirted and ruffled blouse version of native dress as well as her own jewelry, washed the grit from Renee's skinned knees using a bottle of water and some paper towels. Renee had a red, scraped patch on her bare belly as well, and she mournfully held her broken sunglasses in one hand.

"These shoes, no good. You wear flat shoes or boots," the woman scolded her. "You cover your belly."

Renee had no sharp retort for a change. Clearly, she was still shaken by the assault, which Clint hadn't figured on being so violent. He helped her up. Renee drew her dirty-kneed cropped pants down over her wounds and looked at Clint with tear-filled eyes.

"Sorry, babe. He got away. Probably has an accomplice hiding him."

"All that I am was in that bag."

"All that you are is here. You have a roof over your head, food to eat, and me," Clint answered, tipping her head up for a consoling kiss. He stopped and peered closely at her face.

"Am I bleeding?" Renee frantically patted her face.

"Will it scar?"

"No, not bleeding, but you kind of remind me of a Catahoula cur I once owned. Your eyes are two different colors."

"My contacts! I lost a contact. Damn that little bastard! My spares were in that satchel."

"Come on now. You told me once you didn't need them to see. Right now, you got one emerald green eye and one kind of nice gray-green eye with a dark ring around it and full of little black flecks. I like this eye. Pop the other contact out, and you'll be fine."

"You're just saying that to make me feel better."

"Not true." Clint turned to the Navajo woman whom he knew would expect no payment for her act of kindness. He scanned her wares and picked out a thick silver cuff bracelet with inlaid chunks of irregularly-shaped turquoise. It was pricey, and he could have bargained, but he didn't. He turned his back, fished more money out of his belt pouch, and handed it over all rolled up so Renee wouldn't see the amount.

"My best piece," the woman assured him. "You want a bag?"

"No, she'll wear it. It'll make her feel better. Thanks." He clamped the bracelet over Renee's wrist. Buying her something made him feel a little less guilty, too. She'd be on short rations from now on.

"Guess that was our lunch." Clint scooped up the box and fallen tacos.

"Yes."

"Come on, we'll stand in line together, then go find a seat in the shade." He helped Renee along with one hand on her elbow. They passed a small brown boy who wanted to pay for his cotton candy with a fifty-dollar bill. He wore an oversized blue shirt with an advertising logo on the front almost covering his shorts and a small, red cowboy hat. Clint gave him a subtle nod when Renee looked away, but the boy ignored him and continued to demand his change. He was a real pro.

****

Renee downed an entire bottle of water with her taco and felt a little better. Clint started on his second taco and said around a mouthful of fresh, chewy flat bread and lettuce, "Good, huh?"

"Yes, I feel better. Thank you for the bracelet. You didn't have to do that. I know they won't be paying you much here."

"My pleasure. I got to go suit up soon. Will you be all right?" Clint glanced at the arena where they set up for the barrel races. After that, he'd do his demo, sign autographs while the bronc riding went on, then get in the ring with the local boys for the bull competition.

"Sure. I'm tough, remember?"

He looked into her eyes and wasn't so sure. She'd taken out the green contact, and now she looked softer than before. "Say, how about we go back to the Nelle and get a sack of those stuffed toys while I put my gear on. You could give them out while I sign autographs. The little ones don't care who I am and get restless. We can put some antibiotic cream on those scratches, too."

"Sounds good to me."

Back at The Tin Can, Clint smoothed antiseptic on Renee's scratches. She helped him tape his ankles and thighs and pulled up his long dark socks over the bandages. She gave the padding covering his crotch an extra tug into place.

"Don't forget to protect the jewels," she said.

"No, I plan on using them tonight." He drew her in for a kiss hard against his chest protector before he finished strapping on the knee and shin guards. As he pulled on a large shirt slathered with advertising, he looked around the trailer. Something was missing—the small, portable TV that got only one channel out here in the wilderness. That little vermin had come back and helped himself. Thank God, he hadn't taken the bullfighting gear or Renee's fancy boots half-hidden under the leopard throw on the unmade bed.

****

Clint's demo went well despite his sore rear, almost as if the bull had been trained to accept his moves. He made the usual big hit. People lined up for autographs afterward. He moved the line along by sliding the glossy pictures of him walking a bull to Renee, who placed them in a big, white envelope. If she saw a restless child farther down the line, she'd pick out a toy and present it with a few words and a pat on the head. Most of the kids were shy. A few of the older ones thanked her.

She'd covered her scraped belly with the new and freshly washed emerald green top, hoping to reflect some its color up into her eyes, and put on her new jeans and boots. The straw hat had escaped any damage by flying off her head, but her Cassini sunglasses were history. And, she didn't know what she'd do when the last of her makeup wore off. Then, Clint would see what she really looked like, the tiny flaws that squealed she was over thirty, the other imperfections she'd rather hide.

When the bull riding began, Renee took a seat in the bleachers and watched Clint work. He was so deft and fearless it made her heart beat harder. He often stepped aside to let the local boys show what they were made of, and she could see they appreciated that without saying a word. She rested her chin in her hands, never taking her eyes off of Clint in case something should happen to him, and then what would she do? Drive the Nelle back to Louisiana, she guessed, if she could figure out how to get there and scrounge enough money for gas.

All went well. Clint wasn't even sore from his exertions. They strolled around after he'd striped down, taken a quick lukewarm shower, and changed into street clothes. In a tent, a church group sold beef brisket dinners with slaw and a chunk of cornbread for $6.95. They dined handsomely on local fare, as Clint would say.

"I'll get dessert," he said. "Stay right here."

He came back with a choice of temptations—a red candy apple and a piece of fry bread, still warm and dripping with honey.

Renee considered the offerings. "Hmmm, I can break a cap on that candy apple and get some fruit today. Or say the hell with cavities and calories and eat the bread."

Clint took a Swiss army knife from his pocket and cut the fry bread in two, then quartered the candy apple and removed the core. "Now you can do both."

They shared the treats as the sun dipped, the air grew cooler, and people began to depart for wherever they came from. They walked back, hand in hand, to The Tin Can and ended the evening as they were accustomed, this time careful of Renee's injuries and bruised places. Neither missed the television at all.

****

Clint made toast for her as Renee showered in the morning. She usually washed off the make-up she'd worn to bed and reapplied it, despite the poor lighting and bad mirror, before going out to the kitchen for breakfast. Today, she patted her face with the cloth, hoping to preserve some of her coverage. It didn't work. A bit of her eyeliner stayed on, and that was about all. She burrowed into a thick terry robe fairly sure it had come from Bodey Landrum's pool house and brushed her hair down around her face. Keeping her eyes on the floor, she went out to accept the plate of toast with strawberry jelly and a cup of black coffee.

"Soon as we get a signal today, you can use my cell phone to cancel your credit cards and report your driver's license stolen if that's what's bothering you," Clint offered. Guilt crept up on him. He turned his attention to his glass of milk.

"The joke is on them. I maxed my cards out in Phoenix, and my driver's license expired several months ago. I liked the picture and wanted to keep it for a while longer. I was five years younger then. I'll call my father when we get to a town. He's paying my utility bills while I'm gone and collecting the mail. With luck, he'll pay down my cards, too." Renee took a lethargic bite from her toast and chewed it very slowly.

"Is something else the matter, Tiger?" Clint asked. "You feel okay?"

"I'm fine. I need to get to a drugstore, though."

"Hey, I told you last night I got plenty of condoms. Don't worry about losing your diaphragm with that bag."

"I need to get some make-up. You'll have to loan

me the money."

"Sure, but do you really need it?" Clint raised her chin. She shut her eyes. "What do I see here? Freckles. Looks like someone sprinkled cinnamon across your nose. And luscious pink lips. You look good enough to eat."

No way would he mention the small lines in the corners of her eyes. He wasn't an idiot. "Finish your breakfast, and I'll eat you right up before we get on the road."

Clinton O. Beck was always as good as his word.

****

Still, when they arrived at the first small town having a pharmacy, Renee begged him to pull into the lot. He shelled out a twenty and told her to "go to town." He'd wait in the truck. Renee's mouth hung open. The concealer she ordered from Neiman Marcus in Dallas cost three times this amount. She hadn't used drugstore cosmetics in more than ten years, but she got out of the cab to see what she could gather.

A half hour later, she came back asking for another ten, please. He doled it out. When she slid back into the Nelle, Clint looked at the size of the bag and shook his head.

"You know, you don't need all that gunk. I think you look all fresh-faced and dewy without it."

"Moisturizer. I forgot moisturizer. Without it in this climate, I'll crack like a rotten board." Renee snatched the change, ran into the store again, and came back clutching a large bottle of lotion.

"Renee, you have plenty of good years left. Take it easy."

"That's what men always say. They get

distinguished. Women get old."

She'd purchased two lipsticks and rolled one over her lips, making them darker with a bronze sheen. Next, she attempted to smear some potion across her freckles using the mirror on the visor. Not working. The little cinnamon dots still showed, just slightly lightened.

"I can't go out in public like this."

"Sure you can, Tiger. I'm proud to be seen with you." Clint put the Nelle into gear and rolled forward to the next rodeo.

Chapter Nine

The Fourth of July caught them in a small Utah town so tinder dry all fireworks had been banned. Wandering among fair-haired families with enough children to compete with any Cajun Catholic brood, they ate watermelon slices and watched the veterans, trailed by children on decorated bicycles, parade down the main street. Clint lost the seed-spitting contest to the local champ and good-naturedly accepted a second place ribbon. Renee claimed watching the hot dog eating contest made her queasy.

The next day, they were on the road again ending up at a small rodeo each weekend. Clint promised they would hit the big time in Wyoming at the end of July for the Daddy of 'em All, Cheyenne Frontier Days, where he had a big contract to fulfill. He had to say Renee was being a good sport about the situation. In fact, her docility worried him. Casually as they bumped along the back roads, he asked her, "How come you decided to stay with me."

"Oh, that evening you returned to The Tin Can all bruised up it came to me that I'd been acting like a bitch. I mean, I'm always a bitch, but bitchier than usual, and you didn't deserve that kind of treatment. You asked for some respect and to live within your budget. I threw that in your face. I did plan to leave, but I kept hearing these insistent little voices in my head all night long saying I'd regret it if I didn't stay."

"You still hearing those voices, honey, because the heat can get pretty bad this time of year and the Nelle's AC hardly works?"

"No, they went away once I made up my mind to keep traveling with you. Maybe it was my conscience talking. I didn't know I had one."

"Of course, you do. You just haven't put it to good use for a while. Well, I'm sort of glad you stayed and that comes as a surprise to me, too."

Dependent upon him for cash, she earned her keep by making their lunch, mostly salads and sandwiches since her cooking skills were limited, doing the dishes and laundry, and helping out when he signed autographs. She gave a great massage, too, which really counted for something far from whirlpool baths and professional services.

Clint thought Renee finally believed him when he said her eyes were lovely and her freckles added charm to her face. Or maybe it wasn't his reassurances. As she gave out the stuffed toys they garnered at every truck stop claw machine along the way, small children often told her she was pretty and fingered her hair when she bent over to give them a small teddy bear or a yarn octopus. On one occasion when she'd offered to hold a tired child while the parents chatted with Clint, the little girl told Renee she was "comfy" and promptly went to sleep. Even Renee knew that very small children usually called it as they saw it.

She complained only once—about her backside spreading from too much driving and too little exercise. Yes, she knew she wore her clothes a little tight, but her jeans stretched to the point of uncomfortable. Clint had an easy answer for that. They got up at dawn and went running. He needed the workout as well without having access to the machines he used at the bigger venues. Preferring to run on a treadmill in the comfort of a gym, Renee had some trouble keeping up on the rough roads and in the high altitudes. He adjusted his stride and encouraged her each step of the way. He let her use his lighter hand weights, too. To tell the truth, she'd gotten a little less buff, not quite as honed, a little rounder, a little softer—and he liked her that way.

Out in the wilderness, wi-fi hot spots came few and far between. Carefully, he left Renee at the laundromat with their dirty clothes and a few new fashion magazines when he made for the local libraries to check his e-mail, confirm future performance dates, leave instructions for his broker, and drop his mother a line. Snuffy wrote often, asking how the Nelle and The Tin Can were holding up.

A couple of days out of Cheyenne, Renee took off her straw hat to fan herself at a gas station and obviously saw something horrifying the side view mirror.

"Ohmigod! My roots are showing. They've grown out more than half an inch. I can't go back to civilization looking like this, Clint. I just can't. My touchup kit was in my bag."

"Well," he said slowly, "your roots are a nice color, about the same shade as some other hair I'm fond of."

"And that is growing out, too! I haven't had a waxing in ages. Don't joke about it, please! This is a crisis. What if they show me on the big screen while we're in Cheyenne?"

"Keep your hat on. Everyone else does."

"I'm not going then." Renee plopped on the Nelle's running board and crossed her arms. I'll wait here for you, wherever here is."

She looked as stubborn as that little donkey Snuffy used in his act. Clint glanced down the blacktop with a few small stores clumped on both sides, wherever's Main Street, he guess. He hadn't caught the name of the town when they veered off the highway to fill the tank.

"Okay, sit there for a minute while I pay for the gas."

He went into the station with the inevitable sandwich shop attached, paid for the fuel, and picked up two club sandwiches for lunch. He asked the two sandwich assemblers, teen-aged girls, if the town had a beauty shop. They rolled their eyes. Their moms went to Miss Franny's Hair Affair next to the local insurance agency office. Clearly, they wouldn't be caught dead there even on the day of the prom. Sounded good to Clint.

He got the number and called ahead while the giggling sandwich specialists finished his order. Slinging the sack of subs over his arm, Clint picked up his cold drinks, an unsweetened iced tea for Renee and a full octane Coke for himself, and went out to deliver the goods news.

Renee had moved her spreading behind to a picnic table stationed under some dusty shade trees. Sullen for the first time in weeks, she picked through her sandwich, determined to find fault with it. The trouble was they had been together so long now he had gotten her order one-hundred percent right. No mustard, mayonnaise, onions, or jalapenos, but all the rest of the veggies dressed with oil and vinegar. If she had been the one ordering, she knew he'd want the works plus extra jalapenos. They were becoming like some old married couple. Renee shoved her bag of chips, the only thing she could find to gripe about, at Clint when he finished his corn chips.

"I can't afford the calories. I'm too fat."

Clint sidestepped that one. "Hey, Tiger, we are in luck. There's a beauty shop right down the street, and I am going to treat you to an afternoon at Miss Franny's Hair Affair. How about that?"

Renee's mouth dropped open. She clamped her lips shut again and mumbled, "I can wait until we get to Cheyenne."

"Nope, I can tell you are unhappy. I want to fix that right now. Finish up. Miss Franny is waiting for you. I called ahead. It's so close we can walk off those chips."

With the tar bubbles in the deserted road bursting beneath their feet, Clint marched her down the main street until they came to a sign with an eighteenth century lady, hair piled high in silhouette and the words in lurid pink, The Hair Affair.

Full of dread, Renee entered the small shop. The place had only two dryers, two chairs, and one wash bowl. Miss Franny, her hair up in rollers, her chosen tint an *I Love Lucy* shade of red, greeted her warmly.

"It's been slow today, so I worked on myself. We can go under the dryers together," the hairdresser said, friendly as could be. She wore a smock covered with printed pups and kitties over her dumpy body and rocked back and forth on her white SAS shoes as she sized Renee up. "Need a change, do you?"

"No, just a touch up, maybe a small trim, only the

ends, and a blow dry. Clint, I really could wait."

"I heard there's a truck stop at the next exit where I can use a computer. Be back in a couple of hours. That about right, Miss Franny?"

The hairdresser nodded. "You bet. I know what to do."

The man had done more than call ahead. He'd left instructions and promised double the usual fee if she did as he asked. Wasn't like this redheaded woman was one of her regular clients. After today, the two drifters would be gone, and business had been real slow lately what with people cutting back on luxuries like a good cut and curl.

Clint patted Renee's hand as Miss Franny covered her with a pink plastic cape and lowered her head into the washbowl. Then, he ran.

"Let's see." Miss Franny consulted a chart with little tufts of colored hair sticking to it.

"That one." Renee stabbed a finger at a bright red strand on one end of the chart. "I don't suppose this place does a bikini wax?"

"You couldn't pay me enough to fool with a woman's privates. That's why all *those* kind of salons hire foreigners. It ain't American to mess with yourself down there."

Having firmly stated her position on the matter, Miss Franny got out her mixing bowl and concocted a dye three shades darker that should just about match those roots and slathered it on. After the dye had set and been rinsed, she combed out Renee's long hair, still dark from the water, and began to trim.

"Oops, got to straighten that out," Miss Franny said after every snick of the scissors. "You know what would be great—bangs."

"No bangs!" Renee ordered.

"You got a face could wear 'em," Miss Franny assured her as she drew Renee's hair behind her shoulders and continued to clip. The beautician spun the chair to face her, grabbed a hank of hair, and cut. "Wait till you see how cute this is."

With that gouge taken out of the front, Renee had no choice but to go with the bangs. Every time she tried to assess how much hair fell to the floor, Miss Franny said, "Hold your head straight, or I'll never get this right." That kept Renee still as could be, but there would be no tip.

"A blow dry, right? I could put you under the dryer in curlers and give you a good spray that would last the week."

"No, no more. Just dry it, and let me call my boyfriend."

"Whatever you want, hon."

Miss Franny finished just as Clint arrived. "Ain't she pretty now?" Miss Franny asked.

"I think so," Clint answered.

Renee stared at the mirror. All of her siren red waves, gone from her head, lay on the floor. Her hair hung straight, forming a little wedge toward her chin, and a thick row of bangs covered her forehead. The color was a dark auburn, a shade she hadn't possessed since she turned twelve. She'd gotten highlights in Paris, and let her hair grow because Uncle Dewey said men liked long hair. The cut made her stunned hazel eyes seem even larger, her mouth more vulnerable. In the reflection, she saw Clint pass Miss Franny a wad of money.

Miss Franny whipped off the pink plastic cape and dusted Renee's shoulders with a soft brush. "There you go, hon. You can get up now."

Clint helped her from the chair, keeping a firm hand on her elbow, and escorted Renee out and into the Nelle before she could say, "Clinton O. Beck, I'm going to kill you."

Fortunately, Renee's way of killing a man involved lots of punishing sex, more than one guy could handle—almost. All he had to do was run his hands through those straight, silky strands, ruffle her bangs with a hot breath, and say, "I really do love you this way," and she leapt on him again, clawing and biting and riding him hard. Life with Renee was pretty damn near perfect now.

Chapter Ten

"We need to stop at a grocery store, Clint," Renee informed him.

"We got plenty of food, Tiger, and we're nearly to Cheyenne. The traffic is getting thicker—tourists coming in for Frontier Days."

"I want to get a paper bag to put over my head before we get to the big city. Or maybe a plastic one to end my embarrassment forever."

Clint grinned at her, his deep blue eyes full of mischief. "I keep telling you that new do is sexy. Who would have thought Miss Franny could do a precision cut? And if you did wear a bag over your head, you'd still be sexy."

He didn't lie. Many a man would go for that body, face unseen. He told the absolute truth about the new hairstyle, too. It was swingy and sleek, but more wholesome than her usual femme fatale look. If he could get rid of all the skintight clothes, Renee Niles Bouchard Hayes would be fit to take home to anyone's mama. Now, where had that thought come from? His plan had always been to tame her, help her to see herself in another way, and then to cut her loose to roam free. Might be hard to let her go he began to realize.

Renee slumped down in the shotgun seat of the Nelle as if she were hiding. Clint coped with the traffic and got them to the giant arena without a mishap. A small city of motorhomes and trailers had sprung up around the huge venue, homes for ropers and riders, clowns and bullfighters. They weren't there an hour when Snuffy Jones showed up to check on the health of The Tin Can and the Belly Nelle. Renee was lowering the awning, but suddenly got very busy setting up the aluminum chairs. She drew her hat down low over her eyes and pretended not to see the clown. Being Snuffy, he got right in her face.

"Miss, is Clint Beck around?"

"He went over to the arena to check in and get his schedule," she mumbled, turning her back on the clown again.

Snuffy circled her. "I wanted to leave something for him."

"Sure, put it in the trailer. The door doesn't lock." She looked at her boot toes.

"All righty."

Whatever the clown left, he was pokey about it. Clint came back by the time Snuffy emerged from The Tin Can. Renee excused herself. "I'll go and make some lunch."

Snuffy sat down on the saggy webbing of one of his chairs. He spit some of his quid under the trailer. "This is a little awkward. I brought you a picture from Gracie addressed to Mr. Clint and Miss Renee, but looks like you got a new gal along now, so I left it folded up. Did a little inspection tour. Glad to see you're keeping The Tin Can tidy, but don't you ever fold up the bed?"

"Not very often. It gets a lot of use."

"Dumped the man-eater for a sex kitten, huh?"

"No. That is Renee."

"Well, those bazookas looked familiar, but that woman is all round and soft like a ripe peach. In case you didn't notice, this one has freckles, hazel eyes, and much shorter dark red hair. Appears that she makes lunches instead of eating in restaurants, too. You sure you didn't switch her out, Clint?"

"That's the reformed Renee. You know how women like to change their hair styles, and those green eyes of hers were contacts."

"Not real, huh? How about the…" Snuffy made a big circle over his chest.

"Unfortunately, no, but still nice to look at."

"So, how much longer are you going to want The Tin Can?"

"Oh, maybe until the end of August. She'll probably be sick of traveling by then.

"Living so soft in that motorcoach is ruining me. Makes me think I might want to retire, too, and take it easy on the ranch."

"If Ruth Ann can stand to have you around all the time."

"You might have a point. Take care now. Wild cats have been known to turn on people. See you in the arena." After releasing another gob of chewed tobacco under the Nelle as if he were marking his territory, Snuffy headed back to Clint's luxury motorhome.

Clint had some time on his hands before the bull riding events began. He planned to show Renee how to have an innocent good time. They rode the Ferris wheel at night, bumped thighs and locked lips on the Tilt-a-Whirl. He let her win her own prizes on the midway. Without being asked, she put any toys she captured into the bag to be given away. They dined late on chili cheese fries. When Renee upchucked all the greasy food on another spinning thrill ride, Clint got her a cold ginger ale to sip and said everyone should throw up on an amusement park ride at least once in a lifetime. He made a point of tucking her into bed and not asking for sex, but he did gently rub her belly, rising up like a little ball of dough in the oven between those once sharp pelvic bones.

****

Clint rejoiced at getting back into his exercise routine in the great facilities Cheyenne had to offer, but leaving Renee alone for hours wasn't a good idea. He asked Snuffy to take her around with him since Jones distained working out. The clown preferred to work the crowds with Renee trailing behind carrying the sack of stuffed toys.

Snuffy devised a routine to include her, giving her a horizontally-striped clown shirt that made her breasts look as big as carnival balloons and red suspenders that slipped to each side attached to her Daisy Duke short shorts. Below that, she was all long, smooth tanned leg down to her black cowboy boots. Snuffy made her practice saying, "Oh Snuffy, I'd follow you anywhere," in a breathy voice.

They walked up and down the grandstands open to the vast Wyoming sky, and stopped to do their routine when they came across families with small children. Snuffy joked with the kids and ended by saying, "And now my lovely assistant will give you a toy from my magic bag."

Renee rooted in the sack, trying to match the toy to the child—a green plush frog for a rowdy boy, a purple cat with bead eyes for a shy little girl—while Snuffy, pretending to be concerned, asked her if the bag was too heavy.

"Oh, no, Snuffy. I'd follow you anywhere," she answered, fluttering eyelashes greatly enhanced by his clown kit. Then, the clown told the old joke about always leaving women laughing that Renee first heard in Casper, spun his bow tie, and wiggled his eyebrows up and down—a little something to make the parents chuckle going directly over the heads of the children. Renee found she enjoyed playing the bimbo far more than being one.

While Snuffy did his act in the ring, usually with other clowns, she bought postcards of scenes from Frontier Days, filled them out, and sent them off to Eve and Bodey, her parents, sister, and cousin. In the evenings, Clint took her out for some nice meals and brought her home for some leisurely sex. When he had the time, they enjoyed watching the skill of the steer and calf ropers and the hilarity of the Wild Horse Race as teams tried to saddle and ride unbroken horses around the arena in the right direction—which wasn't always possible.

Clint introduced her to the Queen of the Barrel-Racers, Norma Jean Scruggs—older than Renee, he said, and still at the top of her game. Obviously, he and the long-legged, big-busted, black-haired and strikingly blue-eyed Norma Jean had shared some "good times", but as Clint never asked Renee about her past exploits, she gave him the same courtesy. Still she found herself digging her claws into his arm as if he'd ditch her for the barrel-racer any second, and she had to hang onto him. He winced a little and removed her hand.

Norma Jean gifted Clint with a parting squeeze to her ample and probably real bosom, cautioning, "Don't get yourself killed now. Renee, he's a good 'un. If you get tired of him, just send him on over to the Cactus Blossom. That's my rig."

"Not-a-chance," Renee answered with great emphasis.

"Didn't think so. Break a leg, Clint."

That might have been a show biz term for good luck, but during Frontier Days, the possibility remained very real. The rodeo boasted a slate of forty of the biggest, meanest, toughest bulls to be had. Once the bull riding started, Clint routinely returned to the trailer covered with bruises. On the second day of the event, one bullfighter broke an arm, or had it broken for him by a ton and a half of bull.

Renee sat in the stands whenever Clint worked in the ring. She'd never tell him how often her breath caught when he threw himself at one of the monstrous animals or beat another in a race to the boards by inches. She'd never admit being glad this was his last year of bullfighting. When Frontier Days ended its nine day run, she packed with great relief ready to return to the nice, safe small venues where Clint spent more time signing autographs than he did fighting bulls. They were stowing all the loose items and preparing to go on the road when a man rapped on the door of The Tin Can.

"Clint, glad I caught you. Someone's on the phone in the office. You got a Renee Hayes traveling with you?"

"I'm Renee," she answered as she folded up the bed.

"Go in that entrance right there. I'll be along shortly, ma'am."

Wondering why anyone bothered to call now after she'd been gone for nearly two months, Renee started off across the vast lot. Clint detained her guide.

"You have any idea what's going on? Should I go with her?"

"Well, I don't know, Clint. When a woman's daddy calls, it usually means trouble."

Clint finished the packing and moved their vehicles close to the entry where Renee had disappeared. He found the office and Renee with a face turned pale around her freckles. Still on the phone, she took down notes on a piece of paper. "I'll get there somehow," she said before hanging up.

"What's the matter, Tiger?"

"My mother is dead. She drowned in the pool. Probably drunk. The maid found her when she came in this morning. Dad was off at a charity golf tournament all weekend and stayed over to do some fishing. They think she fell in sometime Sunday afternoon. The funeral is on Wednesday. They want me to come."

"Sorry for your loss," murmured the office manager.

"Thank you, we weren't close. Daddy is going to have a ticket waiting at the Cheyenne airport along with a FAX of my passport since my license has gone missing. Clint, would you drive me over there?"

"If I can leave The Tin Can parked here for a while, I'm coming with you. I don't want you to face this alone, Renee."

"That would make a nice change, not having to face everything alone. Let's go."

Renee pressed her face against the glass of the Nelle's side window as they drove to the airport. "I wonder if I'll end up that way—dead over a day and found by a maid or a gardener."

"You aren't a drunk like your mother. You aren't the same." Clint glanced over, his blue eyes full of pity. She couldn't stand that.

"Really? I dealt with my problems by using sex. She used liquor. Not much difference. I can't cry for her, Clint. My mother married for security, not to have kids. When I was a child, she wanted me to be a pretty in pink kind of girl. I wasn't. I liked to ride and spend time in the barns. I'd get filthy following my Cousin Rusty around. When I didn't measure up, she gave me to Uncle Dewey. My sister Cathy was worse than me, but she grew up to be captain of the Mt. Carmel softball team, state champs. She's happily married, has kids of her own. Cathy will die surrounded by family."

"Because you protected her. Does she know?" Clint asked.

"I don't think so. We were close until I went to Paris. Since then, I've felt alone. I had a clique of friends, a new guy every weekend, Bodey Landrum for a while. I guess you knew that."

Clint nodded.

"Sorority sisters, two husbands, but I was always alone with what I knew."

"Not now, Tiger. When we get to Rainbow, you be sure to introduce me to your Uncle Dewey."

Chapter Eleven

Clint took a seat next to Bodey Landrum and Eve, directly behind the family in St. Leo's church. Bodey wore a black suit, dark gray shirt, a bolo tie held in place with a big chunk of turquoise, a business black Stetson and plain black boots. Eve had chosen a simple dress, also black, and a little tight in the bust because she still nursed her baby. Her only accessories were a sterling silver cross on a silk cord and a velvet bow holding back her white-blonde hair. Clint still marveled after knowing Bodey for years and the kind of women he hung with, that the King of the Bull Riders had ended up with this stunning but quietly religious woman. Renee was more Bodey's type, or had been. He didn't like that thought.

As for himself, he had retrieved a tailored suit of deep navy blue and a white dress shirt from Bodey's closet. Clint's striped silk tie, a power tie, had been a gift from his father. He wore no hat, and his shoes were shiny black oxfords. Renee turned to stare when he sat down beside her and raised her eyebrows. He guessed she'd expected him to show up in jeans.

Renee looked wonderful, considering the event, with her simple haircut and less makeup than she'd been wearing when they first met. Still, she'd gotten hold of some gunk to cover her freckles, and the deep red silk tank she wore under a tailored dark suit jacket dipped a little low for a church occasion. She, too, wore a cross, but hers was large and golden and a little gaudy with gems, probably real, not costume. The thing, big enough to ward off vampires, filled the space between her neck and cleavage, a very sexy symbol of piety.

Clint had helped her dress, trying to tug up the rear zipper of the slim skirt matching the jacket. The gadget wouldn't close, so he'd just told her it was closed. After all, the jacket would cover the gap. He wasn't given a say about her jewelry before he went off to claim his suit at the Landrum mansion, but she told him an artist in San Francisco gave her the cross as a parting gift because he owed her big bucks for being his model. He believed her.

The first row of St. Leo's Church overflowed with members of the Niles family. Jed Niles, the widower, sat next to Renee hemmed in by her slim, athletic sister, Cathy, Cathy's husband, and two antsy young nephews. Her Uncle Ted Niles and his lively, fiftyish bride, Mona, came next, then Rusty and his curly-haired wife, Noreen, holding their squirming toddler, Katie. Jesse, their son, old enough to be somber and well-behaved, sat across the aisle with the deceased's niece, Chelsea, in her twenties, fair, frail, and beruffled even in black. A small, blonde woman of middle age referred to by Renee as Ex-Aunt Anna stayed close by Chelsea, a hand placed on her daughter's arm. Uncle Dewey had not put in an appearance.

Two elderly nuns on their knees in another pew prayed privately before the service began. Clint remembered meeting them at Rainbow Liquor and Groceries just before this adventure began, but couldn't recall their names. They gave him a friendly nod after easing themselves up painfully from the kneeler when the music began.

The casket of reddish mahogany, draped in a blanket of pale, pink roses as if it were a winning racehorse, sat in front of the altar rail. Fr. Brian, a young priest with a gentle manner, new to St. Leo's and innocent of knowledge of the Niles family, stuck to the ritual, promising an eternal and happier life for the departed. If he noticed there were no wet eyes in a congregation made up mostly of Jed's business acquaintances and neighbors from Red Horse Acres, he gave no sign.

Knowing the circumstances of the death, he kept his eulogy brief and emphasized God's eternal compassion for the weakness of mortals, whom only He could judge and forgive. Stepping down from the lectern, the priest blessed the coffin with holy water. The pallbearers came forward to take Prudence Niles on her final journey to the spot prepared in the graveyard behind the church.

By the time the family reached the freshly dug hole under the canopy, most of the neighbors and businessmen had taken to their cars and headed for the funeral feast. Catered by Le Rosier Courville and sure to be good, food awaited for the grieving at Tara-on-the-Bayou. Mrs. Parker came from the back of the church and offered to take the restless children over to the house for some refreshments. Renee turned her back on the woman who screwed her father, but Cathy and Noreen gladly handed over the kids. Jesse made a token protest about staying while Great-Aunt Pru got put in the ground, but, stomach growling, gave in to a promise of punch and little sandwiches. Cathy's husband thought he might ride along, too, if his wife did not mind.

Only the immediate kin, Clint, the Landrums, and the two old nuns took seats on the folding chairs for the last of the rites. Under the shade of the canopy, sweat rolled off the mourners as the morning heated up. The whirr of insects in the grass drowned out the words of the soft-spoken priest. As the coffin lowered, the funeral director handed out long-stemmed pink roses matching those on the casket and urged the family to come forward, pitch the flowers into the grave, and say a last prayer if they wished. Whether they wanted to or not, all felt obligated to accept a rose.

As Renee dropped her rose into the grave and bowed her head briefly, a loud voice called from the rear of the line, "Here I am, Pru's beloved Brother Dewey. Made it in just time to say good-bye to Sis."

Renee turned so suddenly clods of dirt came loose from the edge of the hole, and she swayed toward the grave. Clint vaulted over a row of folding chairs, grabbed her elbow, and steadied her, as lightning quick as he would have been in the bullring.

Ex-Aunt Anna placed her small self in front of a suddenly pale Cousin Chelsea, but Dewey didn't appear to notice. He snatched a rose from the undertaker and continued to blunder forward, leaving fumes of whiskey in his wake. Dewey tossed the rose stem first as if he played darts in a bar.

"We had some good times, Pru. Good times. I'll never forget how close we were. Hey, Renee, baby, give your Uncle Dewey a consoling hug."

The scrawny man, his gray comb-over flapping in the light breeze, held his arms open wide and advanced on Renee. He had deep lines etched in his face by alcohol, cigarettes, and sin. Renee retreated, treading on Clint's toes. Clint placed himself between her and Uncle Dewey, not as big, not as fierce, but every bit as monstrous as the bulls he faced each weekend. Clint grabbed the elbow of the man's soiled white suit and turned him toward a nearby iron gate in the fence separating St. Leo's cemetery from that belonging to the nuns of Mt. Carmel.

"You and I are going to have a talk way over there while the rest of these good people finish saying good-bye." Clint marched Dewey toward the gate.

"Do I know you? Who are you to get between me and my niece?"

"I'm Clinton O. Beck, and I fight nasty animals like you."

The smaller man began to struggle, trying to slip out of his jacket, but Clint had him by the neck now. They kept on moving through the gate and past ancient tombstones toward a large monument, ornate with columns and topped by an angel—big enough to block the sight of what Clint intended to do from the mourners. He lifted Dewey over a low wrought iron fence decorated with willows and lambs and bashed him face first against the side of the crypt. Little flakes of whitewash built up over the years fell away like snow in August.

"You with vice? Look, we can cut a deal," Dewey begged, tasting the blood from his split lip.

"I love Renee, and I know what you did to her." Clint turned the man and held him by a lapel as he drew back a fist and plowed it into Dewey's corrupt face. The lapel came lose. The man on the other end of that fist flew through the air and landed on his backside near a small marker where a child lay buried. Dewey scrambled to get up and run, but tripped over the tiny tombstone. Clint's arm jerked him back behind the sepulcher.

Over in St. Leo's cemetery, the priest said the final words of burial, but all eyes turned toward the big tomb on the other side of the fence.

"My God, that cowboy you brought home is beating up Dewey at his own sister's funeral. I've about had it with your men, Renee," Jed Niles told his eldest daughter. "Now I'll have to go over there and stop that."

"No, don't go!" Renee hung on her father's arm.

Jed Niles, tall and heavy from living a prosperous, well-fed life, shook his daughter off. His well-groomed white hair fell across his sweating forehead, and he wiped his red face and wet hands with a linen pocket square before starting toward the nun's cemetery.

"Jesus, Renee, must you always be the drama queen, even at mom's funeral? Why did you bring your latest man toy, anyhow? Have you no respect?" her sister, Cathy sniped.

"I'll take care of it, Jed," Bodey Landrum intervened. "But if Clint Beck is beating a man up, he probably deserves it."

Bodey overtook and passed Jed Niles at the gate. Eve Landrum started after her husband and called out, "Bodey Landrum, remember this is not a barroom brawl, but a sacred rite."

Renee ran after her father, followed by everyone else at the gravesite except the funeral director and the astounded priest. Even the creaking old nuns hot-footed with their canes across the cemetery.

"Hurry, Nessy, hurry. I feel our presence is needed," white-haired Sr. Helen urged as she wobbled along.

The priest shook his head and said to the funeral director, "I've seen things like this happen at wedding receptions, but never funerals. Of course, I haven't been in Cajun country very long. Should I intervene?"

The director raised an eyebrow. "Being a stranger and all, I'd stay on this side of the fence."

The mourners reached the large tomb in time to see Dewey take to the air again from another blow. This time the battered man, adrenaline pumping, managed to get up and make a break, vaulting the low fence like a competitor in the Senior Olympics.

Bodey Landrum stopped Dewey with strong hands to his shoulders and said with a slow drawl, "Now, what's going on here, podner? Clint, what have you got to say?"

"That man sexually abused Renee from the time she turned twelve."

"Then, he's all yours." Bodey shoved Renee's uncle back in Clint's direction.

"His word against mine," shouted Dewey. "And I'm family. Who you gonna believe, Jed?"

"My daughter. Is this true, Renee?"

"Yes," she said faintly, then louder. "Yes, he did, and mother, too, when she was a girl. I'm fairly sure. She was afraid you'd leave her if you knew, and so she said nothing, did nothing, to stop him."

"Your daughter lured me on that trip to Paris, Jed. She begged me to make her a woman. That little tramp was all over me every time I came to visit Pru. I tell you

Renee has suction better than a vacuum cleaner. And this guy is probably taking advantage of that every night, so he ain't no better than me."

Jed Niles' eyes met the steady blue eyes of Clinton O. Beck. "Hold him for me, son."

Clint locked Dewey's arms, and Jed Niles put all he had into a punch to the gut. Dewey retched vomit and blood into the grass.

"May I?" asked Bodey Landrum. Jed Niles nodded. The former bull rider executed a nice upper cut that jerked Dewey from Clint's hold. The man writhed on the ground. The pointed toe of a high-heeled shoe landed between his ribs.

"And that's for Chelsea," swore Ex-Aunt Anna. She kicked him again.

Behind them, a soft chorus rose from the women who had surrounded Renee and Chelsea, hugging their shoulders, touching their hands. "We didn't know. We didn't know," said Cathy and Eve and Rusty's wife, Noreen.

Appalled, Fr. Brian made his way across the cemetery, his vestments flapping in his haste to prevent murder. He overtook and passed the hobbling nuns and held up his hands. "Please, please stop! No matter what this man has done, you must desist and call an ambulance."

"Figures he'd get sympathy from a priest," muttered Bodey Landrum. His wife took a second out from consoling Renee to slap her husband's arm. She'd take the time later to kiss his bruised knuckles at home, he knew.

Rusty Niles, towering over petite Ex-Aunt Anna, held the woman back from doing more damage. Despite being a former steer wrestler, he lost his grip on the little woman who went right back to kicking Dewey and shrieking, "I needed all that child support for Chelsea's therapy, or I would have turned you in years ago!"

"Please, enough! This man needs medical assistance," the priest implored.

Jed Niles took a cell phone from his pocket and punched in a number. "Yeah, I need you to come get a man in the Mt. Carmel cemetery. A child molester. Oh, and he might need medical care."

Jed pocketed the slim phone. "Anyone else want to get a lick in before the police get here?"

Renee left the comfort of the circle of women and stepped forward. She aimed her kick at Uncle Dewey's crotch and hit him where it hurts, way below the belt line. Dewey curled up like one of those big, white grubs that feed on the roots on young plants and vomited some more into the grass.

The nuns arrived panting and limping in time for the finale. Their legs might be feeble, but they both had their hearing. The accusations shouted during the brawl had carried well to their old ears.

"Oh, my!" said Sr. Inez with some satisfaction. "That must have hurt."

"God's will be done." Sr. Helen nodded. "Not that I take any joy in another's pain."

"I think we might just have seen the answer to all our prayers, Sister."

Sr. Helen watched Clint Beck enfold Renee into his arms. Their former student was crying, burrowing into his chest as if she wanted to hide.

"Clint, take me away from here." No one stopped

the couple as they started back toward the church.

"Oh, Nessy, we aren't done praying yet. Before we leave, we must stop at the grave of the Blessed Mother Leontine, founder of our academy, and ask for her aid in bringing about a happy ending."

Neither Renee nor any of the witnesses had an idea what the babbling old nuns were talking about, but Clint gave them a smile over his shoulder as he led Renee away.

****

The two cops assigned to Rainbow by the parish sat at a table in the nearby restaurant. They'd done their duty and run the escort from the funeral home in Lafayette to the church, then chowed down at the café. Reluctantly, they asked for a box to encase the half-eaten big burgers and good, greasy fresh cut fries and a go-cup for the ice cold sweet tea before heading over to the graveyard where an assault seemed to have taken place.

"They tried to kill me," a little man in a bloody white suit writhing on the ground claimed. "Arrest them, officers, all of them!"

"The way I see it, this here child molester, tripped over a couple of tombstones and damaged himself." Bodey Landrum slipped his bruised fist into a coat pocket.

"Yep. That's the way it went down. He tried to get away after my daughter accused him abusing her since she was twelve." Jed Niles used his pocket square to clean his jacket of vomit.

"Anyone else want to say anything?"

The group remained silent except for one of the nuns. "Oh, we were much too far away to see anything.

Just got here, in fact," said Sr. Helen, her blue eyes wide.

A fair-haired young woman in ruffled black stepped up. "Sad to say, I'm his daughter. If you need proof of what he did, get a warrant for his computer! I'll give testimony, too. My therapist has wanted me to come forward for years."

The officers put the cuffs on Dewey, hauled him up and over to the squad car parked in the Academy's drive. They figured he'd live till they got him to the jail.

The group gathered by the big tomb began to disperse. The nuns turned down a ride to the funeral reception, saying they were close to the convent and wished to visit Mother Leontine's grave. Bodey and Eve started after Clint and Renee but did not catch up with them. The other family members took a stricken Jed Niles back to his car that his brother Ted insisted on driving. The last to leave were Rusty and Noreen Niles. Noreen, the family historian, wanted to take a closer look at the sepulcher.

"Well, blood is smeared on the old Niles family tomb, and vomit is in the grass, but no major damage to the structure. I'll come by tomorrow and wash it off."

"Don't. Let the rains take care of it. Thanks to you, I know my ancestors fairly well. I think at this moment, they are mighty pleased one of their own was avenged."

Chapter Twelve

Renee flung expensive cosmetics into a handbag far too smart to take to a rodeo. She'd fixed her eye make-up, not much of a chore as she wore less of it these days. Her suit lay on the bed in her tiger-striped lair. Clint had helped her out of the troublesome skirt with the stuck zipper. She'd packed only an overnight bag to make this trip and was already back into her boots, jeans, and a casual top. Clint watched her with a worried look on his face.

"What's the matter, handsome? Did I tell you how great you looked in that suit before you got blood and barf all over it? I don't know if the blood will come out of that silk tie, though. Frankly, I didn't know Bodey Landrum owned any real ties; he's so cowboy. And you say you borrowed that suit from him, too? Isn't Bodey an inch or so shorter than you? Looks like someone tailor-made it for you. Maybe a good dry cleaner will be able to get the stains out and repair the tears."

Hating her fake cheeriness, Clint answered, "Yeah, I got the suit over at Bodey's. He won't care about the damage. Renee, don't you think you need to have a long talk with your father and sister before you go anywhere?"

"What I need to do is to get out of here. Word about Uncle Dewey will be all over town before we get on the plane. I can't bear the pity. Take me back where

121

no one knows anything about me. Take me back to The Tin Can."

"Oh. The way you were packing, I thought maybe you were planning on going somewhere else."

"Not for now."

The doorbell rang, followed by a fist pounding on the front door.

"Renee, this is your father. Open up. Your Uncle Ted and his wife are out in the car thinking I'll stroke out any minute like he did the year Jesse was born, so let me in."

Clint headed for the living area. Renee bounded after him, hanging on his arm, but she couldn't really stop him. He let Jed Niles in and stepped outside. "Talk," he said before closing the door.

Jed tried to embrace his daughter, but she moved away and hugged herself with her own arms.

"Honey, I'm sorry. I didn't know."

"Because you were always gone, chasing other women, even during the holidays."

"Your mother didn't care for sex. I guess I know why now. She wouldn't let me touch her until after we were married, and then, it wasn't so good. I thought we weren't compatible that way. After Cathy came along, I agreed to take my lust elsewhere, but I promised I wouldn't leave her, and I didn't. Renee, I have the hot blood of the Niles family." Her father ended his plea by holding out his hands to her.

"Uncle Ted and Rusty manage to contain themselves."

"Yeah, well, neither ever had the money for high-class hookers, and both got a woman they love who loves them back."

"Is it true you're seeing Mrs. Parker? Mom said you were."

"A man gets older. He wants a woman he can be comfortable with."

"That hurt her. I don't think she cared about mistresses or call girls, but a woman Mom's own age, and not all that attractive—she couldn't handle it."

Jed Niles hung his head. "You think she took her own life?"

"No. I think she tried to drink away the pain and was too far gone to save herself."

"Cathy said Uncle Dewey didn't touch her because you were always in the way. She says she never knew what she owed you. She wants to be a better sister. Says she'll help you any way she can."

"How nice of her after all these years of avoiding her slutty sister, not even letting me babysit her kids. Not that I cared. I'm not cut out to be a doting aunt or a good mother."

Jed Niles ran a hand through his thick, prematurely white hair. "Don't say that. The man you brought home with you, he might want a family someday."

"Clint? Isn't he just another one of my men toys, as Cathy said? He isn't rich, won't even have a job after this year," she sneered, daring her father to make something of it.

"I like his style, the way he took charge, the way he stood by you. You need a strong man, Renee. If he can get a real estate license, I'll see he gets a job."

"Thanks, Daddy. I'll pass the offer along. Now, I want to get out of here."

"You might have to come home to testify against Dewey."

"If it will spare some young girl the pain, I'll take the stand in her place. Let me know when. You'll have to reach me through Clint. My phone was stolen along with all my credit cards a while ago."

"No new charges have come through. Here, take my phone. I'll have your name put on this card." Jed handed her an American Express Gold card from his wallet. "I want you to be able to come home anytime in case things don't work out."

"Clint takes good care of me, but I contribute."

"I know you do." Jed strained to keep any sexual insinuation out of his voice, an effort not wasted on Renee. "May I kiss you good-bye, honey?"

Renee, her arms still wrapped around herself, stepped into her father's embrace. He kissed the top of her head. Tears gathered in the corners of his whiskey brown eyes. He moved to get out of there fast. Jed passed Clint on the sidewalk in front of Renee's house. He paused.

"You take care of my little girl, son. If you ever need money or a job, call."

"That's not likely, sir, but I do appreciate the offer. Renee is safe with me. My word on it."

The men shook hands. Renee watched from the half-open door as they discussed her. As soon as her father got into the back seat of the car and Uncle Ted drove away to the top of the hill, she opened the door and said, "Let's get the hell out of here."

Chapter Thirteen

Clint was content with the way things were for the moment. He and Renee tooled along in the Belly Nelle, The Tin Can rattling behind them, away from the high country of Wyoming and headed toward Texas. Just the two of them. Each weekend, he'd appear at one of the small rodeos along his carefully configured route. When they reached San Antone, he wanted to visit his mother for a few days before flying off to the big Ellensburg Labor Day rodeo in Washington State.

He had some concerns about Renee being lethargic in the mornings and showing no interest in food, but she usually perked up as the day went on. Clint thought the need for extra sleep and the lack of appetite made up part of her healing process. He prayed to God the symptoms didn't point to depression.

Whenever they stayed in an area with cell towers that blasted phone her father gave to her would ring. Her sister or dad talked until the battery wore down. He'd had to stop at a store and get a charger to plug into the Nelle's ancient cigarette lighter and hoped to hell it didn't ignite the entire truck. They wanted her forgiveness. After the calls, Renee cried as she did so easily lately. If he could find that little pickpocket again, he'd have him boost the new phone and throw it away.

Back in Rainbow, Renee had restocked her suitcase

with a fresh array of slinky clothes and shouldered an expensive leather bag. With her father's credit card, she could buy more anytime—or use it to finance a plane ticket home whenever she became bored with him and their quirky road trip. Just when he thought he'd made some progress again, the old Renee might arise at any moment and take flight with a fancy suitcase full of new duds her guilty father would gladly pay for, no questions asked, no demands she return the stuff. Some people called a fat chance a flying pig. Well, he dreamed of flying tigers not of the fighter plane variety.

Not much sex went on, and that was fine for now as long as it meant she hadn't lost interest in him. Sometimes when Clint held her in the evenings, gentle lovemaking would ensue, all the rage of the tiger gone. Often, Renee simply fell asleep, leaving him in the dark to contemplate his own lies to her and to himself.

He had to come clean soon about who he really was. He had to come to terms with the fact he'd told her pervert uncle that he loved Renee but never told the woman herself. Just what had he meant? That he enjoyed her ferocity in bed? That he admired how she protected her sister? That he saw her as a tough survivor of the ultimate betrayal? All of the above?

Renee dozed against his shoulder when Clint parked at a truck stop outside of yet another small town in New Mexico near the Texas border. They would reach San Antonio tomorrow, but for now, he still pretended to be just Clinton O. Beck, itinerant bullfighter. Renee roused when he turned off the ignition, and the Nelle shuddered as usual. The stop offered all the usual: hot showers, slot machines, huge convenience store with cheap cigarettes, caffeine pills, junk food, and hot coffee. The store fed into a restaurant called Mabel's Good Eats. Clint had passed through here often enough, and he knew Mabel personally.

Mabel greeted him warmly, but Renee showed no jealousy as she had when he'd introduced her to Norma Jean Scruggs. Mabel, short, round, and grandmotherly, had hair obviously dyed black and bright red lips. Dressed in a cotton muumuu with a loud print of parrots and gigantic green leaves, she came running on crepe-soled shoes to give Clint a bosom-crushing hug. He swung her around, which took some effort, Mabel being no lightweight.

"What's good on the menu tonight, dear?" Clint asked her.

"The meat loaf special. Comes with creamed potatoes, green beans, roll, and a trip to the salad and dessert bar."

"That will do for me. Renee?"

"Just the salad bar. Does soup come with it?"

"Two kinds. Help yourself. Clint, you come sit at the counter so we can catch up. I saw that stunt you pulled in Glendale on the TV."

Renee went over to the salad bar. She studied it. A big metal bowl of shredded iceberg lettuce floated on a bed of slightly melted ice. Containers of cherry tomatoes, sliced cucumbers, rings of purple onions, and green olives surrounded it like a colorful wreath. Vats of potato and macaroni salad dominated the display. Renee lifted the lids of the two soup pots. One contained clam chowder, probably not a good choice in New Mexico, and the other a vegetable beef that smelled like canned. She ladled out a cup of the vegetable soup, filled a small plate with lettuce, tomatoes, cucumbers and olives, and added a few packets of crackers from a basket on the side. She drizzled some Lite Italian dressing over the salad.

"Picky eater, is she?" Mabel asked Clint.

"Renee? She's off her feed. Had a lot of upheavals in her life lately and watches her weight pretty closely, too."

"You need a woman with some meat on her bones—like me. When are you going to settle down, Clint?"

"Maybe soon."

"Her?"

"She has her good points."

"Yeah, I see two of them sticking out of her chest. Can't be real," Mabel assessed.

He didn't comment. Renee brought her food to the counter and took a seat on a red vinyl stool next to Clint. Mabel went off to pick up the meatloaf special and returned with a heaping oblong plate and a green plastic basket with two rolls.

"I brought extra bread for you, honey."

"Thank you," Clint and Renee answered simultaneously. All three laughed.

"Got to say you have a great laugh, nice and throaty, Renee. I hate those gigglers. Clint says you're feeling poorly. Try the banana pudding for dessert. It's soothing. Got vanilla wafers in it. My kids always loved that."

Mabel continued to jaw with Clint about her children and grandchildren as he shoveled in the meatloaf covered in brown gravy. Pools of it cascaded down the sides of the mashed potatoes and mingled with the juice of the green beans cooked with bacon. The smell of the mélange of foods drove Renee over to the dessert bar for the banana pudding sooner than she would have liked.

She felt Mabel watching as she put a few scoops of yellow pudding covering lumps of brown banana into a cup. From the limited selection of green gelatin mixed with crushed pineapple and whipped cream or slices of apple pie and chocolate cake, it seemed the best choice for her jumpy stomach.

"You get yourself some of the wafers, too," shouted Mabel from across the room. Renee obediently added a few soggy cookies from the side of the bowl. She went over to the coffee bar and poured hot water for a cup of tea. Mabel watched her closely.

"You sure she ain't knocked up, Clint?"

"Renee? I'd be surprised. She isn't shy about telling me to use a condom."

"Men are always surprised." Mabel waddled off to take care of other customers, topping off coffee and making small talk.

Clint finished up with the apple pie and coffee. He flexed his fingers and challenged Renee. "I think I saw a claw machine on the way in. Want to see who can get the most toys?"

"Sure, but I warn you, I've been practicing when you go to work."

They spent the evening on the simple pleasure of grabbing toys with a metal claw and delivering them to a slot. The business side of Clint Beck knew he could buy a ton of stuffed animals wholesale to give away for half the price, but wouldn't have the joy of picking his target and easing it on over to the hole. He called the penguin in the far right corner, a hard target in the time allotted. Clint got the bird by a flipper, moved the claw toward the slot—and lost the toy at the last second. Renee took her turn, lowered the claw, grabbed the penguin by the head and dropped it in the chute. She laughed as she presented it to him, her hazel eyes shining, her whole face alight, a few cinnamon freckles showing through her makeup.

"I moved it there just so you could get it easy," Clint said.

"Yeah, sure. Sore loser."

Clint leaned over, ran his hands through her silky dark red hair and brought her close for a kiss, a long one with lots of tongue and touchy-feely.

"Get a room!" Mabel called from the entrance to the Good Eats.

"Got one," shouted Clint right back.

He gathered up their prey of penguins, sequined flamingos, and Roswell-style aliens in one arm and guided Renee back to The Tin Can with the other. They made a kind of love that involved much tickling and changing of positions. He'd never tell Mabel, but Renee could giggle if touched in all the right places.

****

What the hell happened overnight? Renee must have gotten up on the wrong side of the bed. First, she'd pounded on the door of the bathroom while he was using the can and demanded he hurry up because she had to pee. Wrapped in the big terry robe he'd gotten from Bodey, Renee came out of the toilet and complained about the eggs he made for breakfast.

"Aren't we out of that bacon grease yet? We haven't had bacon since the first week we were on the road. It smells rancid."

"It's been in the refrigerator. I don't think bacon grease can spoil, but if you want bacon, I'll walk over to Mabel's and get you some."

"Good God, no! Just finish your breakfast and get out of here so I can get more sleep. You kept me up half the night." Renee stumbled over his bag of bullfighting gear on her way to the folding bed and stubbed her toe. Obscenities flowed. "Can't you put this stuff in the back of the truck? I'm always tripping over it."

He'd planned to give her breakfast in bed, but now that deal was off. "I thought you enjoyed last night, lady. But sure, I can move my gear. I have errands to run. Don't know when I'll be back. Sleep all morning if you want to for all I care."

Clint dumped his dishes with a clatter into the metal sink, left the can of bacon grease by the stove, and picked up his bullfighting equipment. He slammed the door of The Tin Can on his way out, but with the lock broken, it bounced open again. Renee snapped it shut sharply behind him. He threw his bag into the back of the Nelle and peeled out, leaving a small New Mexico sandstorm in his wake. He wanted to find a place to hook up his computer and didn't want Renee hanging over his shoulder at the truck stop. His mother deserved a heads-up on the situation.

Renee wiped her face with a wet washcloth. She'd barfed as quietly as she could while running water in the bathroom, and all she wanted now was a hot cup of tea to settle her stomach and more sleep. Clint usually made her toast in the morning and tea if she desired it. Though quite willing to make cold sandwiches for lunch and salads anytime, she remained leery of the propane stove with its big whoosh of flame every time she turned a knob. Oh, what she would give this morning for an electric teapot.

Coming around the bed in the cramped quarters, Renee stubbed her other toe on the leg of the built-in table. Cursing, she rooted for her black cowboy boots and put them on. Ha, no more sore toes this morning! And, she didn't need Clinton O. Beck to make her a cup of tea.

Renee found a small saucepan and filled it with bottled water. She sat the pan on a burner of the tiny stove, lit a match, and stood way back as she turned the knob to release the gas. She heard the hiss and tossed the match under the burner. It didn't quite make it all the way in, but the gas caught and flamed up around the pan. She leaned over to turn the knob lower and knocked the damned can of bacon grease directly into the fire. The melted fat oozed over the knob she needed to turn off, bringing the flames with it.

A big rig rumbled by outside the trailer. The Tin Can vibrated. The door flew open letting in a gust of fresh air that bent the fire toward the thin, greasy drapes over the small window. They caught like dry brush. Renee tried to remember where Clint told her he'd stored a fire extinguisher—in the bench whose cushions had just burst into flames.

She began to cough. Time to bail. She grabbed those things most valuable to her and jumped out the door of The Tin Can screaming, "Fire! Fire!"

Truckers raced for water hoses. Others grabbed their own extinguishers. Mabel called the local volunteer fire department. A group effort kept the fire away from the pumps and the other rigs parked in the lot, but by the time the flames went out completely, nothing remained of The Tin Can but a hollow metal shell with a blackened and barbecued interior.

Mabel guided the shaking Renee into the cramped restaurant office and gave her a glass of water. "What did you save?" she asked Renee as a distraction.

Renee showed her the straw cowboy hat and shook out the two items inside the crown onto a battered wooden desk—a stuffed toy tiger and a very nicely crafted silver and turquoise Navajo bracelet.

"Interesting selection. Guess your clothes are all gone. I got a spare dress in the closet I can lend you until you get something to wear. Can't go shopping in that bathrobe, now can you? Here you go."

Mabel opened the closet door and took out a patio dress with a high, dark green yoke, many gathers, and a big ruffle around the bottom. The pattern consisted of gigantic slices of watermelon. "It's one of my favorites. I'll want it back. Go on, get dressed. It's private here. I'll close my eyes if you're modest."

"Hardly." Renee dropped the robe and in no particular hurry, lowered the muumuu over her head.

Mabel got an eyeful and felt free to comment. "On my best days, and that was before the kids came along, I never looked that good. Sure, you got a little gut on you, but men like some flesh on a woman, no matter what the fashion magazines say."

Renee sat in the swivel chair with half its varnish rubbed off. She crossed her long legs, snapped the cuff bracelet onto her arm, shoved the straw cowboy hat on to her head, and dropped the toy tiger into her lap. She folded her arms under her large breasts. Let Mabel stare all she wanted.

"You had surgery lately or maybe a baby? Sure itches when that pubic hair grows back," Mabel continued, woman to woman.

"My Brazilian wax job is growing out."

"Heard about those in *Cosmo*. Never seen one before. Bet it still itches."

At least the overly intimate conversation with Mabel kept Renee's mind away from the fire and what she'd done to The Tin Can, their home, their only home. What would Clint think of her now? Wearing no underwear and dressed in this hideous gown, she'd soon be on a plane heading back to Rainbow.

The door to the office smashed back against the wall. Clint Beck dashed in and stared at Renee alive, well, and wearing no make-up, but garbed in a dress covered with watermelons, black boots, a straw hat, and jewelry as if she were planning to attend some bizarre hoedown.

"One of the truckers saw the Nelle parked in front of the café downtown and stopped to tell me my trailer caught on fire. Thank God, you're safe—and strangely dressed."

If Snuffy saw her now, he'd find a place for her in the clown truck. Renee couldn't hold it in anymore. Her full lips quivered and tears ran through the soot smudges on her cheeks. Clint knelt and wrapped her in his arms. "Don't cry, Tiger. I'm going to buy you a whole new wardrobe."

She lifted her head and gave Clint a wobbly smile. New clothes, the path to Renee Niles Bouchard Hayes' heart. "There's a Wally World along the way, honey."

Renee began to cry again.

****

134

Clint believed her story about the fire, he really did. For just a moment when he'd first gotten the news, he did entertain the notion that Renee might have set fire to The Tin Can because she'd gotten tired of being on the road, sick of cramped quarters, and was through with him. Sure seemed that way when he'd left in the morning.

He considered the things she'd saved. The toy tiger sat all alone on the dashboard, the sole survivor of the inferno that had burned up its buddies residing in a plastic sack in the trailer because he didn't want them slipping all over the place when he went into town. Renee grabbed without thinking the hat and the bracelet, all gifts he'd given her. His heart felt swollen when he thought about it. She hadn't preserved the three-hundred dollar leather purse holding Daddy's gold credit card. He'd think more about it later, but right now, another problem cropped up. She wouldn't get out of the damned truck.

"Look, Renee. It's only Walmart. I've seen worst-dressed women every time I've been in the place. If I must to go in alone, you'll have to take whatever I pick out."

"I'm not wearing any panties."

"Don't try to tell me this is the first time you've ever gone commando in a public place. I know you too well. Hell, half the time you don't wear anything under your jeans."

"It's this dress. It bells out straight from my breasts. I look like I weigh two-hundred pounds. If a wind comes along, everyone will see—"

"Fine!" Clint stalked off leaving her in the Nelle.

He returned a hot half hour later and tossed a

135

plastic package into her lap. "Now you have panties. You wouldn't believe the checkout lines in there. I tried the self-checkout, but it wouldn't accept my card."

"You are probably overdrawn." Renee tore through the plastic with her nails and held up a pastel pink pair of stretch-cotton bikini panties. She had a selection to choose from. The bag also contained panties in pale yellow, light blue, and mint green. She selected the mint green pair, took off her boots, and shimmed into the panties.

"I hope they fit. I got stretchy ones."

"Clinton O. Beck, are you saying I've gotten fat?" Her eyes weren't that sharp, green glass color anymore, but Renee could still stare a man down and make him feel an inch tall.

"Nope. I'm saying I'm not going into the bra department, so if you want one, you'd better get out of the car."

Renee put her boots back on and slid out of the Nelle. They trekked across the huge concrete parking lot giving off heat like a griddle and into the vast, air-conditioned space of the big box store. Renee headed straight for the clothes, snatched jeans from a rack and a few tops as Clint followed behind. She detoured through underwear and picked up boxes of bras, next stop the dressing room. He waited by door. A few minutes later, the jeans came flying over the top of the divider.

"Clint, these don't fit. Get me another style."

He looked at the tags. Size six. Over at the racks, he picked out an array of jeans in size eight and carefully tore off and pocketed the tags.

"Here you go, honey." He shoveled them under the

door.

"Still snug, but better. You have a good eye, Clint."

"That I do. You need more tops?"

"I always need more tops. Pick out some you like."

He got a few of the ones with crisscross tops and high waists in blues and greens, a pale gray edged with white lace, and one wild swirling lime and hot pink print right out of the seventies. None of them fit tight, but they would show off her breasts without revealing too much skin. After all, their next stop was San Antonio and a visit to his mother.

Renee exited the dressing room carrying a mound of clothes but still wearing the watermelon dress. "If they weren't so hard on shoplifters here, I'd wear an outfit to the checkout. As soon as this stuff is paid for, I'm changing in the restroom."

Clint piled the purchases in a cart abandoned by a rack of cheap purses and started toward the front of the store.

"Wait, wait! This straw bag matches my hat." Renee tossed it into the cart. "It's kind of cute for the price. They have some nice things really cheap."

"Right. What's another $19.95?"

"Are you sure you can afford all this if your card is no good?"

"I'll write a check. And my fucking card is good! It was just the damned machine."

"Now who is the grumpy one?" Renee said, cheery so close to being decently dressed again.

They lined up behind a large, blonde woman with a gap-toothed smile and three small, tow-headed children, all clamoring for candy and bubble gum from the rack of impulse buys. As the clerk swished a huge sack of toddler pull-up diapers over the scanner, the woman asked Renee in a twangy voice, "When ya due, darlin'. You got that glow."

"Due for what?" A waxing, a dye job, a better haircut, what? Renee shot her a perplexed and unhappy glare.

"When's the baby due, sugar? Gonna be a pretty one if that's your man."

"I'm not pregnant," Renee responded coldly.

"My mistake." The fair woman colored up and turned her attention to prying a Slim Jim sausage from the toddler's hand. The other two kids dumped chocolate bars and gummy bears packets on the counter. The mother put back all the chocolate, swiped her card as fast as she could, signed, and made her escape, the children following her like little yellow ducklings.

"Clint, do I look that bad?"

"It's the dress, Tiger. It does bell out. Forget about it. We need to hit the road to San Antone. I told my mama we're on the way."

Renee could not forget. Not when they veered off in Amarillo to cut across central Texas, not when she started seeing signs for Dallas and thought wistfully of shopping in Neiman Marcus, not even as they approached San Antonio, and her hands grew cold at the thought of meeting Clint's mother. No one took Renee Niles Bouchard Hayes home to Mama, even if Mama was just plain folks. If she *did* have a bun in the oven, she did *not* want to know about it right now. Enough stress ahead once they arrived at the family grocery store. Had Clint once told her the Becks lived above the business? Terrified about the meeting, she couldn't quite recall. Her nausea returned. She slowed their travel with numerous demands for pit stops, but inevitably they reached San Antonio. Passing right through the city as quickly as she'd lost her lunch at a rest stop, they popped out into ranch country on the other side. Maybe Clint wanted to show her the site he'd picked for that doublewide trailer he wanted to buy. Any reason not to meet his family sounded good to her.

Chapter Fourteen

Clint brought the battered old Nelle to a stop before a high adobe wall pierced by double wooden gates carved in an intricate, lacy Moorish pattern. To Renee, the entrance appeared as if it pre-dated the Alamo. Clint pressed a gadget on his key ring. The gates swung open on very modern hinges. A paved road wound up a low rise where a sprawling house sat overlooking a wide-bedded creek holding only a trickle of late summer water. Renee knew enough about landscaping to realize the native oaks, clumps of yucca and cactus, and beds of wildflowers gone to seed had been artfully placed to enhance the setting and hide a number of outbuildings. The late afternoon sun turned the clay walls of the Mexican-style hacienda a rich red-gold.

"You live here, Clint?" she asked.

"Rarely."

"I thought your father had a grocery business."

"He does. This place belongs to my mother's family, the Hidalgos. Before we go up there, I should tell you I really *am* the Bean King—the Bean Prince, actually."

"You mean you are related to these people? They let you visit?"

"Any time I want. I'm heir to the whole damned Beck's Beans empire."

Renee's hazel eyes widened with shock. A dozen

harsh questions settled bitterly on the tip of her tongue. They were prevented from escaping by their arrival at another gate, this one of open ironwork allowing a glimpse of a tiled courtyard with a charming fountain surrounded by twelve small stone lions spewing water into its center. Brightly glazed pots of red geraniums circled the fountain and ornamented the sides of cement benches set to take advantage of the shady areas.

An elderly dog, a golden retriever mix, rose up from a cool corner and gave a single "woof" as Clint pressed the key ring again and swung the gate open. The dog waddled over on painfully arthritic legs and collapsed on Clint's toes. He squatted and rubbed her behind the ears.

"How's it going, old girl?" The bitch drooled happily on his running shoes.

"Is that any way to greet your mother, Clinton?" said a small but regal woman appearing in the doorway to the house. She had dark hair liberally streaked with white and pulled back into a classic bun at her nape. Her smooth olive complexion's only wrinkles were the deep laugh lines aside her mouth and merry crinkles surrounding her dark brown eyes. Renee knew for a fact that Madalena Beck had to be past seventy, but she hardly looked her age.

Clint swooped his mother up into his arms and spun her around as he had Mabel at the truck stop, but a little more carefully. "No, this is how I greet you, Mamacita."

"Stop, stop, you make me dizzy!"

Wagging her tail and barking, the old dog got up to join in the fun. Renee simply stood there waiting—for what she wasn't quite sure—an introduction, an explanation?

"And you must be Renee. Welcome to Hacienda Hidalgo. *Mi casa es su casa.*" Madalena Beck's gold bangle bracelets clinked as she took both of Renee's hands and squeezed them lightly with her beringed fingers. Her dangling filigreed earrings swayed as she turned toward the house.

"Let's get out of the heat. We'll have a light dinner, then talk the night away. I am so sorry that Clinton's father is away on business. If we had been given more notice, he would have been here to meet you, my dear."

To inspect her, Renee thought, as she followed Mrs. Beck's low but stylish shoes, and simple but expensive red silk dress, down a dim hallway. They passed carved chests and niches filled with chased silver vases full of fresh flowers and the images of saints on their way. Arriving at a large room where a stone fireplace filled one wall, Madalena Beck gestured to wide, comfortable sofas draped with serapes and a low wooden table set with small bowls of tapas, a pitcher of lemonade, and an open bottle of red wine resting in a cooler.

Clint popped a black olive into his mouth and poured a glass of Pinot Noir. He gestured with the bottle toward Renee. She shook her head 'no' and accepted a glass of lemonade to soothe a suddenly very dry throat. Gulping down wine wouldn't help with first impressions.

"Please, sit and have something to eat," Mrs. Beck said with a gracious gesture toward the offerings.

As Renee sank into one of the sofas, the snap on her new light blue jeans gave way with a pop that Mrs.

Beck pretended not to hear. Renee smoothed the gray jersey top with the lace edging that had been hanging in a Walmart that morning away from her stomach.

She wasn't good with mothers, not her own, not anyone else's. Gerry's mother had been dead, of course. Elias became a heart surgeon because his own mother died prematurely of a heart attack. But, those she had met when seeing other men took one look at her and surmised "slut."

Aware she no longer looked slutty in her very new jeans, almost-demure top, and the black boots she'd worn so often they were scuffed on the toes, gave her a tad of confidence this woman wouldn't condemn her immediately. She wore her only adornment, the silver cuff bracelet, all the rest gone in the fire. At least, she'd had the time to shower off the soot and the smell of ashes from her hair this morning while Clint photographed the husk of The Tin Can with his cell phone and arranged for a tow truck to take it to the junkyard. After the trip to Walmart, she'd returned the watermelon dress with a sincere thanks to Mabel and a silent 'good riddance'.

Okay, she also belatedly thanked Miss Franny of The Hair Affair for a good cut that could be styled with a cheap comb purchased at the truck stop depot and left to dry in the sere New Mexican air. Scavenging around the store, she'd found some cherry-flavored lip balm, but little else to improve her appearance. Sure, they had disposable razors and shaving cream, but completely lacked eyeliner and mascara. She knew of female truckers. They should broaden their stock. If only Clint hadn't rushed her in Walmart, saying his mother would put them up for the coming night and awaited their arrival. They had a long drive ahead of them. Let's go! Now she met this ageless little woman with her own face naked and showing freckles, flaws, incipient wrinkles, and all. Made her want to hide behind her hands.

Yeah, halfway across Texas was a long drive with only a break at an exit with nothing to offer but gas and fast food. All their rest stops fell in the middle of nowhere, and she'd had to go several times. Just once, he could have stopped in a town. But, no! So, here she sat facing Clint's obviously rich and well-kept mother with nothing more than cheap clothes, a clean face, and shiny, cherry-flavored lips.

Renee felt sick with anxiety. She scooped up a bite-sized empanada and nibbled on the edge to settle her stomach. A puree of beans and melted cheese filled the center, which had a small, jalapeno zip to the taste.

"These are very good, Mrs. Beck."

"Lena, you must call me Lena. I am so glad you like them. All of the appetizers are from my cookbook."

Great, Clint's mother turned out to be a gourmet chef, too. Renee thought she'd been doing well to add a can of drained Beck's kidney beans to their luncheon salads for variety. Sometimes, she dumped in Beck's garbanzos and tuna. Speaking of which, a tempting chickpea dip with a hint of garlic and a small pool of olive oil sat ready to be scooped up with triangles of flat bread on the table as well. Renee tried the dip while Mrs. Beck beamed at her. At least, she could show some appreciation by eating.

"Did you have a good trip today?" the elegant woman said, obviously trying to make her guest feel at ease.

Renee swallowed the gob of dip on the end of her flatbread. "I burned down the trailer this morning," she blurted out. "That's why I look this way. All my clothes are gone—and my make-up."

"There is nothing wrong with the way you look, my dear. You are absolutely glowing. But a fire, oh my! I'm glad neither one of you got hurt. Clint, have you contacted the insurance company about your motorcoach?"

"Umm," said Clint around a mouthful of chickpea dip.

"Swallow," his mother prompted.

"It was only The Tin Can."

"Snuffy's trailer? I thought you were driving the Belly Nelle, but I couldn't imagine why."

"We traded off a while back. I guess I'll sign mine over to Snuffy to make it up to him and get myself a new rig. The old one probably isn't habitable by anyone else but him by now. Might fly to my next stop in Ellensburg to save the time."

"But why the trade?"

Renee stood abruptly. Sick in the morning and ravenous at night, she wanted to snatch up a handful of empanadas and run from the room. "I'm so sorry, Mrs. Beck. This day has been awful for me. I have a terrible headache. If I could go to my room, I'll lie down for a while."

"Oh, I so hoped to get to know you better over dinner. We have a nice, clear consommé, cold lamb salad, and pears with cinnamon-chocolate sauce for dessert. I'll send you a tray. Perhaps, the soup will make you feel better."

"Thank you. You've been very kind." Despite

raising a sneaky, lying son who had taken Renee Niles Bouchard Hayes for a ride, literally, she liked the woman and felt no desire to be rude.

At a wave of Madalena Beck's hand, a Hispanic maid appeared to escort the guest back down the long hallway illuminated mainly by the votive candles burning in red glass containers before the statues of primarily female saints. They passed into another wing and entered a room across a smaller, more intimate courtyard where she could see Clint and his mother sitting together, sipping their wine before the fireplace, through tall doors with small glass panes. The décor of the bedroom was Spanish Colonial: heavy carved bedstead, massive dresser, and a smaller table with two wooden chairs. She drew the striped drapes, shutting out the touching family reunion, and threw herself on the wide bed. By blanking out all the deceptions of the last three months, she finally slept. Renee Hayes possessed one great survival skill. She was good at burying the ugly and the hurtful to save herself.

****

The maid woke Renee when she knocked on the door and brought in a tray laden with not only the food, but a pot of mint tea. No sense in punishing herself for stupidity by not eating at all. She'd need her strength in the morning when Clint got around to explaining himself and would most likely end up saying, "It's been fun, Tiger. I'll get you a ticket home when I drive over to the airport." The last year or so she'd heard that sort of statement a lot from men, but none that she'd fallen for like Clint Beck. She had no intention of waiting for that to happen. Better to be the leaver than the one left. She asked the maid for a telephone book and the use of a phone."

"*Si, senora*. May I bring you anything else?"

"No, thank you." S*enora*, proof again she'd gotten way too old, was much too often married, to be a *senorita*—the kind of fresh young woman the Becks would want for their son, the Bean Prince, whatever that meant.

Renee polished off the wonderful meal to the last crumb. She used the portable phone to call home since she'd turned her father's cell to a lump of melted black plastic that morning. Let Clint foot one more bill. "Daddy, I'm sorry but I have to ask you for another plane ticket."

Jed Niles didn't question her reason. "You got it, sugar. Just tell me where to send it. Anytime, anyplace, anywhere, I want to be there for you like I should have been years ago." In the background, someone turned down the TV and moved around the room in Tara-on-the-Teche, Mrs. Parker perhaps. She didn't ask, didn't want to know.

"Thanks, Daddy." She gave him the information. Then, she placed her dishes in the hallway so she wouldn't be disturbed again, and striping down to her Walmart undies, tried to get back to sleep.

She did doze, but voices in the courtyard woke her. Going to the drape covered doors, Renee peeked through a gap in the curtains. Clint and his mother sat nearby on the edge of an old well. Right about now, she wished she could push him in.

Small lights in iron brackets glowed among the trellises of well-watered climbing red roses. An outdoor kitchen constructed between two wooden doors on the far end of the courtyard indicated the family gathered here for barbecues and celebrations. Renee imagined the place strung with colored lights, a mariachi band playing in one corner while their guests danced. The feast prepared would be straight out of Mrs. Beck's cookbook. Safe in the shadows, she put her ear to a glass pane.

"Manuela said she ate her dinner and drank the tea. That's good after all the upsets she's had. I'm worried that she asked for a phone, though," Clint was saying.

"Clinton O. Beck, what have you done to that poor young woman?" Madalena said with a shake of her head.

"Mama, if you had seen Renee three months ago, you'd be telling me I was the one in danger."

"Ah, so she is like Brandy and Ginger and Bess. You find Ginger in an alley, bring her home, and she gives birth in my house the next night. You tame Brandy, and when you leave for school, she won't let another man touch her. Bess eats more than she was ever worth and I must bottle feed her baby. Always, I am the one stuck with them."

"You're going to bring up that old cow, too. Renee is not like Brandy and Ginger or Bess. I was just a kid then, but all of them needed a second chance. You complain, but I know where I got my soft side."

"Yes, always bringing home the needy. Your father won't be pleased with you."

"He never is."

Renee let the curtain drop back. While she took a small bit of consoling pleasure that seventy-year-old Mrs. Beck regarded her as young, being Clint Beck's pity case felt worse than being his practical joke. Renee went back to the bed and burrowed into the covers. She missed Clint's hot, hard body next to hers, but by damn if she would ever tell him so.

****

"I'm getting chilled, Clinton. Let's go back inside and continue this discussion. I believe you haven't the slightest idea what you have taken on this time."

"Nothing I can't handle," he argued as they retired to the large living room. Clint opened the damper in the fireplace and started a small blaze. He knew his mother enjoyed watching the flames in the cool of a desert evening. He poured more wine, hoping to mellow her out.

"What you have taken on is a family. Renee is obviously pregnant and probably hoping you will marry her."

Clint choked on his wine. "Why do women keep saying that? She denied it just this morning when we were in line at Walmart."

"All the signs are there, son. You say she hasn't been feeling well. And her breasts are so swollen."

"They're always big like that. She has implants, Mama. It doesn't mean anything."

"She is glowing—and showing. How long have you been together, Clinton?"

"About three months. I know Renee has put on a little weight since we met, but we spend most of our time driving around in the Nelle." Frantically, he tried to explain away that popping of the jeans earlier in the evening.

"In all those three months, has she asked you to stop at a drugstore for feminine hygiene products? Has she asked you to buy her tampons?"

"Mom, jeez—God forbid that last one! We stop at

drugstores all the time. She buys cosmetics and fashion magazines. Maybe Renee has a prescription for those birth control pills where a woman doesn't get a period anymore."

Clint Beck knew better. Didn't he have her purse with the diaphragm case hidden in the Nelle. Hadn't he been using condoms religiously?

"I am sorry, son. She appears to be more than three months along to me. This cannot be your child. If it was, I would expect you to do the right thing by her immediately. I am old-fashioned that way, as you know. As it is, the decision is yours. Do you care enough about this woman to marry her? Can you raise another man's child and not feel deceived or resentful? Exactly how brave are you, Clinton O. Beck?"

Lena folded her arms and waited for an answer, but her son stalked off to his room without giving her a reply. Whose child did Renee carry if truly pregnant? One of the wannabe bull riders who frequented Bodey's camp, or Bodey himself cheating while Eve recovered from childbirth? The man did have a reputation on the rodeo circuit no matter how much he claimed to have reformed. Could Clint raise a child born with black curls and Irish blue eyes knowing who the real daddy must be? Did he have that kind of heart, that kind of courage? Did he love Renee enough to accept both her and the child? Clint asked himself these questions all night long.

Chapter Fifteen

Renee woke to the sound of mockingbirds quarreling over territory in the courtyard. The hacienda was beautifully antique and that applied to its plumbing also. She'd made the trip down the hall to the bathroom twice in the night and passed other rooms where people tossed and turned as much as she did.

No matter how gracious Madalena Beck could be, she probably spent the evening worrying that her only son would marry this pathetic loser. As for Clint, she'd never known him to miss a night's sleep to anything except sex, but maybe he felt a tad guilty about his deception.

Renee rooted through the oversized Walmart bag a servant delivered to her room. She shook out the seventies-style top with its wild swirls of colors and tied it behind her neck and loosely at the waist. Made of polyester and spandex, the blouse had no wrinkles. Unfortunately, it clung to that definite bulge she'd developed sitting on her tush all day in the Nelle. When had it grown from a little extra pooch of flesh into a noticeable belly?

Still, she wished she owned skin-tight lime green cropped pants to go with it, and ice-pick heels and dangling earrings, so Lena Beck could see the kind of person Renee Hayes was—not a woman who had lost everything and needed care and a home—but a bad, bad girl who could take care of herself.

Sighing, she pulled up the cotton underwear and a pair of too snug blue jeans left partly unzipped and pushed her feet into her scuffed boots. Leaving the silver cuff bracelet on the dresser with the greatest reluctance, Renee set out to find her hostess and Clinton O. Beck.

She heard conversation at the far end of the hall and by taking another right angle passage she ended up in a long, narrow kitchen gleaming with sub-zero refrigerators big enough for caterers to use, stretches of granite countertops, and a professional range with an option for grilling indoors.

The hacienda staff gathered around a long table—maids, yardmen, a few cowboys—each having a second cup of coffee as they polished off a breakfast of warm tortillas, scrambled eggs, and crumbled chorizo sausage. Pots of Beck's Texas-Style Salsa sat within easy reach. Renee recognized the brand. Clint often poured it right from the jar onto his eggs.

"Excuse me. Where could I find Mrs. Beck and Clint?"

The maid who had attended her the night before jumped up from the table. "Come, come. I show you. In the breakfast room, *senora*."

Renee walked the length of the kitchen and through another door opening into a cozy room with a view of the rolling hills, the creek, and on the other side of the water, a small herd of well-bred horses swishing their tails under an oak.

A sideboard held a chafing dish of eggs, a covered dish to keeping the tortillas warm, the expected pot of salsa, and an iron skillet of sausage set on a trivet.

Wedges of cantaloupe and honeydew melon fanned out on a plate in a sunburst pattern with a centerpiece of fresh strawberries. Half a carafe of coffee remained along with hot water for tea, but earlier risers had eaten and left.

Renee waited for her stomach to rebel. When it didn't, she filled a tortilla with eggs and sausage and salsa, made a cup of tea, and heaped her plate with strawberries. Airlines barely fed their customers anymore, and she figured her father, tired of having to bail her out again no matter how much he denied it, had gotten her a ticket in coach. Might as well fuel up for the flight. Gobbling down her breakfast resulted in a belch she was glad Mrs. Beck had not observed.

Finished stuffing herself and hoping the food would stay with her, she wandered into the next room, a dining hall fit for royalty with its twelve high-backed, carved chairs and sweeping length of table ornamented with silver candelabra every few feet. Narrow windows set deep into the adobe walls allowed thin streams of sunlight to enter the room while the glass-paned doors to the left showed off the courtyard still in morning shade. Clint and his mother were neither here nor there.

Renee passed into the large living area where she had been greeted the night before and smelled the scent of ashes from a fire gone cold—still no denizens of Hacienda Hidalgo. She started down the long hallway toward the front door and stopped when she saw Madalena Beck, obviously in prayer before one of the religious statues. A vanilla-scented votive candle burned in the cut glass container and clusters of fresh red roses from the courtyard filled a nearby vase. Dressed in a bright yellow blouse and wearing white cotton slacks and sandals, Mrs. Beck seemed to glow in the dim hallway. The light from the votive candle glinted off her gold jewelry as she crossed herself. Renee moved in to say her good-byes.

"Ah, there you are looking much better than last evening and feeling better as well, I hope. Did you have breakfast?" Mrs. Beck asked most cordially.

"Yes, I do feel better, and I have eaten." Renee suppressed another burp. "Thank you for the hospitality, but if you could ask someone to drive me to the airport, I'll be catching a flight to Lafayette. I own a home in Rainbow, Louisiana, and it's time I went back there."

Lena Beck didn't immediately call for a driver as Renee thought she would.

"I've heard of Rainbow. There is a shrine to Santa Maria Magdalena at Mt. Carmel Academy that I have heard often produces miracles. She is my patron saint, you know."

Mrs. Beck nodded at the statue. "I've often felt she has guided my life. Once, she came to me in a dream and told me that I would have a son at last at the age of forty. I laughed about it with my husband the next day and started with morning sickness the next week. Last night, she chided me for making a poor judgment, saying I would lose something of great value if I didn't repent of it. Renee, you are welcome to stay here as long as you wish, no matter what Clinton has to say this morning."

"Again, thank you, but I must be going. Tell Clint I'm sorry I missed him."

"Oh, he is waiting for you in the outer courtyard. I think he was afraid you might hot-wire the Nelle and leave without him." Lena Beck gave a tinkling laugh.

"How does he know I can hot-wire a car? One of my old boyfriends taught me that in high school."

"Perhaps, you talk in your sleep. I'm sorry. That was uncalled for. I am sure you are very resourceful."

Renee knew her face had gone red. She'd spent years learning to suppress the curse of the redheaded. But, she stood her ground. "I'm no Brandy or Ginger. I am not some pregnant, homeless tramp. I can take care of myself."

"Oh dear, you overheard. Santa Maria warned me. No, not a tramp. I think you are like these red roses, tough and hardy. You find them draped on crumbling adobe walls at abandoned home sites. Pioneer women brought them here to brighten their hard lives. They are beautiful and fragrant, but if you keep them well-watered, they bloom and bloom and bloom. Their hips make a wonderful tea that is curative and delightful. I dug the plants myself and brought them here to the hacienda for our courtyard. I admire their ability to survive. They are part of my home now, one that I love. Please, let Clinton talk to you. Afterward, if you still want the ride to the airport, I will arrange it."

Embarrassed by the flowery compliment just paid her, Renee only nodded and set her feet on the path for a confrontation with Clinton O. Beck. He twiddled his thumbs on a bench near the fountain, all signs of the poor cowboy gone. He wore a pressed pale blue dress shirt open at the throat, ironed khakis looped by an alligator belt, and very expensive running shoes new from the box. Freshly shaven, his short, dark blond hair brushed back damp from the shower, he consulted a heavy Rolex wristwatch for the time, every inch of him a Bean King. He stood as soon as he heard her close the door.

"Renee, I know you are angry with me about lying to you."

"No, I'm not." She had the satisfaction of seeing his jaw drop. "I know my reputation, Clint. I suppose Bodey told you I was on the prowl for my third rich husband. I understand why you hid your identity—because Bodey is right. I would have pursued you for your money."

"Would have? Here I am, still rich, eligible, and if I do say so myself—handsome." Clint spread out his arms to display his charms.

"I know you just wanted the fun and games part of Renee Hayes. That's all most men want. Then, when you found out about Uncle Dewey, you felt sorry for me. But, Clint, I'm no Brandy or Ginger or Bess to be dragged along home for your mother to take care of while you go back to your career."

"Brandy and Ginger and—. They have nothing to do with this." The old dog sitting near Clint pricked up her ears and wagged her tail. Clint rubbed the animal's neck.

"This is Ginger. I found her when I was seventeen and brought her home. She gave birth to twelve mixed-breed puppies the next night. My mother found homes for all of them, but I had to go back to boarding school before they were weaned. As for Brandy, she's buried out there in the pasture across the way."

Renee startled and stared at him as if he might be a serial killer. Clint rushed to explain. "Brandy was a misused mare. Her first owner spoiled her; her second abused her. She was going to end up as dog meat for being incorrigible. The one summer I got to stay home, I worked with her until she turned into a very sweet mount."

"I overheard your mother say she wouldn't accept any other man."

"True, but Brandy did accept our top-notch quarter horse stud. She produced twelve fine foals before she passed away. My sisters' kids still have some of them."

"You called Bess an old cow. Is that how you think of me?"

"No," Clint said carefully. "Because Bess really was a cow. She got mauled protecting her newborn calf from coyotes. My father said to put her and the calf down. I begged him to trailer her in and get a vet. She mended, but my mother did get stuck bottle feeding the calf because Dad dragged me off on another business trip."

"Forgive me if I still do see some parallels here." Renee started to walk past him. She could wait at the end of the road for her ride.

"No, no, listen. I saw a beautiful woman going to waste, that's all. When I had your purse stolen, I was trying to show you didn't need all those props to be lovely, that fun could be had without a lot of money."

"Says the super rich Bean King. I cannot believe you stole my bag. Everything I am was in that bag! Yes, now I'm angry."

"Everything you *were* was in that bag. You don't need the heavy make-up, the green contacts, and the super-sized spermatocide anymore!"

"You—you wanted to keep me plain, naked, barefoot, and—and..."

Here it came, the confession. Clint braced himself,

prepared the words he had rehearsed last night, and hoped they would come to his lips without hesitation.

"Slightly overweight."

"Tiger, I love every inch of you." That wasn't what he meant to say, not what he thought she would say either.

"Well, thanks for letting me know you think I'm fat." Renee put her hands on her hips, which definitely had gotten bigger.

"Honey, you didn't hear me right. I said I love you. Is there anything you want to tell me?"

"Yes. I want my purse. Now!"

"Okay. That's a start. Let's get the purse issue out of the way. It's in the Nelle."

Clint took Renee's elbow and steered her toward the gate where the Nelle sat waiting. She shook off his hand.

"I'm perfectly capable of getting there on my own."

"Of course you are. Watch those cracks in the tiles."

Renee rolled her eyes, then found herself coming to a stop in front of the gate which Clint had to open. He squeezed the door opener on his key ring and let her stalk over to the Nelle by herself.

"Where is it? I've been riding around in this rattletrap for weeks and know my bag isn't under the seats."

Clint felt under the front bumper, found the lever and pulled it. The false back of the cab popped open into the bed of the truck. Miscellaneous boxes of bullfighting gear, mostly running shoes and shirts with logos, tumbled out. In one corner Renee's huge leather bag slouched on top of a Toughbook laptop. Clint clambered over the tailgate and handed the purse to Renee. He jumped down beside her.

"Everything is in there. I haven't touched the bag since I locked it away."

Renee stared at the compartment. "So that's how Snuffy made the miniature donkey appear."

"Don't get upset. Snuffy cleaned out all the donkey dirt before he put the stuff back."

"Now that I have my bag, I'm over being upset. Are you taking me to the airport, or is one of the servants going to drive?"

"I was planning on taking you to Ellensburg with me—in the corporate jet since your driver's license is expired and the passport you picked up at home burned up with the trailer. You won't be able to get on a regular flight without an I.D., but we leave from a private airstrip," Clint said with some satisfaction.

"Is this another trick?" Renee snarled.

"Was I the one who burnt down The Tin Can? Did I let my driver's license expire because my picture was so pretty?"

She noticed a twinkle like sun on the sea appear in those deep blue eyes of his. He would try a new tactic. They had been together daily for so long she could read him the way he read the movements of wild bulls.

"Ever join the Mile High Club?" he asked, grinning.

"Yes." Renee folded her arms. Let him deal with that.

"Fine. Ever do it in a comfortable bed while soaring over the Rockies?"

"No, but the real challenge is using the small

restrooms."

"We have a bathroom on board, too."

"You weren't planning to abandon me here?"

"No, I wasn't. I wanted Mama to meet you, that's all. We still have lots to say to each other. Will you come with me to Washington? Please?" Clint leaned up against the cab of the Nelle with his arms folded as if he could wait all day for her answer.

"Aren't you afraid you are in danger of becoming my third rich husband?"

"Tiger, danger is my middle name." Clint grinned.

"No, your middle name starts with O." She couldn't resist. "Odin, Othello?"

"Nope. Just get in the truck."

"Odo?"

A maid came running toward the gate as Clint lifted Renee bodily into the Nelle.

She held the Walmart bag in one hand and the cuff bracelet in the other. "Senora Beck say you forgot these."

Renee snapped the bracelet on her wrist and accepted the shopping bag. She shoved the sack and her huge, restored purse under her legs, and the maid shut the truck's door.

Clint got in the driver's seat. "You can toss that stuff. I'll take you on a shopping spree when we get to Seattle. Think Nordstrom's, think…"

"I think I'll keep what I have. Just drive. Is it Otho or Odum?"

"No. Nope. You're making these names up, aren't you? You have to wait till my wedding day like everyone else."

The sunlight winked off the emerald green eyes of

the toy tiger on the dashboard. Renee picked up the straw cowboy hat resting beside her mascot. She cocked the hat over her eyes because she intended to be well rested before they flew across the Rockies.

Chapter Sixteen

Renee did punish him on the flight, but in the best possible way with unrelenting sex. Though the jet possessed a very comfortable bed because his father liked to sleep on overseas travel, she refused to use it. The bathroom proved to be much roomier than those on commercial flights. She pointed that out along with the lack of challenge as no one would be waiting in line to take a piss. Positioning him on the commode, Renee spread her legs over his lap, set her knees and did most of the work the first time.

For the second round after a light lunch, she decided on doing it upright with him supporting most of her weight against the wall. Narrower compartments actually made this easier, she felt compelled to point out, as she could have braced her legs on the other side. The third, thankfully, they completed in the bed. Renee appeared to be trying to prove what a total slut she could be, daring him to still care about her, making an effort to tame her. Leopards could not change their spots, nor did tigers their stripes.

But she had changed irrevocably, and Clint knew it. Renee's inner spirit, the one he was sure she possessed, revived in the northwest, or maybe her soul responded to the mountain view corner suite at the Inn in Suncadia Resort that Clint booked. She'd settled into the buttery leather seats of the luxury rental car for a snooze as Clint drove to Ellensburg where she insisted they take full advantage of the vast bed and fluffy comforter again. But to his surprise, she hadn't wanted to stay behind in the morning, soaking in the tub, and ordering up breakfast on a tray and an in-room massage.

Instead, Renee came into town with him and scarfed up a plate of hotcakes and sausage at the traditional rodeo pancake breakfast, passed up shopping in six brick blocks of shops housed in late Victorian buildings, and went along to find Snuffy. Clint found his motorcoach parked in a logjam of vehicles in for the rodeo. Snuffy had made himself right at home apparently. When they discovered the clown at his ease, Jones was enjoying his second cup of coffee brewed from freshly ground beans in Clint's espresso maker. A shining brass spittoon sat handily at his feet.

"Sit yourself down in that nice leather chair, sweetheart, and have a donut," Snuffy offered expansively.

"Too full," Renee answered. "Mr. Jones, I have a confession to make. I take complete responsibility for my actions."

Clint startled, and Snuffy shot him a look. The baby couldn't possibly belong to Snuffy! They'd met Renee at the same time. He figured Bodey as the best possibility. Some men strayed when their wives were pregnant, and the bull rider had a history with Renee. Still, Clint reassured himself again that Bodey was too deeply in love with his ethereal Eve to wander. He waited tensely for the confession.

"I accidently burned The Tin Can to the ground. It's not Clint's fault. He wasn't there at the time. I know how you loved that trailer."

Clint exhaled and dove into the conversation. "I'll sign the motorcoach over to you, Snuff." Not that it would be a big sacrifice. Although Snuffy had gone upscale, dotting brass spittoons all over the place to catch tobacco juice, the flooring had some brown stains—and the air did have that funky smell.

Snuffy flung himself back in his seat and pressed a hand to his chest. "Oh, my heart! And the Belly Nelle? Is she gone, too?"

"No, no, safe at airport parking in San Antone."

"She could be vandalized sitting there all alone."

"Come on, Snuffy, how would you be able to tell? No one will bother the Nelle. After this event, I'll drive her to whatever destination you say. How about your place in Wyoming?"

"Thank you, son. That'd be good. I guess I'll continue to suffer here in this luxurious vehicle because I got no other choice." Snuffy buried his face with its two-day stubble in his hands.

Renee moved over to console the clown. He snuggled into the crack between her breasts and moved a hand around to squeeze her backside. Renee jumped.

"Had you both going now, didn't I?" Snuffy Jones cackled. "I was thinking a while back that I'd gotten so spoiled I was gonna have to buy one of these rigs for myself and retire The Tin Can like a worn out cutting horse. Renee, you want to come clowning with me while this idiot works out on his exercise machines?"

"I'd like that more than anything, but I have to tell you, my short shorts—even if I could get into them— burned in the fire."

"No problem, baby. Clint, you run along. We got a

clown to create.

The next time Clint saw Renee, she was trailing Snuffy with the bag of toys the old clown collected in his travels and answering to the name of Bright Eyes. In a parody of her old make-up, Snuffy had applied ridiculously long fake lashes to Renee's lids and smeared green paint in an arc up to peaked brows far higher than her natural ones. The rest of her face was dead white except for two red circles drawn on her cheeks and a big rosebud of a mouth that seemed to be in a permanent pucker.

She wore the tight red and white striped shirt again. The red suspenders held up baggy pants with large, attention-drawing crimson patches on both butt cheeks. A shaggy orange wig topped her head, and her nose tip supported a pink foam ball. Clint recognized her by the black cowboy boots. Renee and Snuffy were doing the "I'll follow you anywhere" routine and doling out toys to the kiddies. Clint thought she looked happy—or maybe the makeup made her face seem that way.

"I was going to take you out for a fancy dinner tonight, but maybe we should find a Mickey D's and get Big Macs. I can fix you up with Ronald McDonald."

Inside the painted rosebud mouth, Renee smiled showing her perfect, white teeth. "Snuffy says I can shower and clean up in his motorcoach. Hey, he paid me forty dollars for today's work." Renee fished two twenties out of her cleavage.

"And I'll bet he enjoyed paying you, too. Come on, let's get ready to eat."

"Great. I'm ravenous."

****

He must be strict. No sex tonight. Tomorrow at eight p.m., Clint Beck had to be in top form for the PRCA Xtreme Bulls Event, well-rested and centered on his duties. So, they sat out on the private deck and watched the sun go down over the Cascades. Renee decided to get up early to eat more pancakes and see the Yakama Indians in full war bonnet regalia ride into the arena. She wanted to participate in the tribal dancing and win prizes on the midway. He wanted a long nap in the afternoon before he went over to the rodeo to stretch and warm up. Still wearing the hoop earrings with a sliver bucking bull on the loops that she'd bought with her clowning money, Renee fell asleep in her chair.

Clint carried her inside and striped off the inn's thick robe. He laid her beneath the covers and, tossing his own robe aside, took his place next to Renee in the large bed. She automatically fitted her hips against his crotch. Clint put one hand over her protruding belly. He didn't feel any movement. His mother and Mabel and the woman in Walmart could be wrong.

Regardless, when his rodeo duties were over, he'd get a gourmet picnic lunch from the Inn and take Renee for a hike up to Long's Pass. With one of the most beautiful views in the northwest for his backdrop, he planned to get down on his knees in the grass and propose. He'd offer the ring from the parure of Zuni jewelry he'd kept hidden for so long and had transferred to his bag of bullfighting gear for the flight. The old Renee would have demanded a diamond the size of both her former engagement rings combined. This new Renee, the one who put on a clown face to entertain children, would desire a ring with meaning and some history behind it now. He'd tell her he wanted both her and the child, no matter who the daddy really was, even if it drove a wedge between him and Bodey. The best laid plans don't always work out, but he felt fairly sure of the outcome of this one.

Chapter Seventeen

The bright lights of the arena filled the big night sky with their glare, fading out a view of the Milky Way that stretched from horizon to horizon. A breeze ruffled through the stadium. From his spot down by the bucking chutes, Clint watched Renee put on the denim jacket he'd insisted she buy that morning against an evening chill. When the wind pushed the fabric of the wild and swirling top that seemed to be her favorite up against her belly, she did look pregnant, he had to admit.

A dark-haired woman in cowgirl attire glittering with rhinestones took a seat next to Renee. Norma Jean Scruggs, he thought it was. The women put their heads together, not paying much attention to the action in the ring. Maybe, they compared notes about Clinton O. Beck. Women did that. He couldn't worry about it now. The chute would spring open in the next few seconds, releasing another two-ton terror of a bull into the ring.

Next up came Mellow Yellow who always gave a rider a chance for a high score despite his stubby legs. Once free of the man on his back, though, Ole Yeller was fairly docile and had been around long enough to find the exit from the arena with very little help. Clint relaxed. He had the urge to get Renee's attention.

Mellow Yellow's rider hung on for five seconds and went spinning wide out of danger before the buzzer sounded. The mottled old bull looked around for the gate and found Clint Beck instead. Clint took a running leap, and as soon as his hands caught hold of the horns, he wished he'd paused to dust his palms with dirt. His grip slipped, and he came down on the bull's hump rather than behind it. Mellow Yellow lowered his head to shake off the burden, and Clint slid toward the horns and hooves waiting below. He planted his hands, swung his leg wide over the right horn, vaulted off the side of the animal, and stuck a great dismount. The crowd loved it. Clint waved in Renee's direction while the other bullfighters swatted the puzzled Mellow Yellow into the pen. He didn't see her.

Rejoining the group by the chutes, he apologized. "Sorry. I was showing off for my girl. I shouldn't have done that."

"Yeah, you shouldn't have. I think she fainted," one of his bullfighting buddies said as Clint dusted off his hat and put it back on his head.

He found Renee now. Norma Jean had hauled her up and pushed her into her seat, her head lowered between her legs.

"Break's comin' up. Why don't you go see to her, Clint? Women in the family way are almost as much trouble as these here bulls," the third bullfighter added. "Got three kids of my own. I should know."

Her condition had become so obvious even these men could tell. Clint went up into the stands, nodding and slapping hands held out to him, but not stopping until he reached Renee.

Her first words uttered: "Don't fuss. I'm fine. I stood up too quickly. You nearly gave me heart failure."

"Sorry, I made a dumb move. Let's get you over to Mobile Sports Medicine and let them check you out."

"Just to be on the safe side, honey," Norma Jean prodded.

Set up for rodeo participants right down to having cardiac life support, the medical unit wasn't intended for fainting fans, the doctor in charge pointed out immediately. Lean as most of the cowboys, he was just as terse.

"I have one rider back here gathering his chickens after a pretty bad concussion and another with a broken ankle, Clint. Haven't done a gynecology rotation since med school. Take her into town."

"Got more work to do tonight. As a favor to me, Doc, please."

Heavily put upon, Doc Wiley checked her pulse, blood pressure, and flashed a light into the woman's eyes. Satisfied, he told Renee to get up on the table and unzip her pants. He palpated her abdomen, listened with his stethoscope. "How far along are you?"

"I don't know what you're talking about," Renee stonewalled.

"When was the date of your last period?"

"Late May, I guess, but I've been traveling since then. Lots of strange food and water. Sometimes, I'm irregular if I exercise a lot. My mother died suddenly. It was a shock to my system. Could be a tumor." She rolled off a list of possibilities that sounded as if any of them would be preferable to a pregnancy.

Doc Wiley shoved his glasses back up his nose. "That ultrasound machine free?" he shouted to a technician.

"Yes, sir."

"Get a view of her uterus up on the screen for me. Pronto!"

Doc Wiley took Clint aside. "How long you been together, Clint?"

"Little over three months."

"By the size, I'd say she's close to five months gone. Sorry."

"Don't be. Every baby should have a daddy. I'm ready to take that on."

"Clint, Clint!" he heard Renee call.

He came running. The tech continued rubbing slick goop over her belly.

"Don't let them do this to me," she pleaded.

"Ma'am, if this is a tumor it's a mighty big one. I'd feel guilty letting you go without knowing," Doc Wiley said.

Clint took Renee's hand and kissed her fingers. "I promise it's going to be all right, Tiger."

The tech began moving the imagining device over the mound of her stomach.

"Hold it! Would you look at that," the doctor said.

"What! What!" Renee shouted.

Ignoring his patient, the doc looked at Clint. "Congratulations, son. You're the father of twins. One has its back turned right there, but the other seems to have a teeny-tiny penis. I'd say they're just past the first trimester, but find a real obstetrician, would you?"

"Can't be my son if the penis is teeny-tiny," Clint said, absolutely deadpan. Then, he and the doc started whomping each other on the back and laughing.

"I swear, Clint, I haven't been with anyone else. I'll take a test. Anything."

"Joking, Tiger." He smoothed a tear from the

corner Renee's eye.

"Wipe her off and get her up," the doctor ordered. "And you, young lady, don't stand up suddenly. Pregnancy involves changes in the blood pressure. I remember that much. Eat right. See a real ladies' doctor, okay? I got a head case to check."

Clint grabbed a bottle of water and drank it as he walked Renee back to her seat. He should have been riding the exercise bike to keep his muscles warm like the other guys, but some things had to come first. After centering her face with his hands, he said, "I love you, Renee. Everything will be fine. Do you believe me?"

She nodded, speechless and worried. He shared the news with Norma Jean and left Renee in the care of the barrel-racer who exclaimed as he headed for the chutes, "Twins. Now ain't that a double blessing." Clint knew for a fact Norma Jean had raised her four brothers and had no desire at all for children, but she was a good ole gal, and he appreciated her effort.

Lonnie Capshaw, a rising star nineteen years old, stopped Clint before he reached his destination. "I drew Tsunami Sam. I know he's a bad one."

"No way to predict what Sam will do. Only been ridden twice in the past three years, but don't let that shake you. Once you're off, head for the hills. He's a rank one."

"Thanks, Clint." The boy's dark eyes looked large in his fresh, unscarred face. He brushed the curly black hair out of his eyes, put on his hat, and went off to the chutes dragging his bull rope.

Clint took up his position by the gate. The other bullfighters already stood in place. Out in the center of the ring, Snuffy would be working the barrels. All good men to work with. Clint stretched. He felt a little stiff and off-balance. Twins. Who would have imagined twins?

The gate swung open, and Tsunami Sam roared out, a dark wave of bull flesh heaving over the brown dirt of the arena. Lonnie hung on, hardly needing his spurs to urge the beast to perform to the max. The longest eight seconds of the man's life ticked off one by one. The buzzer sounded. The announcer predicted that young Lonnie Capshaw would get the confetti for that ride, even as the cowboy shook loose of his hold on the rope. Not done yet, the bull fishtailed and sent the kid flying toward a hard landing. Stunned, Lonnie struggled to get up and reach the fence. His boots gave him little traction as he stumbled toward the rails with Tsunami Sam on his tail. He couldn't make it up and over—until Clint Beck gave him a boost.

Clint rolled aside as the bull smashed into the space where Lonnie Capshaw had been, but this time, the bullfighter wasn't fast enough. One blunted horn and a big, bony head plowed into his mid-section, ramming him against the boards. Fighting incredible pain, Clint felt his knees gave way. He heard Snuffy taunting the bull to come toward the clown. Through blurring eyes, he saw the other bullfighters swarming Tsunami Sam, literally taking the bull by the horns and turning the monster's head. From the stands, he recognized the sound of Renee's voice, screaming, right before he blacked out.

Chapter Eighteen

A few of the younger nuns dropped gentle hints to the Mother Superior at Mt. Carmel Academy that Srs. Helen and Inez might be ready to return to the mother house and go into retirement. The elderly Sisters hogged the remote control between the hours of ten to eleven p.m. on a Saturday night when, being so advanced in age, they should be napping before midnight prayers. Their order had allowed the purchase of expanded cable for the television in the common area to view more spiritual and uplifting programs than professional bull riding.

"Oh look, Nessy. I think I see Renee in the stands. There, wearing that loud top. Dear, oh dear, she looks as if she's expecting," whispered Sr. Helen.

"Let me get my spectacles on." Sr. Inez found the wire-rimmed glasses in the pocket of her skirt and balanced them on her nose. She hated to admit her vision was failing, but that was a vanity.

"You missed her. They've released another bull."

"I can see that!"

"It's Mellow Yellow, short but mighty. Oooh, there goes the rider. Look at Clint. He's jumping the bull."

"Nearly got himself gored. If you are right about Renee, he should be taking better care of himself. My, that was tense. Oh, they're going for a break. I need the bathroom, Sister. A little too much excitement." Sr.

Inez dug her walking stick into the carpet and wrenched herself up from the sofa. She limped off for a pit stop.

"Take your time. You know the interviews will go on and on before the action starts again. I'll make more popcorn. Anyone else want popcorn?" Sr. Helen surveyed the nuns sitting around the room, reading, sewing, hoping to get the remote control. She pocketed the device and set off for the kitchen. She'd make an extra bowl in case any of the others wanted to join them on the sofa.

Back in their seats, the two elderly Sisters picked around the kernels the microwave always scorched and settled in for the second half of Professional Bull Riders. Sr. Inez overheard one of their more sour compatriots say this wasn't any better than pro wrestling, but she'd given them a bowl of popcorn as an act of charity and forbearance.

"Mighty bulls, courageous men, fine horse flesh, how could anyone equate this with steroid-swollen hulks faking mayhem," Nessy muttered to Helen. "It's the toughest sport on dirt."

"Tsunami Sam is up next. He's a PBR top ten bull being ridden by that sweet-faced boy we saw last week, Lonnie Capshaw." Sr. Helen lowered her voice. "Ignore the other Sisters. They don't understand."

The two holy fans held their breath for the full eight seconds and applauded the ride. "I'm sure he'll score higher than ninety. Oh, no! A bad dismount. Lonnie won't make it to the barrier. Here comes Clint boosting him over. Dear Lord, be with him! Clint is down."

Sr. Helen wobbled to her feet and clasped her hands together. "Blessed Mother Leontine, intercede for this man's life, we pray of you."

"And be with our lost child, Renee. Show her the right path to follow in her time of need. Amen."

The elderly Sisters crossed themselves and sank back into the sofa cushions. They would stay tuned until the end of the program, hoping for an update on the condition of Clinton O. Beck.

****

In the secular part of Rainbow, Bodey Landrum shot to his feet. "Jesus God, that fucker of a bull smashed Clint against the boards! His safety vest can't protect him from that. Eve, say a prayer for him."

The baby in Eve's lap startled awake at his father's exclamation and began to cry. Eve raised Shea to her shoulder and patted him for comfort. "You should say your own prayer, Bodey Landrum. No matter what you believe, your prayers are as good as mine. I sent a message to God the second Clint got hit. And what about Renee up there in the stands? This isn't good for her condition. She needs a prayer, too."

"What condition?"

"Noreen and I are fairly sure she is expecting."

"I thought maybe she was just going to fat."

"Renee? That woman is so body-conscious she will never be fat. Go on now, get on your knees and pray for both of them. Shea and I will join you."

Bodey inhaled, dropped to his knees, and ordered his thoughts. He lacked eloquence for this sort of thing. That's why the world had priests and nuns and people like Eve who believed in miracles. Clinton O. Beck left the arena unconscious on a stretcher. He folded his hands.

"Dear Lord, be with my buddy, Clint Beck tonight.

He's saved many a bull riders' life in his time and now he needs you to save him, especially if he's about to become a daddy. When I rode the bulls, I thought my skill and good luck and men like Clint kept me from harm. Now I know you had a hand in it, too, so I could survive to marry this wonderful woman and raise my own son. If you have another miracle handy, please give it to Clint. Amen."

Eve clasped the baby's hands between hers. "We add our prayers for the recovery of Clint Beck, a good man who is trying to save a lost woman. Let him live to complete this task and see his own child come into the world. And please don't let my son grow up to play around with bulls."

Bodey rose so fast, his bum knee pained him. "Now that ain't fair, Eve. Shea has bull riding in his blood. He's being raised on a ranch that breeds bucking bulls and trains bullfighters. He'll want to have a go at it."

Seeing the stubborn look on Eve's usually serene face, he clasped his hands again. "God, you still listenin'? You tell my wife our boy has to make up his own mind and you'll look out for him if he decides he wants to ride rough stock. Amen."

Eve stood a few inches taller than her husband and leveled her gray eyes at him. "You shouldn't pray for things like that."

Bodey rose up on his toes at little and answered her back. "You said my prayers are as good as yours. We'll see whose get answered down the line."

"Well, our prayers for Clint are the only ones that matter right now. God be with him."

****

At Hacienda Hidalgo, Lena Beck cried, "*Dios mio,* call for the jet, Gunter. We must go to our son at once. I need to go pray to Santa Maria and the Virgin right now. They will help him."

Gunter Beck simply sat there watching his heir being carted from the area like a heap of fertilizer left behind by the bull. "Our son made a poor career choice and he is paying for it. You used all your influence to force me to allow him to follow this path. I should have cut him off entirely, not given into having him sign that foolish contract. So, run to your saints and see what good advice they give you now."

Lena crossed herself as if to ward off her husband's callous words. She took another glance at the television screen where the announcer asked everyone to stand and offer up a moment of silence for the bullfighter. "Look, there is Renee. Norma Jean is holding her up, a good, strong woman to be at her side, but I need to be there, too. I fear for her and the baby she carries. Maybe it is Clint's by some miracle. We must see it has a good home, regardless."

Gunter Beck cleared his throat with disgust. "Stray dogs, spoiled horses, old cows, you expect me to take in another of Clint's misfits. For all that bullfighter's toughness he claims, our son is soft on the inside. Maybe he isn't cut out to be the head of Beck's Beans after all."

Lena's hand came up and slapped his face so hard her bracelets slammed together like a gunshot. "Is that all you care about—your corporation! Clint loves this woman. I will see she and the child are cared for."

Gunter rubbed his cheek where the rose-colored imprint of her hand marked his pale face. His icy blue eyes narrowed. "You were so docile when I married you. Then, you showed me how hot your Spanish blood could be, but not in this way, not by striking me."

"You never deserved it so much before."

"Let me tell you, Lena, this woman Clint thinks he loves is a gold digger. I had her checked out by my investigator the second he started writing home about her. Maybe she's pregnant, maybe she's not. No confirmed word on that yet. If she is, she planned it to force our son or some other man who walked out to marry her. This Renee is a woman of loose morals who lurked about that bull riding school picking up men at random. She's no better than a high class whore."

"They say the same of my patron saint. She became the beloved follower of Christ. There is no reason why Renee cannot reform through her love for Clint."

"Clint is hardly Christ."

"I must go and pray. If you won't summon the jet, I will." Lena left the room taking all of the heat with her despite the small fire that burned in the grate.

Convinced he was right in this situation, still Gunter Beck knew Lena put the only warmth into his life as a cold-hearted businessman. What would he do if she withdrew her love? He'd arrange for the jet, but protect his son and his company as well. All three of them meant a great deal to him whether he said it or not.

Chapter Nineteen

Renee sat by Clint's bed in the ICU. The floor was quiet, the lights dim. Nurses staffed a station that looked as if it contained the control panel for a starship. The only noise came from the humming and beeping machines keeping patients alive and monitoring their condition.

She listened to his regular breathing, thankful they hadn't put him on a respirator like so many others on the floor. The two cracked ribs hadn't penetrated his lungs, but Clint lost his crushed spleen and suffered from a lacerated liver. The body armor worn beneath his shirt had prevented his death as well as quick action by the Mobile Sports Medicine team and the other bullfighters, but still, something could go wrong. She might lose him. Unthinkable. She must stay awake and watch over him. Greater powers were at work, however. Renee's head nodded in the gloomy silence.

When she forced her eyes open again, a nun in the old style penguin habit stood by Clint's side. The woman clasped her hands in prayer. Renee had thrown a few prayers into the wind herself on the frantic race to the hospital with Norma Jean Scruggs driving like she rode her barrel horses, fast and close to anything in her way as they followed the ambulance. Renee called on Lena Beck's namesake, St. Mary Magdalene, to save her man, hoping that after being estranged from the church for so many years, heaven would hear her pleas.

She felt grateful to have Norma Jean on her side, too. The moment Clint said he loved her all jealousy of the flamboyant black-haired woman vanished like a vision and left space for friendship. When the hospital staff sought to bar her from the ICU as a non-relative, the barrel racer got into their faces. A riled Norma Jean had the power of a Texas twister.

"This woman is pregnant with that man's twins. If that ain't family, I don't know who is. You go on in, honey. I'll be in the waiting room if you need a ride, coffee, food, or anything else."

True to her upbringing, despite the many headaches she'd given the nuns at Mt. Carmel Academy, Renee waited respectfully for the nun to finish her prayer. The robed woman at last raised her head and turned stern gray eyes toward Renee.

"Thank you for your prayer, Sister," Renee whispered into the hush of the hospital room.

The nun, who looked strangely familiar, unclasped her hands and pointed a long, strong finger at the pregnant woman. "Marry this man or burn!" she commanded.

Mute and astounded, Renee jerked upright in her chair. The room was empty. She'd been dreaming of course. That's what too much Catholicism did to a person. Suddenly wistful, she thought marrying Clint Beck might be her idea of heaven on earth, a heaven she didn't deserve. "He hasn't proposed, Sister," she murmured, offering an excuse to the spectral nun. "And he shouldn't just because I'm pregnant. I'll ruin his life exactly like I always ruin mine. You have to understand."

The best she could hope for would be generous child support, not that she deserved to be a mother either. He'd be a great dad, maybe not around too much since he'd be living in Texas, and according to him, running the business he'd long evaded because he always kept his word. But, he might keep in touch, stop by and take the kids for a nice vacation, teach them to ride, stay in their lives, be a real father who noticed what went on with them. The night grew long, and she slept again.

****

Renee woke with a stiff neck and a full bladder. Another person stood in the room. Not the scary nun, thank heaven, but brightly-dressed Madalena Beck. She looked as cheerful as a bouquet of daisies in this sterile place where flowers weren't allowed and gave Renee a friendly smile.

"I got here an hour ago but didn't want to wake you or Clint. The jet has gone back for his father who had some paperwork to complete before coming. Snuffy and Norma Jean are out in the waiting room. They tell me you're going to be the mother of twins."

Instantly defensive, Renee straightened in her chair. "They belong to Clint."

"Of course, they do. Santa Maria Magdalena promised me a wonderful miracle would occur if I could take you into my heart. I have done so. What could be more miraculous or wonderful than twin grandbabies?"

"Right now, having Clint open his eyes, hearing his voice again, knowing he will have a full recovery."

"Also true."

Whether their voices wakened Clint or whether

Renee had received her own small miracle, the man in the bed groaned and opened his eyes. Their deep sea blue appeared glazed by pain or drugs, but he opened his mouth and said in a dry croak, "My two favorite women together. My kind of vision. Had one earlier. This tall, old nun prayed over me." Clint coughed. "Thought I was dying."

"Did she speak to you?" Renee poured a glass of water and held it to his lips.

Clint swallowed. "No. Not a word. Just got a weird feeling I had to wake up and do something before things went wrong."

"Sounds like the nuns I grew up with. Do it their way, and do it now. Rest Clint, and get better. Don't worry about it." She stroked his hair.

"I'm not worried. I know what I need to do. First, tell me what happened."

"Tsunami Sam nailed you to the wall after you helped Lonnie over the barricade."

"Yeah, right. Then what?" Clint glimpsed down at the tubes and wires attached to his body.

"Son, they had to take out your spleen and repair your liver," Mrs. Beck said gently. "Two ribs were also broken, but your lungs are fine."

Clint came back stronger. "Broken ribs are nothing. I guess I can do without my spleen. As long as I'm able to say 'I do', Renee and I can get married. You were right, Mama. She is pregnant. I know Renee looks big for three months, but we're having twins. Great, huh?"

Clint had this loopy look on his face prompting Renee to say, "Thank you for the lovely proposal, but you might want to rethink it when you aren't drugged up."

"No, no. I feel like shit, so it can't be drugs. I planned a picnic with a great view and a nice ring. Honest to God, Renee, I was going to ask you. I want to be sure the babies have my name and my fortune in case... Well, people do die in hospitals. Mama, find a priest and get the paperwork started no matter what Renee says."

A nurse, the picture of efficiency, briskly entered into the room. "I see Mr. Beck is awake and talking far too much for his condition. Everyone out for now. We have some routine maintenance to do here."

Shunted into the hallway, Renee gave Lena Beck an embarrassed glance. "I really need to use the restroom."

Mrs. Beck smiled. "I remember the feeling, and I carried only one child at a time. Go get some breakfast, too. I will remain by Clinton until you return."

Getting the bathroom business out of the way very quickly, Renee poked her head into the waiting room where Norma Jean Scruggs lay stretched out, full length and asleep, in a recliner. Snuffy Jones, curled up on a sofa like an old dog on a favorite rug, snored loud as a buzz saw. He must have come over as soon as the bull riding event ended. Good people, both of them. The growling of her stomach grew so loud she was surprised it didn't waken them.

Whatever people said about hospital food, after weeks of barely keeping down tea in the mornings, Renee wolfed a ham and cheese omelet, two slices of whole wheat toast, and a fruit cup. Trying to remember the last time she'd craved cow juice, she sucked up the last drops in a carton of milk. Not for years, though Clint drank it by the gallon. As if thinking of him summoned up his mother, Madalena Beck took the seat across from Renee and stirred two little pots of half and half into her cup of coffee.

"Shouldn't you be with Clint? You're his real family."

"They've given him drugs for the pain and put him back to sleep. He fought it off while trying to give me a to-do list." Lena showed Renee a sheet of paper torn from an address book. "By item number four, he was out."

Renee looked over the list with its cryptic abbreviations.

Get priest

Do paperwork

Take Renee shopping, w.d.

Jewelry

"I don't want to go shopping. I have clothes back at the Inn and more at home. He doesn't owe me a new wardrobe. I keep telling him that."

"W.D., Renee. He wants you to have a wedding dress."

"Mrs. Beck, you ought to know I've been married twice before. I've had the big white wedding at the cathedral in Lafayette. I've done the destination wedding in the Bahamas. My first husband divorced me for adultery, and I killed my second husband with sex."

Mrs. Beck nodded. "He was elderly, your second husband, but you were fond of him. Clinton and I keep in touch through e-mail when he is on the road."

"Ah, yes, the hidden laptop. Then, I suppose you know I am tainted, too."

"I know about your uncle, yes. The fault was not yours. You saved your sister from that evil man."

"I could have saved more girls if I had spoken up sooner—Uncle Dewey's own daughter, who knows how many others. I didn't want anybody to know what he did to me. If Clint hadn't forced the matter at my mother's funeral, I would never have spoken out. I am a coward." Renee kept her eyes on her empty plate. Her stomach churned.

"Not any more. You will testify against this terrible man. And if you feel yourself falter, Clinton has courage enough for both of you."

"That's true. Mrs. Beck…"

"Le-na, please, or Mama Lena is what my sons-in-law call me." She patted Renee's clenched hands with her be-ringed fingers.

"Lena, Clint is the kind of man who will marry me because of these babies. Not so long ago, I would have jumped at the chance for another rich husband. When we first met, I was bored. I went on the road with a simple cowboy for a lark—and to shock my family and friends. I've been doing that for years. If I'd known he had money, I would have dragged him to Vegas for a ceremony. I can't do that to him now."

"You are wrong about the babies. Before you left Hacienda Hidalgo, Clinton told me he would marry you even when he thought you carried another man's child."

Renee gave her a wavery smile. "That's Clint. Always putting himself between trouble and a person who needs protection. But, I'll be fine, really."

"You know my son is brave and kind of heart. You should also know he is very, very stubborn, like his father, and could not be forced to marry anyone. Clinton is the man who tore up his Harvard MBA in front of my husband, told him to stuff the family business, and ran off to join the rodeo. They didn't speak for months until Gunter offered him a contract stating Clint would have ten years of complete freedom and financial support if he returned to the Beck Corporation at the end of that time. The time has come for my son to settle down, and he wants to do that with you. Believe me, if Clinton did not love you, he would see that you and the children were cared for, but he would not put a ring on your finger."

"That's another thing—about caring for the babies. I doubt I can be a good mother. My own wasn't much of an example."

"Nonsense!" Lena Beck exclaimed. "Clinton has told me how well you got along with the children at the rodeos, how kind you were to Gracie Jones. He says you would protect your children with the ferocity of a tigress."

"That's certainly true. I'd never let someone hurt my children the way Uncle Dewey hurt me. I'd see the signs. I'd know and prevent it. As for other children, they don't judge a person. A big smile, a comfortable lap, a very big chest, and a few soft words wins them over—along with a large bag of toys."

"Exactly. You see, you already know some of the secrets of motherhood. My daughters and I can teach you more. You will not be alone in this. And if I do say so, Clinton will be an excellent father having learned from Gunter's mistakes."

"You don't have a happy marriage, Lena?" Renee asked, twisting the straw of her milk carton between her fingers.

"Gunter and I have been together for fifty years, my dear. Considering how we met, we have been very good for each other. I grew up at a private school run by nuns as you did, but I was very obedient. Then, Papi sent me to a women's college for the rest of my education. I was so sheltered it makes my daughters laugh. Shortly after my graduation, young, handsome, and very Anglo, Gunter Beck, came to arrange contracts with my father for agricultural products that have been raised on Hidalgo land for centuries. Papi invited him to dinner at our hacienda. With Gunter so very stiff and proper, my father allowed him to walk with me in the courtyard when Gunter asked him so very seriously if he could do so."

Lena Beck wrinkled her nose. "I secretly hoped for someone with more fire who would come to my window at night and ride away with me like all romantic young women. We did go riding the next day with two of my father's *vaqueros* right behind us. The courtship progressed very slowly, very formally. We were never left alone. Gunter asked my father for my hand before he asked me. I begged for time to consider the offer. I wanted to turn him down, of course. I could not imagine spending my life with this staid man. Papa approved of an alliance with the Beck family as good business, but he would not have forced me."

"Yet you have been married for fifty years," Renee marveled.

"That night, Santa Maria Magdalena came to me in my dreams and told me Gunter Beck had a great need for warmth only I could fill. The passion I craved lay just below his cold exterior. One does not ignore a saint. I discovered the truth of that on my wedding night. I do not believe Gunter has ever strayed, no matter how many foreign places he visits. When he teases me about getting messages from saints, I remind him he owes our marriage to Santa Maria." Lena returned the smile she'd made blossom on Renee's face.

"So, along came our daughters, Marisol and Annalise, then an ectopic pregnancy. I lost an ovary, nearly bled to death, and was told my chances for having more children were very slim. Gunter worried so about losing me that I started using a diaphragm, which failed to work when I was forty. Another vision told me I would have a son, a wonderful son. Renee, you must never turn down gifts from God."

Renee touched her belly. "I haven't. Even when I suspected what might be wrong with me, I did not consider abortion." She laughed ruefully. "I guess the nuns got to me after all."

"Yes. They have a way of doing that. So, only one question remains. Renee, do you love my son?" Lena looked directly into the eyes of the often-married Renee Niles Bouchard Hayes and waited.

Renee took a deep breath. "I love him so much that I know he should have a better bride. The best I could do for Clinton O. Beck is never to find out his middle name."

Madalena Beck threw back her head and laughed. Her dangling earrings swung merrily. "Oh, that! Not only will you find out his middle name at the wedding, but my Gunter will insist the first boy born to you have it as his middle name. He is so very proud of his heritage. And now, since you and Clinton love each other, I suggest we go wedding dress shopping.

Chapter Twenty

"With that dark auburn hair, green is definitely your color, Renee. The gray silk was very attractive, but this is much better." Madalena Beck nodded her approval.

Renee checked herself in the mirror of the nurses' lounge. A shade of blue-green the color of butterfly wings, the wedding dress wrapped around and under her breasts, then belled out slightly to her knees. Lace dyed the exact color extended the length of the gown to mid-calf in a many-pointed hem. The sleeves were extended from her elbows to her wrists with the same lace. The fabric had some body, unlike the gray silk which clung to her belly. They'd found it on a mother-of-the-bride rack where styles for heftier women prevailed. She had no intention of standing in front of a strange justice of the peace looking pregnant. Ellensburg proved to be thin on Catholic priests, at least of that variety who would perform a rather irregular marriage without banns being read for a divorced woman who had married again without obtaining an annulment from the Church. They'd had to go with a civil ceremony performed by a justice of the peace only too happy to oblige the famous Clinton O. Beck.

Her hair hung straight and silky to her shoulders now, and her complexion did glow so much she had used little makeup—just a touch of smoky eye shadow with a hint of green, a bit of liner and mascara, and a lush, dark coral lipstick. She was as ready as she ever would be to marry Clinton O. Beck.

"And you, Norma Jean, should always wear blue with those gorgeous eyes of yours," Lena Beck told the cowgirl more used to jeans than dresses.

Norma Jean Scruggs, so relaxed on a barrel horse or in bed with a man, squirmed in discomfort, and Renee laughed. "You do look wonderful. Thank you for being my bridesmaid."

Norma Jean tugged at the skirt of a dress with a tighter fit and total lack of embellishments that suited her long, lean frame. "I'm kinda old to be anyone's maid, but thanks for not makin' me wear lace. Never been in a weddin' before. Women don't seem to like me as much as men do."

"I know that feeling," Renee assured her.

"I'd only do this for Clint because he's the best." Norma Jean squirmed again.

"He is, he definitely is. Are we ready, then?" Renee asked eager to go to Clint's side.

"Oh my, no! We haven't put on the finishing touches yet." Lena Beck opened a long, flat box and unfolded what Renee mistook for a tablecloth. She shook out the swath of creamy lace and draped it over Renee's hair. "The Hidalgo wedding veil worn by my grandmother, my mother, myself, and both my daughters. Here, let me pin it into place. We have hand-tied bouquets of yellow roses for both of you, and an extra yellow rose for your hair, Renee."

The bride didn't have the heart to tell her future mother-in-law that she would rather be bareheaded. "Funny, the Niles family has some history with yellow roses. My cousin's wife would be so thrilled."

"Yellow roses for Texas, of course," Lena Beck amended. "I know they should be red. I think of you more as a wild, red rose like the ones in my courtyard, but we are too far away to use them. Gunter suggested the yellow roses and they do blend better with the dresses. And now for the jewelry. Clinton wanted you to have this set."

She held out a box containing the Zuni parure. "Evidently, he has been carrying this around with his bullfighting gear since you left the hacienda. I hope it hasn't been damaged. Snuffy had to go over to the arena to retrieve it along with Clint's other belongings."

"I can't believe Clint bought it for me. I saw this set at a stop we made our first week together, and he refused to buy it no matter how much I pouted. The only piece missing is the ring."

"Snuffy has the ring since he's acting as best man today. Let's get you decked out in this. Then, I'll go tell the men we are ready." Lena fastened the gorgeous silver and green stone sunburst around the bride's neck. Renee snapped on the bracelet—even though the lace of her sleeve hid it—and placed the earrings in her lobes.

Lena gave her a big, encouraging smile and scurried off in her festive red suit, her jewelry a-clanking. Norma Jean followed doing a fake bridesmaid's walk down the hall, twitching her tail at the interns and orderlies she passed. Renee took a moment by herself. With the addition of the Zuni jewelry and veil, she now resembled a hybrid Hispanic-Indian pregnant bride, not her best look of the three weddings, but each item was filled with meaning and goodwill. So what, no photographers lingered around.

Clint had been out of the ICU for only a day. Fortunately, the clerk who handled marriage licenses, a big rodeo fan, came personally to the hospital for the groom's signature and expedited the paperwork after getting a signed glossy from the Bull Bomber himself and a great tale to tell around town. Being at the hospital every day, they'd had no trouble getting blood tests. All that Renee Niles Bouchard Hayes had to do was sail smoothly down the hospital corridor and claim her happy ending.

The lounge door creaked open. Gunter Beck, Clint's father, entered. He wore an expensively tailored gray business suit with the signature Texas yellow rose in the lapel.

Taken up in Lena's whirlwind of preparations, Renee had met him only briefly. He'd been busy elsewhere and apologized very little for that. She saw where Clint got his chiseled good looks, though Gunter's eyes were a lighter, colder blue, his lips thinner, and his blond hair long ago faded to white. At seventy-five, the man's erect posture had not given an inch to the passage of time.

"Did you come to walk me down the aisle?" Renee asked with a smile on her lips.

"No. We have a small matter to discuss before the nuptials take place, some papers to sign. Please sit down, read over these documents, and put your signature here, here, and here." He drew large X's with an expensive pen.

"A prenuptial agreement?" So, Clint's notation about paperwork concerned more than getting a marriage license. She recognized the form well from her first two marriages, which she'd left with nothing except a few luxurious gifts. Why should now be any different? Why had she believed it would be?

"Of course. Clinton's brain may be addled by years of playing with bulls, and once Lena gets a message from her saint, she cannot be stopped, but I must look out for my son and my family business. Having been married twice before to wealthy men, I am sure you are familiar with the procedure. The first set states you will have no claim to the assets of the Beck Corporation, family lands, antiques, or heritage items should you divorce my son. Considering the circumstances I have added two riders. Please read over them carefully."

Renee flipped to the first rider and read aloud the key phrase buried in legalese. "In case of divorce, the undersigned will relinquish full custody of any children produced by the marriage to Clinton O. Beck, who shall determine the amount of contact, visitation, and shared vacation to which any offspring will be exposed."

The second rider appeared to be more of a chart spelling out how much the undersigned would receive in alimony according to a sliding scale adjusted by the cause of the divorce and the years of marriage. The lowest amount, still a comfortable living for most people, mentioned divorce for adultery within two years. Desertion came second. Mutual consent topped the chart with the biggest bucks, but this was subdivided by the years of marriage completed. Renee dropped the fine Mont Blanc pen Gunter presented to her onto the stained plastic table of the lounge.

"I wouldn't balk at this point, Mrs. Hayes. Should you walk out the best you can hope for is child support—if you can prove the children belong to Clint. If they do, we shall certainly sue for custody based on your past lurid sexual behavior. My private investigator had no trouble gathering sworn testimony from the personal trainer mentioned in your first divorce. Your adult former stepchildren were quite helpful in pointing out men you associated with after their father's death. Oh, your family closed ranks, and Bodey Landrum, whom I should have thought would want to help his friend, tossed my man out, but we have more than enough witnesses to your foul morals to win a custody battle." Gunter Beck offered the pen again.

Numbly, Renee took it and signed her name three times.

"Shall we go? The justice is waiting." Gunter offered his crooked arm.

"I'd rather walk alone, thank you."

He nodded sharply, as if he had just concluded a hostile takeover of a sauerkraut company, and marched off to join the wedding party clustered in Clint's hospital room. Renee stilled her shaking hands and wobbly knees. She could leave right now and count on several miserable years of ugly litigation, or she could go through with the wedding because that would be best for Clint and the babies. Afterwards, she would be alone once more with her miserable self, no happy endings for those who did not deserve one.

Despite her turmoil, Renee managed to smile when she set eyes on Clint dressed in the top half of a tuxedo, yellow rose in his lapel, and any number of tubes and wires poking out from under the sheet that covered his bottom half. Snuffy had managed to get a rented tuxedo and a clean shave. Norma Jean kept watching the clock as if gauging the amount of time left until she could put her jeans back on. Lena Beck cried happy tears into a hankie. Gunter Beck presented a face of stone to the others.

The justice of the peace was bald, fat, and genial. Clearly, he would enjoy relating this extraordinary story over a nice meal served with wine. He strove to make the service a happy occasion peppered with short analogies equating marriage to bullfighting: its give and take, its need for finesse and great care. Renee heard very little of what the justice said until the he came to the vows. She repeated hers softly, "I, Renee Marie Niles Hayes, do take you, Clinton…"

Clint said his vows with gusto, pausing for a brief moment before stating his full name. "I, Clinton Odulf Beck—"

"Odulf!" The ridiculous name lifted Renee from her depression for an instant. She pressed her lips together, but the giggle came out.

Gunter Beck bristled. "Odulf is a fine Teutonic name meaning 'the rich and heroic'. Odulf Beck founded our company along with his brother Wilhelm in—"

"*Ja, ja*, Odie and Villie had no talent for raising cattle, but they sure could bake a bean, Renee," Clint quipped.

Snuffy nearly gagged on his chaw, which so far, he had kept discreetly stuffed in his cheek. Norma Jean sing-songed, "I know Cinton's middle name, I'm gonna tell-elle."

Madalena Beck laid calming hands on her red-faced husband, and the officiator begged, "Please, we are in the middle of a solemn ceremony."

The service continued. Snuffy found the ring at the right moment and a water glass to spit into in the nick of time. Norma Jean did her duty by holding the bouquet. Somehow, they finally reached, "You may kiss the bride."

Clint smiled up from the bed. "You'll have to do the honors, Tiger."

Renee raised the hand she had been holding and brushed his fingertips with her lips. Bending over the bed, she took her husband's face between her hands and kissed him with such tenderness and longing that even the hardened Norma Jean sighed.

Lena Beck began snapping pictures with a digital camera she had kept hidden in a perky, red leather handbag. She arranged and rearranged the wedding party: the bride and groom with and without attendants, with the justice, with her and her husband, Snuffy taking that last picture. Several nurses hovering in the doorway took their own souvenir snapshots. Renee managed to curve her lips for each pose. When the photo frenzy ceased, she asked, "Are we through now?"

"I've made arrangements for a wedding dinner at a wonderful restaurant. My dear son, I wish you could come with us, but you must stay here and get better. When that day comes, we can have your vows repeated within the Church and will have a big fiesta with all our friends and relatives at the hacienda. You do look tired. We should go."

"No, I feel fine, Mama. Can't eat much of anything for a while, anyhow. Come back later with Renee."

Meanwhile, his bride took off the heirloom veil and folded it neatly. She placed it on the foot of the bed. Then, she removed the Zuni parure, all but the ring, and laid the jewelry on top of the veil.

Zeroing in on Gunter Beck, Renee said, "I

wouldn't want to be accused of making off with any family treasures. You may pick up the babies in six months. They will be in Rainbow, Lousiana. Oh, and put me down for the least amount of alimony. I am sure I can live up to your lowest expectations."

Out she walked, directly to the elevators. Chaos and discord exploded behind her. That was what Renee Niles Bouchard Hayes Beck did best—create havoc and misery. She heard the shouts, recognized the various voices, following her down the hall.

Clint shouted, "Where the hell is my wife going!"

Lena Beck, who knew her husband well, said shrilly, "Gunter, what have you done?" She followed that up with a string of Spanish words, some of them not too nice.

"The patient's blood pressure is spiking! Sedate him." The nurses ordered everyone from the room. Renee stopped in her tracks. Should she return and explain, try to calm Clint with the icy logic of her decision? No, he remained in the best of hands with excellent medical care, family, and good friends by his side. She wasn't part of all that. Never had been, never would be. Her past could not be erased by love, but perhaps by selfless acts, letting Clint raise the children who would not have a mother that shamed them. He'd find someone else, someone better to help raise them, someone he trusted enough to marry without a draconian prenup worse than any of her others.

Snuffy and Norma Jean and the justice started after her, calling her name, but by that time, the elevator doors were closing, shutting out the uproar. Renee stood in a void without sound thanking heaven no cheery elevator music played. If she could only maintain this same stillness for the next six months, she would survive yet another devastating crisis in her life. The wild red rose must spring from its roots after being chopped to the ground again.

****

Snuffy returned puffing. He'd taken the stairs down and come back in the elevator. Clint had already been stripped of his wedding finery by a nurse, the tubes he'd torn out trying to leave the bed put back into place, and wore a hospital gown once more. Whatever the staff had given the patient to calm him down went into effect. His eyelids fluttered. He stayed awake by sheer force of will.

"Where's Renee?"

"Norma Jean caught up with her. She got those long legs, you know. She moved pretty fast considering the tight dress. They were talking it out when I started back. I figured it's a woman thing, hormones or something. Your parents left?"

Clint nodded, sank farther into the pillows. "Arguing. Some mess."

Norma Jean slunk in, two wilting bouquets still in her hands, and threw herself into a bedside chair.

"Renee?"

"Hell, Clint, when I heard what your father made her sign, I let her go. You'd better mend real fast, bullfighter, because you got one mean situation to handle."

Chapter Twenty-One

Mrs. Renee Beck drove directly to the modest motel she had checked into that morning to be closer to the hospital. She hadn't mentioned the shift from her plush digs to anyone. Changing into her jeans, one of Clint's bullfighting jerseys with an advertising slogan splaying across her belly, and her scuffed boots, she gathered up the rest of her Walmart clothes in a bag and laid the wedding dress out on the bed, a gift for some lucky maid to find.

Then, she hesitated. The fabric was so beautiful, the lace wonderfully lavish. If one of the babies should be a girl, she might want the dress some day. Renee put the gown back on its padded hanger and slipped it inside the zippered bag. Even with this extra baggage hanging from a loop in the back seat, she traveled light. Renee stuck her straw hat on her head and put the toy tiger on the dashboard. Grateful she had the rental car with the big engine and wide leather seats Clint had leased upon their arrival and would not have to fight the gears of the Belly Nelle, Renee slipped the luxury vehicle into drive, set the cruise control at eighty, and began the three day drive back to Rainbow.

****

Just her luck that Rusty's goody-goody wife, who had never slept with anyone but her own husband, was the only person available to come get Renee at the airport after she'd turned in the rental car. Renee got into the mom-mobile with three-year-old Katie of the coppery curls strapped into a car seat in the back, slouched down in the front seat, and hoping to avoid conversation, stared out the window. No luck with that either.

"So, how is Clint? We all saw him get hit by that bull. Everyone has prayed for him, even Bodey."

"Must be working. He got out of ICU and was mending three days ago."

"You and he are expecting twins. That's wonderful."

Renee closed her eyes and compressed her lips. She kept her eyes on the scenery. "How did you know?"

"Well, Eve and I thought you looked a little plump at the funeral, and we sort of guessed you might be expecting because you never let yourself go that way—unlike me. When Bodey got in touch with Snuffy to see how Clint was doing, we heard the news. He said you two were going to get married in the hospital."

"We did—for the sake of the babies. It was a marriage of—what do they call it in those old novels? You're the history major."

"A marriage of convenience? I don't believe that, not after the way Clint beat on Dewey for doing—you know."

"Look, Noreen, you believe in soul mates and all that crap, and hell, Eve believes in miracles, but it's not like that. I had to sign papers saying I'd give up the babies to the Becks. It's the best for all of us. What kind of mother would I be anyhow?"

"A good one if you tried. Rusty and I will vouch

for you, Eve and Bodey, too, if you want to fight for custody."

Noreen had that pitying stare on her face, Renee knew without looking. "What would your testimony be—that I helped you sneak around with your boyfriend until you got pregnant—that I slept with Bodey at the age of seventeen and a few times after that."

"You helped bring about a reconciliation between the Niles and Courville families."

"I made trouble. That's all I ever do. I'm no good. Stop praying for me. I cannot be redeemed."

A small voice came from the backseat. "Auntie Renee, don't cry. We can get some ice cream to make you feel better."

"Thanks, Katie-bug, but ice cream won't help this time." Renee regarded her belly pushing against the fabric of Clint's bullfighting shirt. "It will only make me bigger sooner.

****

The terrible drive over at last Renee refused any help with her scanty bags and let herself into her house. If Noreen got in the door, she'd insist on staying and talking. First thing she did was turn the thermostat down to seventy from its setting of eighty. Louisiana—still hot as Hades in September. She threw open the living room curtains hiding the view the garden. Le Grand Pisseur still tinkled mightily with his oversized dick into the birdbath, not as amusing as he used to be.

She straggled back to the bedroom past the parade of partially nude male portraits she'd done mostly of former lovers and into her lair. Instead of finding comfort in her home, all seemed wrong, unsuitable, out of joint. Renee jerked off her boots and stretched out on the tiger-striped comforter. She couldn't rest. She'd had her own bedroom suite when married to the heart surgeon who came and went at odd hours. Dear, sweet Gerry had taken himself off to a snoring room after he completed his business. Except for Clint, men rarely spent the night with Renee. She missed his warmth, the steady sound of his breathing, the arm always ready to enfold her if she had one of those wretched dreams of Uncle Dewey entering her room.

Renee tossed, finally found a comfortable spot, and let her mind drift. Maybe if she got rid of the erotica, Clint would allow the children to visit sometimes. She closed her eyes. A short nap might help to banish such ridiculous sentimentality from her mind.

The doorbell rang. Someone persistent outside laid on the bell. She wished they would go away. Close to eight o'clock, darkness fell. Her stomach rumbled and her bladder ached. Pregnancy was a real pain in the—belly.

The visitor couldn't be the one person she wanted to see. She'd seen him last tied to a hospital bed by tubes and wires a thousand miles away. A scowl on her face, Renee stalked down the hall and flung open the front door. There stood Eve Landrum, tall, pale and pure, the mother goddess holding a hot covered dish by its handles.

"If you've come to save me, you're too late," Renee snarled, ever ungrateful for pity and comfort.

"I believe you have to save yourself, Renee. I've only come to feed you because I know you rarely cook. Let me put this down. I have groceries in the car."

Oh, how she wanted to slam the door in Eve's face, but steam escaped from under the lid of the covered dish. A rich, cheesy aroma filled the air. Renee's stomach betrayed her with a loud growl.

"Come in if you must. I have to pee." She stalked away and let Eve do as she wanted.

By the time Renee returned to the kitchen, Eve had filled a dish with a generous portion of shrimp fettuccini, the kind made with cream cheese and Velveeta and featured at every church social. She had shaken salad from a bag and added a tall glass of milk poured from a gallon container for a beverage.

As Renee sucked up tiny pink shrimp embedded in noodles, Eve put away the contents of a dozen plastic bags from Rainbow Liquor and Groceries. She filled a bowl with fresh fruit: grapes, bananas, apples. She stocked the empty vegetable drawer with tomatoes, green peppers, carrots, and celery, and threw away a sealed bag of moldy cheese cubes.

Holding up a loaf of seven-grain bread from the Herbarium, Eve asked, "Should I leave this out, or do you want to refrigerate it? No preservatives. It goes bad fairly fast but makes great toast. I put a dozen eggs in the rack, and there's sliced low-fat ham in the meat keeper. Say, your answering machine is blinking. Should I turn it on for you?"

"No! I'll get to that later. Look, Eve, I appreciate this. I really do. But, don't you have a baby to nurse or something?"

"I pump breast milk and put it into bottles so Bodey can help out at night."

"Too much information!"

"Don't you plan to nurse?"

A lump formed in Renee's throat. "Implants, remember? I don't think I can even if …" For a moment all she could recall was Clint doing his yokel cowboy routine about her not being able to feed his babies with those breasts.

Eve watched her face and changed the subject. "Why don't you come over and go for a swim with me tomorrow? Afterward, we could paint together in my new studio."

Renee licked cheese sauce from the corner of her mouth. "My bikinis won't fit anymore."

"There wasn't much to them in the first place. Just let it all hang out. Bodey won't mind."

"Okay, after all that driving I could use some exercise, but I'm not sure what I'm allowed to do."

"Swimming is great for pregnant women. I swam in the pool the day before I had Shea. But, we need get you set up with Dr. Maddox in Opelousas. He is wonderful. And we must shop for some really stylish maternity clothes. Does that cheer you up?"

"Oh, I don't need them yet. Besides, my cards are maxed out." Renee glanced down at her full stomach and realized she still wore Clint's bullfighting shirt, stretched out over her breasts and belly and defaced by a fettuccini noodle, along with an unzipped pair of jeans. She wanted to cry about losing her figure, but mostly about losing him.

"Hey, finish your salad, and there's frozen yogurt for dessert," Eve said a little too brightly.

"Maybe later. I think I want to lie down again."

"You will come over tomorrow. Promise me. You need good food and exercise for the sake of the babies. Your figure will recover faster if you stay in shape, too."

"Fine, I promise. Go home to your husband and

son."

As soon as she got Eve Landrum out the door, Renee turned on the answering machine clogged with messages—Clint in a slurred voice asking her to come back—Mama Lena, no, that would be Mrs. Beck, telling her she would make Gunter fix everything—Snuffy saying he sure thought Clint might heal faster with her at his side—Norma Jean claiming other women, those damned nurses, would cut into Renee's territory if she didn't get her ass back to Washington now that she'd showed 'em she couldn't be pushed around—Sr. Helen telling their former student that she and Sr. Nessy prayed for both her and Clint—and Clint again and again and again. She erased all but the ones with Clint's recorded voice and played those over and over until she got to sleep.

Chapter Twenty-Two

The phone rang in Bodey Landrum's house, interrupting Daddy time. Bodey switched off an old CD of his bull riding triumphs and settling Shea firmly in the crook of his arm, got out of his leather recliner and glanced at the caller I.D. Clint again.

"Howdy, Clinton. She's fine. Can't go out on my own damned patio, but Renee is fine."

The baby smiled and waved his arms at the sound of his father's voice, and Bodey grinned right back. Shea's eyes seemed to get bluer with each passing month, and judging by the way women doted on him, he had the Landrum charm. Yessir-re!

"So what's wrong with your patio?" Clint Beck's voice asked from far away.

"Not a thing. Eve and Renee are swimming laps, and Renee doesn't want me to see her *that way*." The baby made a grab for the phone. Bodey raised the receiver higher.

"What way?"

"Wearin' a maternity swimsuit and all swollen up with your babies. Hell, I saw Eve swimming all the time while she was expecting Shea and there is no prettier sight than a wet woman carrying your child. If you ever tell another man I said that, you're bull bait."

Clint laughed as Bodey hoped he would, then got serious. "Put Renee on the phone."

"Now you know I can't do that. Eve says if I trick her into talking to you, Renee won't trust us anymore and we won't be able to help her. My wife did get her to cash the check you sent—for food and medical expenses only. Renee sold that obscene statue she had out in the yard to those two gay guys, Archie and Roger. Got a bundle for it, too, so she's okay financially for now. Eve and Noreen make sure she gets to the doctor and eats right. That's about all I can tell you—except I wish you'd come for your woman because me and Rusty had to spend all last weekend strippin' wallpaper over at her place. Seems she wants to redecorate half her house before she gets too big and is doing it herself to save money. She did order in ribs from the Rainbow Café for us, though."

"Bodey, I'd be there if I could. I'm still locked up in San Antonio. Hacienda Hidalgo might as well be San Quentin. They won't let me drive, limit my exercise, watch my every move. I have to get in shape for the Dickies National Championship Bullfighting competition at the end of October."

Bodey could tell he had one frustrated man on the end of the line. "Maybe you should think twice about that, Clint. Doesn't do to come back too quick from an injury and hurt yourself again."

Clint snorted. "You should talk. I know you rode with a bad back and a bum knee. I need to get Renee's attention. She won't answer my calls or my e-mail messages."

"Been there—know the despair," Bodey said. "Those old nuns say time and prayer takes care of everything, but in my experience, the good Lord moves mighty slow. Still, Sr. Helen and Sr. Inez have been on

208

their knees prayin' for you two so much both of them will soon need knee replacements, and I guess I'll be stuck with the bill."

He got another chuckle out of Clint. "You praying for me, too, Bodey?"

"Sure, every time Eve drags me to church and I got nothin' else to take up my spare time. Get well, good buddy."

"I need to get out of here to do that. My dad is sleeping in a guestroom. I guess I know now how Mama got him to let me keep on with bullfighting. My sisters are over here constantly trying to 'affect reconciliation', they say. Everyone yells, half the time in Spanish. So many candles are being lit to the saints they could burn this place down. I'm telling you, Bodey, I'd be better off in the bullring. Just get Renee to watch the championship competition, would you?"

"I'll do my best. Take care now, you hear? Shea wants to say bye-bye."

The baby grappled for the phone again. Bodey let him have it. The receiver went directly into Shea's mouth and was immediately covered in slobber. Bodey wiped it off against his shirt and hung up. Imagine having two of these little dudes to contend with. Now that would be a handful.

The door to the patio opened. Eve entered toweling her long, fair hair. Renee followed wrapped up in one of the thick terry robes Bodey kept for guests. She was way shorter than Eve, and much bigger at five months. Guess twins did that to a woman. Eve, now, she had gotten her figure back quickly, and her breasts stayed even bigger than before.

"Have a good Daddy time?" Eve asked.

"Sure did. I showed Shea, here, how to stay on a bull. What's for lunch?"

"Chicken salad with mandarin oranges and pecans in a light dressing. Pumpkin bread. Iced tea."

"Girl food."

"Yes, take it or leave it. Renee and I plan to paint after lunch, but we'll keep Shea, so you are free to roam, cowboy."

Bodey sighed internally. He knew better than to let it out. Since Renee returned home, his sex life had been seriously impacted. No more afternoon romps while Shea took his nap.

"I think I'll mosey on over to Rusty's place and get a burger on the way. We have some things we need to discuss, a few plans to make. You girls have a good ole time." Because I won't.

****

Rusty Niles sat settled in front of the television to watch a World Series playoff game when Bodey walked in and stretched out on the sofa next to his recliner. Russ held up his bottle of beer. "Want a brew?"

"No, thanks. Just had lunch at the café."

Bodey could hear Noreen tapping away on the computer in the kitchen alcove. Noreen and Bodey had never gotten along that well because Bodey tried to break up her and Rusty on more than one occasion before their marriage. Still, Noreen was now Eve's best friend and the wife of the man he regarded as a brother, so both of them made an effort to get along.

"Noreen still workin' on her book?" Bodey asked, taking an interest.

"You bet. Once she got that mini-grant for DNA

testing to prove that the Niles family and her branch of the Courvilles were descended from the same man, she got a contract from the university press to write *Sundered Hearts—the True Story of the Niles-Courville Feud.* She still had all her research from the high school project she did at Mt. Carmel that won the state social science fair. The nuns wouldn't let her use the adultery angle, just the star-crossed lovers stuff because we found those letters. The university nixed a last chapter on reincarnation. Not scholarly, they said. She was pissed, but really wants her book published so she had to go along."

"So no one but Noreen, you, me, and Eve will ever know you really possess the tragic soul of Rufus Courville?"

"Go ahead and mock me. I think Noreen has convinced my dad and Mona they are reincarnated, too."

"Who were they in their past life?"

"I don't want to go into it." Rusty took a large swig from his beer bottle.

Little Katie appeared, her small arms overflowing with stuffed toys and dolls, which she arranged in a semi-circle in front of the TV.

"Where's baby Shea?" she asked Bodey. Katie loved playing with Shea, putting bows in his black, curly hair and giving him dollies to gnaw on, all of which made Bodey kind of uneasy.

"He takes his nap after lunch, Little Bit."

Katie went back to her room for a second load of toys.

"And with Renee around all the time, his daddy doesn't get to play with his mommy in the afternoons anymore."

Bodey Landrum should have watched his mouth. The clacking of keys had stopped while he spoke to Katie. He realized Noreen stood right behind him. Without turning, he could imagine his friend's wife with her arms crossed and a frown her face. Here it came.

"Bodey Landrum, you dense side of beef! How can you be so self-centered? Not only does Renee need our help and support, but you probably haven't noticed that Eve has been sick and tired. She's been trying to keep the fact that you've gotten her pregnant—again—already—quiet in order not to depress Renee who believes she isn't going to be keeping her babies."

Bodey Landrum felt and probably looked as if he had been struck by lightning while riding a bucking bull in a thunderstorm when he turned to stare at her and could see Noreen took a great deal of pleasure in that.

"Can't be! She hasn't said... Eve is nursing. I thought monogamous married men didn't need to use condoms."

Noreen smirked right at him. "You know Eve is more Catholic than any of us. She wouldn't ask you to use a condom now that you're married. You should have taken more care, you dick head. Now you have a second baby on the way, and..."

"I do! That's great!" Bodey held out a flat palm for Rusty to high five.

Russ gave him a good slap, but mumbled under his breath to Bodey, "Thanks a heap. Noreen has been hinting around for a third child with all of her friends busting out with babies."

"That would be terrific! You, me, Clint, we could

all be daddies the same year."

Noreen gave Bodey the friendliest smile she had ever bestowed on him. Katie returned with a pile of plastic teacups and placed one in front of each doll and teddy.

"Have a brew," she said. "Unc Bodey is a dick head. More babies." Katie giggled.

"See what you've made me do! Men! No, honey, Uncle Bodey is a really good guy." To prove that statement, Noreen patted Bodey on the head with a heavy hand.

He ducked down on the sofa. "Look, I only came over here because Clint called and asked me to get Renee to watch the National Bullfighting Finals in a few weeks. It's on after the Professional Bull Riders Finals. I thought I'd invite everyone to a party at my house to watch."

"Won't work," Noreen said. "Renee will figure you'll spend the whole evening praising Clint Beck, saying what a great guy he is. She knows that already. The darned prenup made her feel worthless again. She'll avoid a situation like that. Hmmm, maybe we should get the Sisters involved."

"Now what could Sr. Helen and Sr. Inez do about this? They barely met Clint," Bodey countered.

"They know of him and have been praying for him. And it seems to me, the good Sisters were the ones who brought you and Eve together again. Let me talk to them."

"Go ahead, then. Let me know if I can help," Bodey conceded.

The front door burst open, and Rusty's son, Jesse, ran in holding up a string of dripping bass and catfish.

He was followed by his grandfather Ted and Mona Niles loaded with more fresh-caught fish.

"Fish fry tonight?" asked Bodey hopefully.

"Grilled fish," answered Rusty. "Renee is coming over. You and Eve are welcome, too.

"No, thanks," said Bodey, a gleam in his eye. "I think I'll stay home and make love to my pregnant wife."

Chapter Twenty-Three

Renee Beck double-checked her house again for any object that might be offensive to nuns. The semi-naked male paintings had gone along with Le Grand Pisseur to the little gallery Archie and Roger had opened. She'd told them to get whatever price they could for her art.

At Eve's suggestion, she'd started a new series of children, not pretty, prissy little girls decked in Sunday dresses or clean, tidy boys scrubbed for their portraits, but scruffy kids having fun. The first was a self-portrait at age ten done from an old photo. She wore her hair in a messy auburn bob, all of her freckles showed, and her eyes shone wide and gray-green. A young Renee Niles leaned her head against that of her favorite horse, a little red mare named Ruby. The child that she had been, pre-Paris before Uncle Dewey, radiated happiness. She'd hung that painting close to her bedroom door as if it would ward off the bad dreams.

In the bedroom, the ceiling mirror had vanished. She'd discarded the tiger trappings, painted the room a deep green, and edged the ceiling with die-cut tropical leaves. The spread was scarlet and silky. Tall red and deep yellow vases from local potteries glowed against the dark walls. A small toy tiger peered out from behind an orange pot filled with lucky bamboo on the top of the dresser. A straw cowboy hat hung from the bedpost.

The effect was something like the painter Rousseau's idea of the Garden of Eden with the live plants still clustered by the windows overlooking the patio.

All sex toys had been removed from both her bathroom and the one for guests. She'd packed them away on a high shelf children couldn't reach. Someday, she might want someone besides Clinton Odulf Beck, but not now. He'd bound her to him with his tricks, made her into a person she barely recognized and did not know how to use. He'd given her no instruction manual typed up on a computer like the prenup for his creation, Renee Beck.

Renee gazed at herself in the powder room mirror. A gauzy sea-foam green maternity dress hung straight from her shoulders. Personally, she thought she looked like an overweight housewife, but she'd dressed up the outfit with the inexpensive silver earrings she'd gotten in Ellensburg and a new pair of suede slides because her boots fit too tight now. She wore the Navajo cuff bracelet every day whether it matched her outfit or not. She'd surprised Noreen and Eve by passing up the tight, stylish tops and dresses that would show off her baby bump. Why flaunt what you couldn't keep? Better people thought of her as fat than expectant. Enough of the self-pity. She moved on.

Renee thought she'd show the Sisters the guestroom, now painted in pale green and yellow stripes. Alerted by Noreen, her father and sister had shown up for the wallpaper stripping and painting party. Cathy brought along the pieces of the two sturdy oak cribs that had held her close-born sons at one time. Bodey and Jed and Rusty put the cribs together with the help of lots of beer and an excess of swearing. When they were finished, her father unloaded from his SUV two new identical wooden rocking horses with thick manes and tails of real horsehair exactly the reddish color of the mounts favored by the Niles family. For now, that was all the room contained. No sense in adding more until sure the Becks would allow the children to visit at all after she and Clint divorced.

Forget the exercise room. The more strenuous machines gathered dust. Mostly, she went swimming with Eve in the Landrum's heated pool or walked on the treadmill for as many miles as her legs would carry her.

Along with all the sharp-cornered glass tables, the sofa resembling a pair of puckered lips had gone to Goodwill, surely one of their more unusual donations. A comfortable overstuffed couch, where a man could stretch his legs or children bounce around, and two matching armchairs gathered around distressed wooden tables, the better to hide the inevitable nicks and scratches kids made. The television and sound system had been stashed in a matching corner cupboard.

The kitchen remained the same, mostly unused, as her friends kept the refrigerator stuffed with easy meals to heat in the microwave. She had stocked up on soft drinks for her guests and invested in a popcorn popper to make healthy snacks. All was well—or as good as it could be.

The doorbell rang. Renee went to welcome Sisters Helen and Inez. The elderly nuns entered, their canes thumping softly into the carpet. One held a jar of Orville Redenbacher's popcorn, the other a pound box of butter. Behind them, Eve Landrum stood in the doorway.

"They insisted on stopping at Plato's Grocery before coming over."

"Good popcorn and real butter," Sr. Nessy said. "Not like the microwave stuff they have at the convent."

"It was the least we could do for your letting us come over for the PBR finals. The other nuns, they simply don't get it. To watch this event with someone who has been on the rodeo circuit—what a thrill," breathed Sr. Helen.

"I was merely a spectator taken along for the ride, I assure you. Eve, aren't you coming in?" Renee asked with a hint of desperation.

"Sorry, no. I promised to watch at home with Bodey and Shea." Eve lowered her voice. "Bodey tends to use words like 'mean fucker' when he gets excited, so I couldn't invite them over to our house. Noreen and Rusty were going into Lafayette to pick up something. Thanks for doing this."

"Ah, happy to have them, I guess. Please, Sisters make yourselves comfortable. I'll take the goodies and start a batch of popcorn. Something to drink?"

"Would you have any wine, dear?" asked Sr. Nessy.

"Sorry, no, I'm not supposed to have it. Root beer, Diet Coke, Sprite, lemonade."

"Sprite then."

"A lemonade for me." Sr. Helen sank into the sofa, her toes barely touching the floor.

For the next two hours, Renee ferried refreshments and assisted the old nuns in getting to the bathroom. They amazed her by knowing the names of the top ten bulls and riders. When Tsunami Sam leaped out of the chute, they booed.

"That is the animal who injured your poor husband, isn't it, Renee?"

"Yes." She strained to see if Clint stood among the bullfighters, hoping he wasn't there when Sam threw his rider at the five-second mark and went rampaging around the arena. It would be like Clint Beck to honor a contract no matter what his condition, but she didn't see a sign of her husband. The PBR might have asked him to be a commentator at least. Then, she could have seen if he was well, hear him say so in his own voice.

After two tense hours, the experienced and flirtatious Pedro Sanchez was crowned the new king of the bull riders. "What a remarkable comeback," the announcers said. Sanchez rode with a knee brace, delaying surgery until after the finals. But what about Clint? Shouldn't they mention how he'd saved Pedro and given the crowd an update on the bullfighter's condition? No, they moved on to mentioning the second place winner. Young Lonnie Capshaw came in third, an excellent showing for his first year at the highest level of the sport.

Sr. Helen sighed. "Never say prayers aren't answered, Renee. No major injuries, and our sweet boy, Lonnie, did very well for himself. Did you notice how he kneels and crosses himself after each ride?"

The announcer urged fans to stay tuned for an exciting extra, the Dickies National Bullfighting contest featuring the seven best contenders in the U.S. of A.— among them, the amazing Clinton O. Beck, recently recovered from a severe accident.

"Oh no, no!" Renee clutched the arms of her chair. "He shouldn't be there. He isn't well enough."

"We'll pray for him." Immediately the nuns folded their hands and closed their eyes. They finished in time to see Clint speaking with an attractive woman holding a mike to his lips.

"I'd like to dedicate my performance this evening to my beautiful wife, Renee, who is carrying my twins. I wish she could be here tonight. I know she's watching."

"He can't know that," Renee fumed.

"Oh, maybe he can," Sr. Nessy speculated.

"Tell me, Clint," the floor commentator asked, "are you fully recovered from your injuries and up to competing at this level against the other six invited outstanding bullfighters?"

"I'll do my best. That's all I can say."

The screen showed Tsunami Sam slamming into Clint from several angles while the commentator made remarks and Renee covered her eyes. Finally, they stopped analyzing Clint and went over the rules of the competition. Each bullfighter was allowed forty to seventy seconds to complete his routine which would include showing control of the bull, making contact with the animal, jumping the bull with precision, and handling the barrel.

Clint went last. He lured the bull to him, swatted the animal as it passed. He set up his jump, flipping onto the bull's back and off again. Calling the beast, he made for the barrels, dove in and snaked out, leaping the bull sideways, and finally led the animal back toward the gate. Pale and sweating, he waved to the crowd and pointed toward the big screen. "Love You, Tiger!" flashed on the set.

All three women sitting safely in a living room in

Rainbow, Louisiana exhaled.

"Oh, Renee, dear child, what more could you want from your husband?" Sr. Helen said.

"Some common sense for one thing. He shouldn't be competing so soon after his injuries. What, what—second place! No way!"

"Well, that other young man did jump the bull three times," Sr. Helen said.

Sr. Inez got to her feet as the doorbell dinged. "I'm up. I'll get it. Must be our ride."

She hobbled into the foyer and opened the door. Noreen stepped inside leaving the door cracked a little way.

Renee still talked to Sr. Helen. "And trust. I'd want him to trust the woman I've become and forget the woman I was. I'd like him to tear up that hideous prenup and come for me."

She buried her face in her hands, hoping the tears would not escape between her fingers and the nuns would leave without any more talk. Something flickered past her face, slid down her belly, and landed in her lap. Renee opened her eyes. Pieces of a legal document scattered all around her like the confetti floating down on the World Champion Bullfighter. She looked at a fragment containing part of the sliding scale for alimony.

Behind her, a man's voice said, "You do know that competition was taped, Tiger? You can get anywhere in this country in a corporate jet in a few hours."

On the television screen, Clint congratulated the winner. In Rainbow, Louisiana, the small town where miracles sometimes happened, he placed his hands on his wife's shoulders.

"You should have won."

"No. The winner has to stay behind for a ceremony and interviews. I had some place else to be."

"You mean you threw the competition for me."

"Just left out that third jump. I was getting tired anyhow, and I've won before several times. It doesn't mean as much to me as you do."

Sr. Helen got up from the sofa, making room for Clinton Beck to sit beside his bride. She pegged across the room and joined Noreen and Sr. Inez by the door.

"I guess we should leave now," she whispered.

"No, no! I want to hear if all our prayers have been answered," Sr. Nessy said.

"Be quiet, then," Sr. Helen prompted.

Clint picked up some of the torn papers. "You know I had nothing to do with this. My father drew it up, and he is still paying the price. He says he signed a legal document when he married my mother. She shouts at him that the agreement had only to do with the hacienda and Hidalgo land. Anything more would have been an insult. If you forgive him, Mama might take him back."

"I like your mother, Clint, but I don't know if I'll ever warm up to your father. He probably has six more copies of that prenup, you know. What if you become like him when you take over the family business?"

"Not a chance in hell, Tiger. I've already told him I don't plan to be an absentee father or one who drags his son around on business trips. We have computers and teleconferencing now. Furthermore, the Beck Corporation needs to give more to charities, support the arts—and sponsor professional bullfighting. I hoped you'd help with that."

"I would. I could—if you can trust me enough to know I won't go back to my old ways."

"I'm right here saying that I do. I heard you redecorated the bedroom. I'd like to see what you've done with the place. I have some fine memories of your old boudoir."

"Oh," Renee looked down at her bulging belly, five months and she was as big as seven. "I'm not too attractive or gymnastic right now."

"How about horny? I know I am. I'll show you my new scars if you'll show me your stretch marks. You know, they're both badges of honor."

"I am horny, and I do have stretch marks to show. Cocoa butter just doesn't work the way they says it does." Renee swiped at her eyes careful not to smudge the little makeup she wore. "Oh, Clinton Odulf Beck, I do love you so. Just help hoist me out of these cushions."

He did. Renee took his arm and they walked down the hall toward the new Garden of Eden room.

"I think this is where we leave, Sisters," Noreen Niles prompted.

"Oh, yes. We mustn't miss midnight prayers."

"We have so much to be thankful for," Sr. Nessy agreed.

Chapter Twenty-Four

Clint stayed with Renee in Rainbow. He approved of her new décor and appeared genuinely touched by her preparations for the babies. He didn't press her to go to Texas and face the stone cold blue stare of Gunter Beck, though she often thought she'd like to have Lena around, especially when the babies began kicking in earnest. How her mother-in-law would have loved that. Clint did. His hands seemed to be always on her belly. His love-making became tender and gentle and so very careful that at times she wished they were back in The Tin Can tearing up the sheets.

Most important of all when Uncle Dewey's trial date was set and the prosecutors wanted to depose her in detail, Clint went along and held her hand. Her courage transferred Dewey's daughter who stiffened her fragile spine and agreed to testify, too. Lest the occasion of their molestation be too far in the past, two young Hispanic women not yet out of their teens came forward to tell their tales. After being kicked out by his wife, Dewey moved into an apartment in their complex and courted their mother in order to get to her girls, aged ten and twelve. He earned their trust, offered to stay with the children when the mother worked nights to make sure none of the teenaged boys hanging around got in their pants, he said.

For all his current scraggly looks, Renee knew

Dewey possessed ways of making an immature girl feel pretty, desirable, ready for sex. He'd see them through this rite of passage and make sure they knew all they needed to know about men, he promised them. That line worked well on an insecure tomboy once upon a time, and he still used it, evidently. By the time girls reached the age of eighteen, he generally lost interest and let his victims go, though he'd tried to get at Renee during holidays long after she started college. "You were always my favorite," he'd whisper while carols played obscenely loud in the Niles home, her mother drank herself into a stupor with well-spiked eggnog, and her dad spent the evening at a gentlemen's club in Lafayette. She'd push him away.

She told all when called to the stand: the trips to France, the things he'd made her do and threatened to tell her father. Her agitation caused the babies to kick furiously in her belly as if punching her from the inside out of anger. She looked to Clint in the seats beyond the lawyers for reassurance and found a face made unrecognizable with hatred, his blue eyes lasering fury directed at the back of Dewey's head which should have exploded under that gaze. Her problems had done this to the kindest man she'd ever known. Again, she feared she only brought trouble and chaos into the world, not love. Her knees wobbled as she made her way back to his side and grasped his hand like a lifeline rescuing her from dark seas of her past.

Her cousin Chelsea gave similar testimony, only having no Clint in her life or layers of tough hide built up over the years, broke down and cried on the verge of hysteria. If possible, her story was worse. At home and handy, the blonde woman who so resembled her mother got no trips abroad, only promises that Dewey would tell Anna what Chelsea begged him to do to her. If that failed and his daughter seemed to waver toward confession, he hinted that her mother might have a fatal accident so the two of them could be alone together forever. She had no idea he'd move on as she matured.

Against the advice of his attorney, Dewey wanted to tell his side. His perversion went so deep, he perceived his actions as normal and easily explained. Mounting to the witness box, he swore to tell the truth—as he saw it. The lawyer made sure his client appeared well-dressed, nicely groomed, and completely sober, a tidy disguise for a scrawny and disgusting middle-aged man, a retro-vision of the man Dewey had once been before paying life's tolls for heavy drinking and his secret debauchery of girls.

"See here," Dewey began. "I want to set the record straight. I never molested any child. These here girls all bled before I touched them. That's nature's sign they are women and not children anymore, the getting of their period. In a lot of cultures, they'd be ready for marriage. All I did was train them for that. Their husbands should thank me one day."

Clint surged to his feet. In the row behind him, Bodey Landrum set hands on his shoulders to push him down again, but Clint shook him off as easily as a bull did even such a skilled rider. He took a few steps before a huge bailiff got in his way, and he lowered his head as if he'd butt the man in the gut to get at Dewey. Calmly, the officer of the court asked him to return to his seat. That didn't really change his mind about vaulting the barrier between him and Dewey and beating this terrible man to a pulp again, but Renee's hand on his arm and a soft request to stay by her side did. Clint settled against her, hip to hip with the babies in her belly kicking against his side, but she felt his pulse racing beneath her fingertips.

Her uncle pointed a finger in their direction. "See there now, that's the guy who beat me up. Broke two of my teeth." Dewey showed the unrepaired damage of his ragged dentition to the jury. The female members turned their heads away. "Stove in some ribs, too. He's the one should be on trial."

Ex-Aunt Anna stood with a fist raised in the air as if to make herself appear taller and more noticeable. "Liar! I kicked your ribs in Dewey, and you know it. Give me credit for something."

"I was married to that woman. She got a mean temper. You see why I turned to my daughter for comfort, don't you?" Dewey turned to the jury for sympathy. Even the men looked in another direction. His attorney buried his face in his nicely manicured hands.

Not a stupid person considering what he'd gotten away with for years, Dewey noted their reaction and changed his tact. "See, I got a condition. It's called hebephilia. Now ain't that a mouthful? It means I have a yen for girls who just became women, you know, around eleven. That's what the shrinks tell me. I'm pretty much done with the gals around sixteen when it becomes ephebophilia, except for the redhead over there. She kept coming back for more Dewey years past that age. Really, I only need court-ordered therapy, not a jail sentence."

He kept an eye on Clint who stirred in his seat, but gave the jury an ingratiating broken-toothed grin that failed to charm, so he returned to his first weird defense. "Like I was saying, I trained those girls good. Always used a condom till I got them on the pill and never gave a one of them any diseases. I kept away the boys who might have knocked them up. Like my niece, Renee. Her feller put her in a family way long before they got hitched. Thought I taught her how to avoid that, but she turned into a real slut, not like my other pretty girls who still remember Dewey's lessons."

A woman seated near Anna with the other two witnesses, her dark-eyed, wounded daughters, began cursing in Spanish and spit on the courtroom floor. Clint bolted to his feet again. This time Bodey locked his arms around his friend, not to save Dewey but to protect the bullfighter from arrest.

Chelsea began to scream, "Yes, I remember your lessons—so well sex repels me. I'll never have a normal life, never!"

The gavel pounded. "Clear the spectators, bailiff. Whatever anyone thinks of the accused, I will not have pandemonium in my courtroom." Despite her words, the judge, a woman, looked at the victims with compassion on her face. "The law will deal with him."

It did. The verdict came in guilty, very guilty, after only a half hour of deliberation The judge assigned the maximum sentence on their recommendation, adding years for each of the four known victims. If Dewey ever got parole, he'd be a doddering old man wearing diapers by the time he got out.

"I'm glad this is over," Renee said as they walked from the courthouse. The November air cooled her skin, and she hoped Clint's temper. "I despise what he did to me, but I hate what he did to you in there, Clint. You would have killed him if he'd gotten off."

"I can't deny it."

"If I turned you into a murderer, I couldn't live with myself anymore."

"It would have been Dewey who did that, not you, Renee. Never blame yourself again for any of this."

"Hell, I'd have helped you hide the body," Bodey said. Having no wish to expose Eve to this lurid trial, he'd left his own pregnant wife at home. "Let's vamoose and tell the ladies waiting at home the good news that Dewey won't be around anymore."

"As long as he's locked up, I'll get over it like the bulls that lose all their fury once the rodeo is done. But, that pervert does deserve to die," Clint said, meaning every word.

****

Others agreed. Uncle Dewey didn't thrive in the penal system. Nor did he serve out his sentence. An inmate shived him the shower in the most trite of prison deaths. The warden personally called Chelsea to express his regrets about not being able to protect her father and to ask what she wanted done with his body.

She gave a short answer. "Cremate it. I'll come to get the ashes."

Chelsea asked Renee to ride along the day she received the cremains of her father stashed in a plain cardboard box. Clint spoke out against it, but Renee insisted on honoring the request. Just the two of them would go together and see Dewey to his end.

"She's not strong like me. She doesn't have a person like you in her life. I can do this for her, help her gain all that closure my therapist always talks about. For me, the circle is almost completed. Let me see it through to the end," she argued.

He let his wife go with reluctance. She held Chelsea's hand as the warden presented the box and again expressed his condolences.

"I don't need kind words. Just tell me exactly how he died," Chelsea insisted.

The head of the prison, an older man, had the demeanor of a kindly grandfather despite his high-ranking position in the prison system. Known for being compassionate, he never let a prisoner walk that last mile alone. "You really don't want to know that, Miss. Better you remember your father as he was."

"I want to hear every detail." Eyes hard as blue pebbles reinforced her words.

"Okay, then. Cons don't take to child molesters. They raped him with a broomstick before stabbing him in the gut and trying to saw off his genitals with a piece of sharpened plastic. He didn't die right away, lived long enough to know he'd been mutilated. Lots of internal damage carried him off in a few hours. We did do our best to save him and find the culprits. No one talked."

"I appreciate your telling me, Warden," Chelsea replied with a soft voice and perfect good manners. She stood, shook his hand, and exited with the small brown box tucked in her capacious handbag.

Back in the car, she turned to Renee. "Maybe now I can sleep at night knowing he'll never creep into my bedroom again. I'm glad he suffered."

Renee couldn't say she grieved for Uncle Dewey, but the manner of his death shook her a little. Loving Clint Beck made his wild red rose grow back with fewer thorns. "Chelsea, call if you want to talk. Only I can totally understand. What will you do with the ashes?"

"Pull over at the next gas station."

"We don't need to fill up yet."

"I'll only be a minute."

Presuming a rest stop, Renee steered into the first station off the interstate. Well, these days she could always use a bathroom. A six months, the babies enjoyed bouncing on her bladder. Chelsea got out lugging her heavy purse, but didn't veer toward the restrooms. She made her way to a dumpster with Renee following, raised the lid, and chucked the brown box full of ashes into the bin among the used menstrual pads from the ladies room, half-eaten sausage sandwiches, and a multitude of flies. The heavy lid clanged down like iron being forged into a chain link.

"Garbage," her cousin said. "Just garbage, and this is where he belongs."

Renee didn't disagree, though she would have used the word, "Closure."

Chapter Twenty-Five

Renee Beck, big as a cattle barn, knew she made Clint's entire family nervous. They'd given her the end seat in their box at the Heart of Texas Coliseum in Waco so she could overflow into the aisle and get up easily for bathroom breaks. That hadn't been necessary as she'd been sucking only the ice chips in her drink since their arrival at the Texas Circuit Finals Rodeo. Renee knew she had been willful about coming along for Clint's last performance as a bullfighter, but they'd wanted to leave her safely behind in San Antonio. She wasn't going to miss his big moment, not for anything.

Clint took her to Texas for Christmas despite the reservations Dr. Maddox had about late term travel. The flight in the corporate jet had been swift and smooth. Forgiving Gunter Beck was tougher. Standing stiffly before a roaring fire in the living room, her father-in-law officially burned the last of the prenuptial copies and gave her a brief and formal hug as a welcome to the family. Lena Beck kissed her husband and ran her be-ringed fingers through his white hair—welcoming him back into the family, too.

The next night on Christmas Eve, a party very like the one Renee imagined on her last visit to Hacienda Hidalgo followed a trip to Mass. Candelaria lined the drive upon their return. Guests, drinks in hand, swarmed the inner and outer courtyards with tiny white lights illuminating their way among swathes of red, pink, and white poinsettias. A mariachi band played outside in the clear, chilly air. The inner courtyard with its adobe walls radiated the warmth of the day and retained the heat of the outdoor kitchen stocked with cast iron kettles of Beck products. The vast dining room table with all its candelabra lit held an array of foods from Lena's recipes.

Clint's sisters and his seven nieces and nephews plied her with tidbits, though at this point Renee had to admit she couldn't hold very much of anything, not food or fluids. She stayed in the rocker by the fire and admired the tall Christmas tree with its interesting combination of antique German ornaments and colorful Mexican decorations of pressed tin and straw since everyone seemed to fear she'd drop those babies right out on the floor if she moved. Guests came to her to be introduced to Clinton's new and very pregnant wife.

They spent Christmas as a quiet family day. Clint presented his wife once more with the Zuni parure, hers to keep forever, and a platinum wedding band with a channel of deep, green emeralds. A big Christmas dinner followed, then afternoon naps for the elderly and expectant. Grandchildren ranging in age from eight to fifteen ran amok everywhere. When Clint came to the quiet bedroom wing and laid down beside her, his hand on her belly, his babies kicking inside, Renee slept peacefully during a holiday where no Uncle Dewey prowled the halls seeking the moment when he could molest his niece.

On New Year's Eve, Gunter Beck brought his daughter-in-law a flute of ginger ale to toast the coming year. He clinked his glass against hers and said, "*Prost*

Neujahr", then looking at her belly, *"Zum Wohle!"*— Happy New Year and To your Health—old German sayings that passed down in his family. The severe old man smiled when she repeated the words after him.

All cordiality between them vanished the next day when Renee announced she would attend Clint's last bullfighting performance in Waco and his induction into the Texas Sports Hall of Fame with the rest of the family. Gunter Beck grew red in the face and rocked back on his heels.

"Stay here and rest. You should not be gadding about when you are so—so…"

"Huge? Go ahead and say it. That won't keep me from going. I'll rent a car and come after you if I must," and she stamped her foot.

Clint and Lena gasped as if her action would bring on labor that very moment. It hadn't. Noreen once commented that Renee must have inherited the child-carrying ability of the legendary Ramona Niles who had given birth to twelve, including one set of twins, with no trouble at all. Renee's twin pregnancy had been free of problems, and she wanted to see Clint perform if she had to hitchhike to Waco. In the end, the Becks rented a limousine, and they'd gone in style and comfort.

Renee experienced the first labor pain just past Austin. After that, the pangs came irregularly and without any agony. Nothing to worry about. They would probably stop soon. The pains didn't cease. They increased as she climbed to the box. By the time Clint performed, and the camera switched to his family after he'd jumped the bull in three different ways, she had to paste a brilliant smile on her face to disguise her clenched teeth. Wearing darkest green and the Zuni parure, she surely looked like a gigantic black hole in the universe surrounded by glittering stars on that big screen. Lena assured her she had a radiant glow. Liar, sweet liar.

His post-performance interview seemed endless. Clint waved for her come join him. Nice that he wasn't ashamed of her size, but oh, the agony of getting down those stairs to reach his side. She'd stayed there, tucked under his arm and grinning like a politician's wife until the commentator moved away.

Through gritted teeth, Renee said, "Clint, the babies are coming."

"Wheelchair! Over here!"

She'd married a man of decisive action. Clint whisked her to the medical area where Doc Wiley took one look and said, "You! No way! This is not a delivery room. There's an ambulance right outside."

Renee stood up. "I need to push."

"Don't!" the doctor ordered—and her water broke over his shoes. If she hadn't been in so much pain, she would have enjoyed the expression on the man's face.

"This is why I prefer cowboys and broken bones," Doc Wiley muttered. "Get up on the table. We'll have a quick look. Then you go to the hospital."

The doctor pulled off the fluid-soaked green lace bikini panties and bravely faced a well-waxed crotch. "Ah, durn it, the first one's crowning."

He snapped on rubber gloves in time to catch Clint's son, delivered with a hard push and a long scream. Injured bull riders in nearby cubicles shuddered. The medics from the ambulance arrived to do the rest of the dirty work—deliver the afterbirth and the second twin, who had remained coyly hidden behind her brother on all of the ultrasounds. They cleaned up the mess, too, and allowed Renee a few moments to admire the twins wrapped in light blankets and tucked in her arms while the Beck family gathered around.

"Very small and redheaded," assessed Gunter Beck.

Doc Wiley, cordial now that the medics had taken over, said, "Good-sized for twins. I'd say five-pounders. Nice color, breathing well, but we need to get them out of Sports Medicine now. All this screaming and crying is unnerving the bull riders."

"They are beautiful," said Lena Beck. "What will you call them?"

Clint cleared his throat. "We decided on Ty for the boy." No sense in explaining that Ty was short for Tiger. His father preferred very traditional names.

"Ty—a cowboy name. Ty what?" his old man asked severely.

"Ty Odulf Beck." Clint shook his head. Sometimes, you had to give in and get on with life.

"And our little granddaughter?" Lena inquired.

"We picked Serena because that's the kind of life we want our daughter to have, serene," Clint said.

"Serena Maria Madalena Beck," Renee added.

"Perfect."

Epilogue

Twelve years later
Mount Carmel Academy, Rainbow, Louisiana

Serena Maria Madalena Beck, who was neither calm nor saintly, stamped her foot on the shells in the oval drive and pouted. "I don't see why I'm the one being sent away to boarding school when Ty gets to stay at home and play cowboy."

"Being educated at Mt. Carmel Academy is a privilege. All the Niles girls attend here. As Grandfather Gunny would say, it's an old family tradition," her mother answered firmly.

"Family tradition is why my brother has a dorky middle name like Odulf. Besides, I am not a Niles. I'm a Beck," Serena claimed, her sea-blue eyes turning dark as a storm passing over the ocean. She tossed her auburn hair. The cheeks of her fair, flawless, and freckle-free face reddened.

"You're a Niles girl, no doubt about it. You and your mother are the prettiest women here today," her father told her.

That made Serena smile and blush again. At age twelve, she was still more concerned about her horse, now stabled in the Academy barn, than about boys, but she recognized a grand compliment when she heard one.

"You'll get a wonderful education and be completely safe here," her mom assured her. "We'll only be a phone call away, and the Sisters will take good care of you. You have Auntie Noreen and Auntie Eve and Grandpa Jed living just down the road. There's a shrine here to your own special saint where you can pray, but don't go into the woods alone. Remember the two old nuns I used tell you about? I am sure they are both your guardian angels now—along with St. Leontine—but I wouldn't bother her too often. She tends to be rather severe when people don't want to obey her." Renee Beck finally ran out of breath.

"As if I'd ever tell anyone my mother thinks she had a vision commanding her to marry my dad."

Her mom worried way too much about her kids. Serena guessed that was why she'd never had any more children, that and giving birth at a rodeo, which must have been very embarrassing. She'd never understood why any woman would have to be ordered to marry a handsome, rich, wonderful guy like her dad.

Might as well let the rest of it out, Renee Beck thought. "You might hear stories about me from the other girls. I went to school with their mothers and…"

An eye roll from Serena. "I'm to tell them you reformed, turned your life around, are a better person now. I'm supposed to study hard and get good grades even though you didn't. Yada yada."

"Someone has to run the Beck Corporation after I retire, and it doesn't look like Ty will be the one. He has bull riding and bullfighting on the brain." Clinton Beck gave his daughter a wide grin full of perfect dentistry.

In a light gray business suit worn with a deep blue

tie the color of his eyes, her dad was easily the best looking father at orientation. The sunshine picked out the silver strands in his short dark blond hair and made it shine.

"Yeah, Uncle Bodey says Uncle Rusty blew it when he had another daughter the year I was born because his sons and Ty are going to rodeo together. Aunt Norma Jean says she could train me to be a barrel racer. Sarah Beth Niles could never do that. She's too puny." Serena dismissed her second cousin with a wave of her hand.

"Listen to me, Rena. I want you to be kind to Sarah Beth. She'll be in all your classes." Do as I say, not as I did. Renee gave a slight shrug.

"Sarah is weird."

"You might be, too, if you'd nearly died when you were six. Sarah is pretty and very talented, just rather shy."

"Shea told me she did die. They had to bring her back to life with artificial respiration and those paddles, and that's why she's so different, but he and his brothers watch out for her. Shea told me he'd be happy to punch anyone who was mean to me, too."

"Great." Clint Beck smiled as his wife and daughter duked it out. "That will be like having three brothers living nearby. All of them go to St. Leo's."

"For the time being," muttered Renee. "They were nearly expelled last year after putting that yearling bull in the vestry and almost giving Fr. Brian a heart attack. He could have been injured, not to mention the damage the animal did to the vestments. Bull poop everywhere. The animal must have been in there for hours. If Eve weren't so active in the church, those boys would have been out on their asses."

Serena had to giggle over her mother using poop and asses in the same speech. Her mom tried so hard to be proper, but sometimes the wild woman everyone said she'd been came out.

"Not so funny, young lady. Uncle Bodey and Uncle Russ had to bring over horses and ropes and a trailer to get the beast, and meanwhile, it was flinging around the holy vessels."

"A good bullfighter could have done that with his bare hands. Bodey did pay for the damages. I wonder how the boys got the animal all the way over here," Clinton O. Beck speculated. "Speak of the devils and here they come."

Sauntering through the wrought iron gates of Mt. Carmel Academy came the Landrum brothers, Shea and Ben, a year apart in age and alike enough with their mischievous bright blue eyes and dark, curly hair to be twins. Ten-year-old Rick had his mother's light coloring and long legs, making him nearly as tall as his siblings. No wonder their mother's pale hair got whiter by the year.

Ty in the midst of them was as happy as could be because no one planned on sending him off to some snooty school. He'd soon be back in San Antonio practicing his rodeo skills. His floppy red hair combed back with water and his freckles apparent even from a distance, he waved to his family.

"Wasn't Aunt Eve going to bring you over in time for the orientation Mass while we were settling Rena in her dormitory room? I didn't see you at the service, son." Renee Beck stared her boy in the eyes, hazel like her own. He attempted a wide and innocent gaze and the goofy grin that usually won his mother over.

"Ah, Aunt Eve had to come early to help with the registration, and Uncle Bodey kind of forgot about Mass, so Uncle Rusty picked us up just now. But we're here in time for the brunch. Aunt Noreen said there would be cinnamon buns. Her and Uncle Rusty and the girls are right behind us. We had to park about a mile away. Aunt Noreen said they have been oriented enough since Katie has gone here for years, but she promised to help serve the meal. Can we go eat now?"

"Y'all run along—and don't be a nuisance. Clint, you'd better go with them and keep them out of trouble. I want to wait for Noreen." Renee shaded her eyes, looking for her friend. She really should put on sunglasses to prevent any more wrinkles from forming.

"I know how to herd young bulls, Tiger. I'll save a place for you." Clint followed the boys stampeding toward the cafeteria. His daughter took to her heels, parochial kilt swinging, and raced after them kicking up puffs of dust from the circular drive and passing, lickety-split, the statue of the Virgin and Child in the center of the lawn.

Renee let Serena go. Her daughter was spirited, bold, and undamaged, and she hoped Mt. Carmel Academy would keep her that way.

Wearing the school uniform of white blouses and blue kilts, Katie and Sarah Beth Niles turned in at the gates. Not as striking as Serena, both were still very pretty girls. Katie had her cascading red curls pulled back and held in place with golden barrettes. Sarah, her straight blonde hair hanging over her large, light eyes, walked along studying her shoe tips.

"Your brother Jesse couldn't make it?" Renee

asked Rusty's daughters.

"No, ma'am. He's already at college. I can't wait to get out of this place and leave for the university. Two more years," the leggy sixteen-year-old sighed, heaving a nicely rounded bosom.

"I remember that feeling, but believe me, once you are out in the world, this place will seem wonderful."

"I guess," Katie said, trying not to sound rude.

"You don't have to stand here in the broiling sun with me. Serena and the boys have gone ahead. Go and join them."

Katie started up the drive, but Sarah hung back. "I'll wait with you, Aunt Renee. I don't think Serena likes me very much," the child said softly. Small for her age and still flat-chested, she could not compete with Serena's budding figure.

"Honey, if you stand up to Rena, you'll win her respect. Remember that, and don't let her bully you. She's too used to getting her own way. I hear you have a beautiful singing voice and play the piano so very well. I'll tell you a secret—my daughter can't sing on key to save her life and has no musical talent whatsoever."

Sarah looked up through her long bangs and smiled timidly. "Thanks for telling me that. I thought Serena could do everything."

"No one can. I hear you have three knights in shining armor willing to defend you." Renee stooped down trying to get the girl to raise her head.

"Uncle Bodey's boys, just Shea really, but his brothers do what he says. They aren't very much like knights—more like cattle rustlers, my dad says. I'd like to have a real knight to fight for me like the ones in *Le*

Morte d'Arthur." Sarah looked up now, gray-blue eyes filled with light.

"I can see you are ahead of Serena in reading, too, but she's very good at math. You should help each other."

"I will if she'll let me."

"Go along and save some places at the table for us."

The child went, dragging her feet, scuffing her new school shoes in the shells, and looking back over her shoulder for her parents. Rusty and Noreen finally appeared, Noreen puffing as she held on to her husband's arm. She'd never lost her baby weight after Sarah's birth and remained much rounder than she should be, while Rusty was still so tall and lean and distinguished now with those white streaks in his hair. Renee knew Noreen wore the black dress with three-quarter sleeves to look thinner, but orientation day at Mt. Carmel always meant a hot and sticky affair, a part of living in Louisiana. She'd worn sleeveless white cotton with a few colorful accents, herself.

"Hi, Renee. You look great as usual." Noreen smiled, doubling her chin.

Her big, brown eyes were as lovely as ever though. She held out her chubby arms to give her friend a hug, and Renee noted her curls were still dark without the aid of dye. She felt a little pinch of envy at that. Like so many of the Niles family, she was going white early and had tinted hers back to the shade Clint loved.

"I'll tell you a secret. I cheat."

Noreen grew horrified. "Not on Clint!"

"Oh, no, no. I meant I look great because I had a breast reduction and a lift. Makes me look slimmer.

Clint said I didn't need any surgery, but that was all I wanted for our anniversary, to keep looking great for him."

"I'm so relieved. Maybe I should get liposuction now that we have money," Noreen said, whispering.

"I think Rusty loves you just the way you are."

"Honey, I'm going ahead to walk with Sarah, okay?" Rusty asked.

He was very aware of the forlorn looks his daughter cast over her shoulder. Because of her delicate health, she'd been home-schooled until this year. Maybe they should have enrolled her sooner, but there had been the money issue until recently. Katie had that nice scholarship and thrived at the Academy. Sarah Beth would be fine, too. He knew she would if she could simply get over her fears.

"Sure. Renee and I will have a nice chat. See you in the cafeteria." Noreen watched her husband move away, her smile now small and secret.

How fortunate those two were to find each other at such a young age and to love each other still, Renee thought. How lucky she was to have found Clinton O. Beck at all. Or maybe not lucky. Sr. Helen and Sr. Inez always said all things came with time and prayer. That had certainly been true of Noreen and Rusty, of Dudey and Eve, of herself and Clint.

"Looks like you finally got a petite, blonde Courville in Sarah. I was beginning to think there was no such being," Renee joked.

"I'm not sure how I got her either, but I always wanted to *be* one. You know, like that portrait of Marie-Celeste Courville my parents have, so feminine and golden."

"Don't put yourself down, Noreen. You have more important qualities. So, how do you like living out at Frenchman's Bend now that the decorator has finally sold it to you?"

"For a pretty penny though we talked him down a million. I know you think I'm nuts, but I feel as if I belong there, that I've lived there before."

Renee refrained from commenting on that last remark. Noreen had stood by her when she thought she'd lost both Clint and her babies. She would never make fun of her again. Who knew? Maybe Noreen was right about all that reincarnation junk.

"No one deserves that house more than you and Rusty. You were the one who wrote the book on the Niles family that brought in enough money to buy that marshy, old thicket where the Rebs sneaked up on the Yankee army at the Battle of Frenchman's Bend."

"Well, we had to do something. They were going to drain the area and put up more houses. It's sacred ground."

"Right. My dad had a fit when the land deal fell through after your appeal to the owner. And then, you go and discover oil down there and buy the plantation house, too."

Once upon a time, Renee would have envied her friend for more than her natural hair color, but she had Clint, a very fancy roof over her head called the Hacienda Hidalgo, and all the beans she could eat. Her life was good.

"I'm starting another book, one on Wild Billy Niles and Owney Maddox and what happened to them based on my senior thesis. Could I stay with you when I come to Texas to do research?"

"As my mother-in-law used to say—*mi casa es su casa*. I'd like some female company now that Serena is away at school. It's just me and Clint and Ty and grumpy old Gunter now. I miss Lena so much. Why did she have to be the one to pass away? And it seems odd being here at the Academy again without seeing Sr. Helen and Sr. Nessy bumping around on their canes and trying to fix everyone's lives." Renee glanced over toward the nun's graveyard full of simple markers for the Sisters who had served and died here, overwhelmed now by the large shrine built above the grave of St. Leontine.

"I'll bet Mother Leontine hates all that folderol. Must be a pain being a saint and having people begging for stuff all the time," Noreen remarked.

"Only you would think that or use a word like folderol, Noreen. Love that about you. To think I didn't recognize her in my dream when Clint was injured. I spent enough time in the Mother Superior's office being chewed out for my make-up, my rolled up skirts, and my attitude problems with her portrait glaring down at me."

Renee gestured in passing toward the historic brick convent with the wavy old glass in the windows and small ferns growing in the cracks of the plaster, two women over forty and still loved by their husbands.

"You did write up that testimony about your vision, and it did help Mother Leontine become a saint. I'm sure she has forgiven you."

"Mama Lena pushed me to do it. I'll never be as good as I should be."

"Oh, you've come a long way. Better pick up the pace or all the cinnamon buns will be gone."

****

Over on the top of Mother Leontine's shrine, the spirits of Sr. Helen and Sr. Inez watched their former students walk away. They no longer needed their canes, but had chosen not to appear any younger than they were at their deaths only days apart several years ago. Old people were a less threatening form if they had to materialize.

"I hope Mother Leontine doesn't mind our staying here to help," said Sr. Helen. "We do have another generation of Niles girls to look after."

Sr. Nessy stretched out across the top of the shrine while Sr. Helen dangled her skinny legs over the edge of a parapet. "Which one do you want?"

"I think I should devote myself to the timid child, Sarah, since I am more in tune with the artistic." Sr. Helen bobbed her head.

"Fine, I'll take on Serena Beck. She's going to be a handful. As for Mother Leontine minding—I think this is all part of her plan."

A word about the author...

Once a librarian, now a writer of romance, Lynn Shurr grew up in Pennsylvania Dutch country. She attended a state college and earned a degree in English Literature. Her first job really was working in a burger joint. Moving from one humble job to another, she traveled to Europe and across the United States, finally buckling down to get an M.A. in Librarianship.

She found her first reference job in the Heart of Cajun Country. For her, the old saying "Once you've tasted bayou water, you will always stay here" came true. She raised three children not far from the Bayou Teche and lives there still with her astronomer husband.

When not writing, Lynn likes to paint, cheer for the New Orleans Saints and LSU tigers, and take long road trips nearly anywhere. Her love of the bayou country, its history and customs, often shows in the background for her books.

She is the author of the Sinners sports romances, a new series, The Roses, and a single title romance, *A Trashy Affair*.

Contact Lynn at:

www.lynnshurr.com, lynn.shurr@yahoo.com

or

lynnshurr.blogspot.com